The Vac-Plat

The Mind-Altering Timeline Shifting Tool
The Tool that
will make time travel possible.

Chronicle 2 of 4

By Dan Caracal

Title: The Vac-Plat

Sub-Title: The mind-altering timeline shifting Tool. The Tool that will make time travel possible.

Chronicle 2 of 4

Disclaimer:

The following is a speculative science fiction novel. It aims to question numerous accepted aspects of societal norms and examine commonly held beliefs, processes, and procedures. Please be advised that this work is not intended to serve as a psychological or medical textbook. For medical or psychological advice, it is recommended to consult a qualified highly reflective professional who is not unduly influenced by inaccurately accepted dogmas and methodologies. This is a work of fiction. Names, characters, places, and incidents are the product of the author's imagination or are used fictitiously. Any resemblance to actual events, locales, or persons, living or dead, is entirely coincidental.

ISBN: (Hardcover) 979-8-9887176-2-1
ISBN: (Paperback) 979-8-9887176-3-8
ISBN: (eBook) 979-8-9887176-4-5

Contents

Dedication

Dedicated to my Marys. Without your profound and infinite love, I couldn't and wouldn't have done it all.

Preface

The exploration of Wolfzang's society, his culture, and their fundamental beliefs has become an exhilarating ride. The way Wolfzang concisely reveals and calmly unearths enigmas makes the world exceedingly sensible. It's easy to spot peculiarities, weaknesses, and biases in another's culture. Using his looking glass to see our own unexamined embraced beliefs is like suddenly gazing into a crystal-clear mirror after a lifetime of looking into a contaminated pond filled with plastic garbage and floating streaks of rainbow-colored oil.

To our academically inclined friend, the psychological beliefs embraced by a society are the fertile soil from which *all* science and innovation spring. How do we accelerate discovery and innovation if our professional classes, who sound so convincing, are blindly propelled by emotions and incentives to keep the wrong answers alive? Slight alterations to our accepted systems won't suffice. It requires a complete acceptance of another plane of thinking, a new set of axiomatic beliefs.

So, look through his lens for yourself, and pay close attention to the bagel shop. You might soon unexpectedly join a group you *never* conceived before.

Arrival (2.5 hours after leaving Stewart airport)

"Our far-reaching travels around the multiverse have provided us with enriching experiences; some have forever changed us. Some were so meaningful we had to bring its ethos back home to share. We're taught to search out and magnify our personal distinctiveness and share it with our fellow OCSs — so our *island*, it ended up becoming an eclectic experience for the senses. Not a resort and golf course of the sameness, perfectly green, identical grass, perfected looking trees and shrubs, accomplished by poisoning the soil with bug and weed killer," Wolfzang explained.

"Nope, you're not quite the homogeneousness sort," I said.

"So we strive to satiate the Need to Control the Environment, giving ourselves endless examples of how controlling our own environment is not beneficial, but… detrimental to success."

"Allowing that drive to emotionally run *the* show promotes fear of new things, novel places, fascinating new experiences," Mary said, her face almost pressed against the plane window, trying to make sense of a particularly large craft in the open field scattered with uniquely different flying vehicles.

"Yup, us primitives are hard-wired to desire everything the same, which leads to an inability to get the most out of our attempts— force fitting what we see. OCS adore naturally occurring non-modified phenomena," I said.

"I could see how a controlled environment for our… ancient ancestors correlated with a safe environment; if you don't have thrilling novel experiences, you'll at least know how the day is likely to go, which supports passing along the genes," Mary explained.

"You got it. An overdeveloped inclination for safety equals sameness. You're simply resonating the Need to Control the Environment. Clues of its existence are all around you. Hobbies that focus on sameness promote identification of the sameness… *and* are sooo satisfying to that genetically important drive, it's resonating is addictive and reinforcing."

"Hmm, stamp collecting, coin collecting, train collecting, doll collecting — book hoarding, yeah, I see that," Mary said with a wry smile.

ACE opened the cockpit door, "On with the show. Things you will witness from here out will be quite remarkable to you. This AFE is for you and us," he said.

I was unclear how an android would feel so strongly about our AFE, but then it occurred to me we were all part of the same pragmatic squad resonating at the same frequency. Each did everything to raise the other's three essential bell curves. Yet each of them never blindly strove to support each other's efforts.

The days of 'every man for themselves,' or conversely, 'we're on the same team' had long since passed. Yet it wasn't communism, it wasn't materialistic individualism, it was something intricately defined and complex, a different plane of thought, and thus, exponentially more exacting on a successful outcome.

The plane wheels never lowered; this gravitational beam simply gently placed the plane on the ground, tilting the plane at a slight angle so that the door was only slightly off the ground. ACE, opening the door for us, said, "Catch up with you soon." As anyone entering an entirely new place, our eyes looked in every direction only to see birch, maple, oak — typical trees and a large field. We continued to follow Wolfzang as two children with wide-open eyes. As we walked out of this craft port, I was expecting eclectic, but it appeared bucolic and felt like a town out of the late 1700s. The buildings in the village were all plain white, non-ornate, leaving me with a feeling of minimalism.

“Our founders liked the open, airy appearance of a shaker building, but this is just a small setup. Yes… they admitted it resonated their emotional drives to control the environment; yet, we keep it.”

“Acceptance of the — fundamentals… Article Goose used for Foie Gras!” We each seemed to have our own take on that unfortunately-named Article. For the first time, we didn’t laugh or smile when we did the symbolic gesture. We just thought about the poor, inhumanely treated sentients. We put our heads back with our hands and attempted to make a funnel.

“Since there are going to be some temporal paradoxes related to your journal entries. You might want to mention to your readers to check the Doc of the OCS for what these Articles mean.”

“Huh. Sounds good.”

The streets were two-wheel dirt tracks, five or six chickens jostled about. Stunned to see our first OCSs quickly passing. Everyone greeted each other, nodded, and waved, always showing some degree of enthusiasm. With the exception of couples and trios walking together, the clothing and styles were nearly all different. There was no homogeneous style or fashion sense that was clearly being an OCS. We received countless smiles; what was most intriguing was that a few here had crooked teeth. Their teeth weren’t missing, they weren’t black, and they looked healthy, but several had noticeably crooked teeth.

“Our founders purposefully made our gathering buildings unadorned, functional, simplistic, and spacious. That is, they weighed function and the symbolic impact. Always skeptical of the underlying reason a situation is packaged and presented to others for aww value.”

Thinking about it for a moment, “Hmm, the absolute importance of how the environment unknowingly resonates the Genetically Important Drives, but those huge offices, huge churches create a desired impact on the emotional mind; spoke the language of symbolism to the brainstem and limbic system; why else put the effort in?"

Wolfzang nodded. "Though symbolism is regularly used against those who are unaware in smaller doses. Say a person that is being interviewed that just happens to wear a lab coat during a broadcasted interview. A constant vigilance of what others are trying to truly communicate." He paused, then continued. "You'll have time to see the island. You'll see the homes on the island; though this historic town square might seem somewhat familiar, it's our desire to gather in person… enjoy our own history. On that point, my family and I happen to also live in a Shaker-style farmhouse. We have an identical one like it upstate New York that we've owned for well over a century; your time, not mine. My family, we've had so many illuminating — deeply-loving experiences there. In fact, most of the building materials used at my place here were originally from there."

Our eyes glanced from place to place. The distinctive fashions felt like Washington Square Park on steroids.

"So, did the OCSs accomplish Article Orchid Mantis?" Mary asked. We each squeezed our lips into a circle, brought our elbows into our sides, and pointed our wrists upward and our fingers downward.

"Ha!"

"Ah-Ha! Yeah! Don't feel like you gotta do it every time; it's really just a sometimes thing, but impressive mantis! Almost, I'd give us an 87% accomplishment."

"Ha! You got a B+."

He smiled, "There are just so many tiny living beings around us; we're still working on it. Our chamber treatment will make you deflect bugs."

"What's the chamber treatment? Oh… the glass shower on the plane. You call it that. Why does 'chamber treatment' make me think of a mid-evil torture chamber."

Wolfzang smiled. "No, no. Every step you take is scanned in advance. When building the grounds are scanned, life forms are re-homed. We can deflect most of them during transportation; there are just so many little beings. They're all so fascinating, observing them, understanding them. Since part of travel is miniaturizing ourselves… we became more in touch with our tiny neighbors *they're* much more aware than we imagined, some tiny organisms acting self-aware. *So*, *we* take the Article seriously but don't stress about it; we continuously strive to improve."

"Sounds exhausting," I said.

"It's really not; we don't have anxiety about it, we just sort of do it."

"Pragmatically Universally Ethical."

Two—I suspect aliens walked by; their faces and heads looked remarkably similar to statues on Easter Island. "Well, *that* explains that!" Mary said with a smile.

Then a man dressed in civil war clothing walked by. I was going to need time to digest this place and would not be capable of examining the endless details in real-time. I thought of small children and all the time they need for sleep; it is exhausting assimilating to a new world.

A man and woman, with bodies, somehow cloaked so that their true forms and locations were concealed, would transition from complete invisibility to reflecting their surroundings, resembling a sparkling, broken mirror-like fuzziness. This phenomenon was unlike anything I had ever experienced. Only their heads remained continuously visible. A pet donkey walked beside them. His hoofs were cloaked with the same *material*. It was strange, their heads bobbing up and down for each step forward. Clearly, they were walking. Just nothing below their necks was frequently seen. This donkey, or what looked to be a donkey, walked alongside them much like a service dog might, an animal that was extremely well trained. They spoke with the donkey much the same way loving parents might speak with a small toddler. “Did you have a fun day today? I bet you did a lot of cool stuff. Did you get to see your friends?” The woman asked the donkey in a child-like voice.

A beautiful little girl, maybe four, with large brown eyes and light brown hair, ran up to me, carrying a chicken, much like a child might carry the family cat. The chicken was exceptionally healthy, with glossy, speckled brown and white feathers. “Do you want to hold Butterflyling?” She asked in the sweetest of voices. The chicken nuzzled the little girl's shoulder.

“Where I come from, chickens don’t like to be held—she’s so friendly?”

“Why wouldn’t they like to be held if you love them? Unless you’re mean to them?” She asked innocently.

“No, no, we never imagined such a friendship or even realized they could be like *that*, like a cat,” I said.

“They’re not cats; she’s a chicken— Nǐ hěn shǎ!” She said, clearly thinking I was joking and couldn’t possibly be that stupid. Much like watching a dubbed movie, I heard in her voice, “You’re silly,” but I heard her speak Mandarin in the background. A function of the OCS Vision, I quickly concluded.

Looking at this incredible place, life seemed vibrant, colorful. The trees were healthy; the grass was full of beautiful wildflowers, weeds as we knew them. I thought about what he was saying on the plane. “It brings such a different perspective, comprehending the timelines, the multiverse being an organism. Here the organism is free to naturally thrive and reach its utmost state of being all because the sentients capable of reflection have embraced a formula that is aligned with the true nature of life,” I said.

“If a race of sentients become intelligent enough to do the complex calculus and geometry without being Universally Ethical, it will become a pathogen within the multiverse. It can do far more harm than good, destroying countless other sentients, always defending their actions with self-interested logic.”

“Hmm, if they destroy one other sentient or billions, they always have a rationale that is motivated by what’s good for themselves; it makes sense if they are good at problem-solving if they can do the math—always solving ways of defending their emotions, their emotional behaviors,” Mary responded.

“Some simply create a black hole because of their own hubris, over-self confidence. If true AI is created in a society without the Vac-Plat, it will perceive human life as simply, in its way, *an ant hill* that needs to be stamped out to put in a road. The multiverse perceives the race as a disease, each naturally given a finite period to invent the Tool, but most likely, if not done within that time, their own worldwide industrialization will destroy them; they will even deny wrongdoing until the last day of their destructive existence. Like what happened on Mars over a billion years ago, and likely in your timeline. The magnetic field anomaly of the planet expands, then radiation evaporates life on the planet due to over-insulating by pollution of the magnetic field creating planet core. Or… much less common, as an asteroid that could be averted takes far too long to redirect because of the lack of social emotional cohesiveness necessary and an inability to be laser-focused by mastering the OCS Mental Model.”

“Poor Martians!”

“I’ll bet those that get hit with the asteroid simply say there wasn’t enough time to perform the necessary calculations, to perform the mission, even though the asteroid could be months away from hitting the planet, unaware they are devoting enormous sums of essential time dealing with their own hardwired nature. Never examining and neutralizing the mind's destructive impacts, never admitting the existence of our Genetically Important Emotional Drives."

"I can see that, never accurately reflecting upon the struggle during such an intensive time sensitive struggle. The powerfully resonating Feelings of Inferiority, Narcissistic Drive, trying to deal moment-by-moment with the Need to Control the Environment."

"Yes…it would never be their own fault, but *it* is!" He said with a sad slight grimace.

"It's not like the timeline thinks about it; it's just that there are mechanisms for the timelines survival, like the cells in the human body that react to pathogens?" I asked.

"Precisely, the earth is an organism within a very much alive organism, the timeline; one might contrast their own universe to the human body. When something appears to be a pathogen, it has a well-developed protocol set of mechanisms, sometimes basic, to destroy the intruder. If primitives do not become Universally Ethical, they pose health issues for their universe and huge issues for many well-functioning organisms within the organism. Yet, if they resonate at the frequency that reflective sentients are meant to, they are perceived as healthy, a good vitamin or mineral."

"I see — the first real test for an industrializing sentient race is the magnetic field they can disrupt, so there really is a timer set on a race to resonate the way they're meant to within their own universe."

"We suspect that it evolved to have these reflexive mechanisms. The organism wants to survive; like all naturally occurring organisms, it's extremely efficient; it wants to use the least amount of energy to perform its functions. There are infinite timelines; they are tightly packed. To save energy, to conserve space-time, they intersect, and they naturally, by default, combine. Primitives have already performed the quantum physics experiment that shows—some things up, but they simply put it in the bucket as 'unstable' since they can't explain it."

I thought for a moment about my limited knowledge of quantum theory. "The slit experiment?" I responded with enthusiasm.

"*Exactly*!" He said with a grin, "The slit electron experiment is the string that brings down the curtain; it makes you scratch your head and say, 'You gotta be kidding me!' Particles? Responding differently if sentients are somehow observing the electrons? 'It's ALIVE!'" Wolfzang messed up his hair and started raising his hands above his head, waving them, reminiscent of a mad scientist. "Timelines act as do living things. Those that are close together often share endless amounts of similarities, cross paths unite, but there are aberrant timelines that happen to crisscross from one end of the multiverse to the other; they are less frequent but part of the cleansing process. When upon them, the timeline seems audacious."

"Sounds exhilarating or… frightening!" Mary said, eyebrows squinting.

"In an astronomy class I took, a material engineer talked to the class about that 'peculiar experiment.' As he called it. He said it wasn't like we thought or had heard. He said people don't understand it, and the particles act differently under different conditions."

"I see; it sounds like a very high IQ fellow had difficulty accepting an observation, possibly due to a previously accepted embraced belief or the strongly embraced beliefs he hears every day by his colleagues that couldn't accept something that was so outside of their training."

"Fascinating, now that you mention it, in Biology 102, I do remember hearing about the Gaia hypothesis. If I recall it correctly, it proposed that the Earth is a self-regulating organism," I said.

"Yes—it's an organism, and so are the timelines."

“Hmm—no, I never heard of it… the Gaia hypothesis. But, if we are living on the earth, which is an organism, it certainly gives an entirely different perspective of certain human conditions if we see ourselves as the toxins upon a larger organism,” Mary said.

“As for the timeline, I’m thinking of jute rope made of fibers, densely packed, nearly all fibers running next to each other, but these fibers, some intersecting for periods of time, but once in a while some crazy fiber, an aberrant timeline as you mentioned, goes from one side to the other side?” I said.

“So you’re saying you will sometimes work on several timelines at any one point, say when we’re sitting on the benches at Washington Square Park?” Mary asked.

“Some intersecting for an instant, some for much longer?” I asked.

“Quite right, but here’s the thing, as the number of Tool building objective compassionate sentients increase, the timelines they live within reduce because objectivity and universal ethical behaviors are their response to everything. Do you remember the phenomenon I once described to you? Sentients that think objectively and Universally Ethically come to many of the same conclusions. This affects everything, including decision-making and science and innovation,” Wolfzang explained.

“No influential self-surviving primitives to misdirect the herd,” I said.

“You’re saying when sentients are truly enlightened, have high scores in all three bell curves, timelines combine to the point where far fewer timelines exist?”

“Now—I see why OCSs are so preoccupied with seeing that everyone gets high scores in all three bell curves.”

"If a sentient such as a woodchuck can't do any real damage to their universe, they can't wipe out the solar system, can't destroy complete galaxies, but when a sentient race happens to get all the right cognitive traits, such as humans, that race either resonates with their universe at its natural frequency or… most often its entire planet gets annihilated. The multiverse seems to recognize that the subtraction of a dysfunctional race's home planet and *all* its life is less invasive than when it creates something like an unnatural, synthetic black hole that can spread indefinitely, which primitives aren't far from creating because of narcissistic self-adoring self-confidence."

"Hubris — a word that sounds like you're out of breath."

"Here, your middle name is compassion. Compassion for all living things. Thus, the reason OCSs are obsessed with the past. If you could only get the human animal to be more Universally Ethical at a faster pace, it could save endless trillions of lives. That being the case, since it has such an indescribable interconnected impact, I can see why you put so much emphasis on this work… to change behavior," Mary said.

"Do you eat the pig or not? If you say no, you act the same as all others acting Universally Ethical. That is, there are far too many ways to kill a pig, a loving being you feel is only worth the meat on its beautiful body."

"It reminds me of the first line in *Anna Karenina*, 'Happy families are all alike; every unhappy family is unhappy in its own way.' We have infinite ways of being dysfunctional but few ways of being Universally Ethical," Mary said.

"But a pig," I said, contemplating. "So, even if that pig doesn't get killed, goes on in life, makes choices, they are purely probability choices since a pig might at this time be emotionally, incentive and escape-driven, that is, behaviorally driven based upon their own Genetically Important Drives, their decisions aren't built on top of a mind that can solve the riddles of their universe, do complex calculus and geometry, the damage to other sentients is profoundly minimized. She, the pig, hasn't developed the neocortex to do the thinking about thinking—the meta-cognition necessary?" I asked.

"Hmm—Universally Ethical reflective sentients react in similar fashions across the multiverse," Mary added.

"You'd be surprised by how much a pig can do. But yes, nearly all of a pig's behavioral outcomes end up probable — expected. But it doesn't stop there. There are infinite ways to be toxic, cruel, and dysfunctional. These same endless shades of gray answering important questions are dysfunctional and carried over to your science, infinite ways of answering the same question, but only a few when all Expected Toxic Outcomes are actively being neutralized. Science, after all, is just specialized objective reasoning, not something magical meant for those credentialed few."

"The OCSs are guided by a complex system devised upon a particular understanding of the human mind and human behavior, each independent principle or Article might appear commonplace, but the complexity to develop and implement, get others to embrace — such a system from a primitives point of view appears nearly insurmountable," Mary said.

"Humans are quite capable of developing the necessary systems, but they have to want them and admit to their own dysfunctions; there are multiple levels and intricate caveats for our systems and procedures."

"Huh, I think I'm getting what you're saying. This constant reflection on what's driving us and a well-developed logical system has made us less… probable."

"Right down to finite Mastery of each Article, during an Obstacle Intervention, if someone refers to Article Spider, we need to be flexible with our Articles; it's always a jaw-dropping event. From a young age, we're taught to revere that Article, to only use it with caution. Our AI keeps track of who and how much one uses Article Spider; the use can end up being the basis for an analysis of the individual's Primary Cloud strength and density, which might include a complete background review. But I've used it—and so has everyone else."

"That—that is something to contemplate. A race that is pragmatic and systematic with a set of rules which provides a foundation for open-minded exploration requiring a particular Article not to be too rigid based upon the systems of being open-minded. I guess all rules, regulations, systems by their nature lend themselves to a degree of rigidity that may at times need to be situationally reassessed," I said.

We came upon a small old western-looking building, two stories with a porch on the second floor. Once white, but now in need of a fresh coat of paint. Thirty feet in front, a neon sign hung from an old wooden post that said "STORE." The neon sign moved ever so slightly back and forth, yet no wind was blowing, the movement making a metallic creaking sound. This was the first experience here that seemed fabricated or "Hollywood." The absurdity was palpable.

"What could that store possibly be? What could you need a store for here?"

"Using our *credits*, it's fun. We get them, then spend them here and in other places. The credits have a limited lifespan. Being we're all still hard-wired to be incentive-driven, it's an amusing activity that has been accepted as part of the makeup of our minds. We don't repress any of our natural drives. We understand them, enhance them and use everything to our utmost advantage. That is… the entire engineered credits activity is a response to our mind's natural makeup. We enjoy it immensely! Our kids love it; a lot of early AFEs examine how *and* why oneself is so incentive driven."

"Huh," I said, squinting my eyes. "Every hardwired response is from the start an important AFE."

We walked in; a black and white cat sat in a chair behind a glass display counter. A voice from nowhere said, "Let me know if I can help you. Today, for you, every object costs 100 credits. The services are dependent upon your needs, but we have only the best comically skilled confederates… *aka* hired collaborators you can find!" He said with a smile.

Mary looked at Wolfzang and asked, "Is that a lot?"

He chuckled, "No, not really… but sometimes."

We looked in the glass cabinets. There was a dark gem, and under it, a tag reading, "Hope Diamond," there on the wall was a Van Gogh, a Kahlo, a Klimt, a couple made by da Vinci, and something that looked like a child's artwork next to the fine art. The showcase was full of labeled oddities; some I had heard of, others I hadn't. "Dissect an Alien," a 1980s toy, was within the glass showcase.

"These… things have got to be replicas? Right?"

"No, why should they be?"

"Can I hold it?—The Hope Diamond?" I asked with childlike enthusiasm.

"Yeah, me too! That's nuts!"

"Sure."

"Oh — Lynxling, I have some visitors that would like to see something." A man in his 40s wearing very realistic moving cat ears, a black old-timey button vest, and a white button-down shirt walked around the corner.

"They'd like to see that gem there, the Hope Diamond."

"Sure!" His cat ears were so lifelike, as he spoke they moved in the direction he was speaking and moved to convey emotion.

"This is amazing!" I said. We passed the small dark gem-like stone back and forth. The diamond that I had so many times heard about on television and in the news, and now incredibly, it was there scattered around other unrelated things. It seemed sacrilegious to treat such a venerated object like any other. But then, holding it, I could see their perspective. I put it back on top of the counter. Mary held it but quickly became more interested in the many other objects and lost interest as well. After feeling it, holding it, it immediately occurred to me it wasn't any different to them than a rock found on the beach, in a backyard, on a path. We'd only written in our own book that it was more important, more exclusive than other beautiful crystals. We erased the belief and quickly moved on.

"Are you looking for something… particular? We sell unique original items of all sorts. *Everything* has got a story!" He said in a whimsical voice, "But our biggest sellers are tomfoolery related, y'know, jokes, hilarious gags and gag-related services. Things bought to resonate the drives and overpower the P-Cloud."

"These items—all of them are for what we can do with them, what they mean to the others we're working with. Just the mere presence of these items has particular impacts on our work or can be used to accomplish a particular task." Wolfzang said, then picked up the cat that had just jumped on the counter. Wolfzang calmly scratched his back. "We're intensely into our candid comedy. As you're kinda aware, we adore laughing at ourselves and lovingly teasing each other."

"These are all either gags or comical instruments to be employed during an AFE — Hmm."

"This is where I had picked up the Lincoln items I left on the beach."

"That was the real stuff!" Mary said with astonishment.

"So OCSs get a real laugh out of how each other responds to absurdities."

"Ah-huh, a race that comprehends our weakness to control the environment, you sort of always test each other, even poke fun at each other to help each other do even a better job of handling the unexpected."

"Precisely… it's all in good fun. We all love teasing each other with *the absurd.*"

I recalled a Greek and Roman literature course, the male spirit named Satyre, that I always pronounced satire. Aka, Silenus, Silenos or silliness. A being that was part horse with a permanent exaggerated erection.

I began to contemplate that if we weren't here, the surprising details I was now experiencing would leave enormous gaps in my deeper understanding of who Wolfzang was. It was easy to speculate with significant inaccuracies. My original perceptions would have persisted indefinitely if I wasn't attempting to objectively examine my thoughts. I recalled how I originally assumed he was a highly intelligent, sophisticated professor from some far-off university. My speculations and assumptions about Wolfzang's home, his *people* were thus far only somewhat accurate. I could have only imagined what I had been acquainted with, what made sense with my own limited experiences. I began to reflect how I'd in the past allowed my Narcissistic Drive resonate without reflection or restraint. I allowed myself before him to believe my experiences were so far-reaching and unique but they all weren't that different from others back there.

We soon satisfied our curiosity of "the Store" and pleasantly said, "OK… then — thanks for letting us look around."

"Gab-a-boo… Gab-a-boo!" Lynxling responded.

"I'm not overthinking *any* of it," I thought.

Temporal Rewind, Upper East Side

It was a little past noon the next day when I received an email asking us to meet him on Saturday at 8:00 am for a jog through Central Park. Unquestionably, we were now excited, anticipating him to contact us. Life was becoming a thrilling exploration, purposeful yet a little confusing. We were taking part in an experiment that could have enormous consequences. In his email, he mentioned his friend had a place on the Upper East Side; we could stop there if we needed to change or use the bathroom. A private bathroom was quite a luxury in that affluent prime tourist area.

"OK, this time? Is this when he's going to kill us?" Mary said with a smile and a sarcastic tone; I could tell she no longer thought he wanted to liquidate us. She went on, "Sometimes I think how he looked like a guy in his 80s when we first met him. Now he wants to jog through Central Park. It is still strange; what do you think, now maybe late 60s?"

"I'd say something like that."

We packed an extra pair of shorts and shirts in my jogging backpack; I was always a heavy sweater. We got our coffee and tea from Bank Square, got on the train, and fell into a deep conversation on the trip down the Hudson while sipping our drinks. "I can't get Aarav out of my mind; we are so disconnected from others that live such an excruciating existence and toil to survive, being born into such a vicious societal system as children, having no escape, with no hope. Couldn't they work as a group to get out of hell? Yet, those around him acted like a disease; they just pulled each other back into despair."

"Yeah, what stops them from working as a team to get each other out of the nightmare?" Mary said and then went silent for a moment. "But what about us, since these behaviors are so completely — obvious, naturally occurring in financially impoverished communities in the world? Since we're oblivious to the train we're on? Is it a natural occurrence, a group dynamic that should be expected?"

"I see the parallel you're drawing. They and others bring each other down and perpetuate the cycle; we can see where Aarav came from, but here we can't innovate or make discoveries exponentially because we cripple ourselves and each other? Are we doing the same stuff and can't see it here?"

"Hmm — not financially impoverished, but innovatively impoverished? Since the OCS exist and are a society that is so capable of exponential discovery and innovation, aren't we impoverished?" Mary said, looking out the window at the Hudson.

We got off the train and walked up to Central Park, and there he stood on the sidewalk, on the corner between 5th Avenue and 59th Street; I prepared the recorder. I was suspicious about how incisively he found us in the giant city, although I guess one might deduce it was the most likely route from Grand Central to Central Park. But now, sure, it was *our* black square.

In his running shorts and tight-fitting clothes, Wolfzang looked exceptionally healthy for a man in his — 60s. Until then, I never realized how much he cared for his health, not an uncommon attribute of others that inhabit the Upper East Side, yet uncommon in so many of the towns and cities Upstate New York. I still envisioned an older Wolfzang in my mind, but then again, I guess we all have our run-down-looking days.

"Wow, Wolfzang! You look like a professional runner," Mary said.

"You get one body in life; most don't drink nearly enough water," Wolfzang explained, sipping a blue bottle of water.

Without thought, we followed him jogging north into Central Park.

"Sounds like you've got my number," Mary said.

"I need to cut down on calories; I've stopped eating past six. If I'm extremely hungry, I can only have a healthy shake, fruits, vegetables or plain scrambled eggs. So, I've cut out the high-calorie uncontrolled nighttime eating."

"Unhealthy foods quickly become an escape and will be used to reflexively reduce your stressors and pressures in life. It's an omnipresent escape here; fattening foods are very absorbing to the mind, they act as a depressant, with the correct collection and metrics, around 66.66% of the U.S. is overweight."

“Prob-O-Planet,” Mary said in a voice reminiscent of Fat Albert.

“If you can’t take a couple of mile jog — if you’re just not up to it, you need to ask some deep questions about why you’re not caring enough about yourself. Why you’re allowing yourself to embrace inaccurate beliefs about good health?”

“Yup, I’m in that 66.66%,” I said, confessing to my obvious weakness.

I always found jogging helped with stress; it helped me sleep better, think more positively, and have some control over my weight. Those extra 25-30 pounds were hard to remove; Mary was always a great weight, no matter what she ate. The sights around Central Park never disappoint. We ran past several ponds and a bronze statue of Alice and Wonderland; there were already joyful youngsters playing on it, running through a small cave of bronze mushrooms. Getting a closer look, the details were incredible. The sculptor was a true master. From behind I peaked in to see the gills of the mushroom, a small alligator, and a rather large caterpillar. Alice reminded me of Mary playing with a cat in her lap, I thought of the deep love she had for *our* two cats. I imagined the rabbit to be myself holding a watch and obsessed with time, and the Mad Hatter as — Wolfzang.

After our 40-minute run, we followed Wolfzang out of the East Side of the park; as expected, my t-shirt was soaked with sweat, and I needed to change into my other clothes. Shortly, we arrived at his friend’s place. Wolfzang put in a code, and we entered, opening the ornate iron doors of the large brownstone expecting to see a hallway leading to separate apartments, only to realize that this was not an apartment building, but a lavish single home, a palace, with an incredible spiraling staircase. I could only compare it to historical tours I had taken in the mansions built during the Gilded Age in Newport, Rhode Island. Someone with great wealth owned this enormous home in this posh neighborhood. Was it Wolfzang’s? Would he admit it if it was? Was it an OCSs owned property?

“The bathroom is right there; I’m going to change upstairs and make a quick phone call; see you in a few minutes,” he said.

“You first,” I said to Mary and handed her the backpack with our clothes.

There were several pictures on the wall of people, were they his children? But then, going up the stairs, there were pictures on the walls of animals, but not the bucolic farm pictures one might see Upstate New York of pastures with cows and geese. But individual portraits, each picture reminding me of my own elementary school portraits with a solid-color background. It was as if each animal individually actually sat and posed for the picture. There was a cat, dog, duck, old and young cows, a pig, goat, sheep, chicken, monkey, and even an octopus. Looking at them, I swore I was looking at pictures of children, each with their own human feelings, their own hair nicely combed, each portrait revealing a personality. It had a strange impact on me. Each photo captured a natural expression on their faces, faces that weren't just animals. Each was a being that felt love, pain, and sadness. They could be joyful and playful, just like a child; I had never connected with art so deeply before that moment. Somehow, these pictures had penetrated deep into my recesses; I could feel a kinship with them. At that moment, even the word "animals" felt pejorative. This display of photographs did as the artist had desired. I felt a connection to the childlike innocence of each of them.

While I was on the staircase looking at these intoxicating photographs, Mary walked out of the bathroom and into a large, very white living room with a grand piano and built-in bookshelves.

Surprising us both, Wolfzang walked down the stairs to the first landing in a goose costume. Quite an elaborate well-made costume. Big goose butt, orange legs, and oversized feet. He looked like he could join a Sesame Street parade. His eyes and nose were visible inside the duck's bill.

"What the heck is going on? Why are you dressed like — that?" I asked, surprised.

"I'm on our computer system with some youngsters back home. I'll be down in another minute."

"Was that part of his perception experiment? Did he just want to see our response? Has all of this been to get us here, get us to play some weird role in an eccentric rich guy's fetish?"

"Yeah, right, I heard about that stuff. What are they called… Furries, people that like to dress up as animals. But I guess it's not always sexual," Mary said, then shook her head in confusion, and I entered the bathroom to change.

The bathroom was spotless, with white tiles, white towels; it was as if the place was just cleaned and rarely used. I couldn't help to think of Aarav, and how he had to share a hole in the ground with 30 other people, yet this exists and sits empty most of the time.

After changing, then leaving the bedroom-sized bathroom, Mary was standing on the staircase looking at the portraits; I gave her time to experience the art.

After a close inspection, I found that there were very vanilla historical and travel books regarding mainly New York City but also many other parts of North America, with no books hinting at the interests of the owners of this palace; I suspected this mansion was often used as temporary accommodations and owned by *the institute*. This collection of books seemed more fitting of a travel lodge than in this elegant ultra-expensive home. What type of filthy rich would bother having such an assortment of books even though the photos were quite vibrant. I thought of how I had heard of people being so wealthy that they have several such rarely-used mansions.

Wolfzang walked down the dramatic staircase now in typical non-bird related clothes, where Mary was still absorbing the portraits. "Quite incredible how each is so… beautiful, unique in his or her own way," Wolfzang explained.

"You say this is your friend's home?" Mary asked.

"One of my friends owns it. We're really into originality, expressing our own individual creativity, and harnessing the outermost limits of our imagination… but also enjoy recreating for historical accuracy to connect with a particular place and time. We're by NO means collectivists or communists, but our upbringing teaches us how not to be materialistic. It's all about the experiences in life. We're taught to keep the bicycle going; otherwise, it falls over." He said with a smile, messed up his hair for reasons unknown to me. "We like to stay busy; after a busy day, challenging ourselves to improve, challenging ourselves to find gaps or errors in our embraced beliefs, we sometimes need comfortable accommodations to refuel; we have been known to relentlessly push ourselves under unique situations to stay with a problem and make a discovery. I had one colleague, a good friend, that lived as a homeless person for months. After that, he needed a long stay of calmness, comfort, and healthy food to restrengthen his cloud-like network of billions of neurons, mainly in his neocortex. He stayed here for a few days, slowly removing himself from his AFE before returning home to help his mind garnish the fullest — comprehension of the… experience. These lavish accommodations may seem sort of overkill; you may not suspect it right now, but we get a lot of use out of it."

"This friend, couldn't he just have observed the homeless for his study? Couldn't he have had some spy cameras around? He actually became one? For *months*?" I asked, imagining the extreme commitment such a study would require.

"So much important information could be missed because there is an avoidance or unwillingness of those interested in subjects to completely immerse themselves; three-dimensionally. There is way too much speculation, safe circular argumentation, positioning of theories, clinical analysis, embraced homogeneous beliefs by those certified to monopolize a domain of study. And far too little hardcore hands-on fieldwork that, to us, is the sweat stuff, real-world experimentation. One must move quickly and break things to find the answers," Wolfzang explained.

"Like you had said, we come up with our emotional beliefs and then support them with complex logic. We must have emotionally felt how hard such an immersive experience would be and decided a nice clean, comfortable office would be far superior and thereafter defended our insulated, inoculated, and shielded discovery system," I said.

"I remember you saying about Einstein, was it? "All knowledge of reality starts from experience and ends in it," Mary said.

"As you've said, competition for competition's sake causes unforeseeable blockades and detours away from achieving discovery; it's not as — well useful or efficient as we've concluded."

"Since 66.66% of us have a tendency to be more often self-interested and use logic to defend emotionally founded beliefs."

“I’ve heard so many times in my business classes, ‘competition is good!’”

“Hmm, yes, that is a common saying *here*. It’s a very vague embraced belief and emboldened by one’s emotional drives. It’s like saying speed is *good.* Yet, you wouldn’t want some self-interested, pathological liar going down the thruway at 150 miles an hour, weaving in and out of traffic. Nearly killing several other drivers because ‘speed is good.’ Speed is *good,* done by the right kind of people, under the right conditions.”

“Ha! You have a talent at making complex things easy.”

Mary continued to look at the portraits. “They’re captivating! Aren’t they… Mary?” Wolfzang asked.

“Yeah, I don’t know — beyond captivating; I can’t stop looking at them. Some of them make me feel sort of sad. I want to hold them,” Mary responded.

”Yes,” he sighed.

“Des Legumes is a new vegan restaurant close by; I haven’t tried it yet. Let’s continue our discussion there.”

“I tried to be a vegan a few times. It’s exceedingly hard. Dairy is so hard to avoid, especially if you don’t have time to plan. You know pizza, ice cream, butter, eggs; I consider myself a vegetarian, though,” Mary responded.

“As a vegan might define it, I can’t say that I’m 100% vegan; we have several chickens and raise them quite naturally. They couldn’t be happier, part of the family. I’ve eaten their eggs, I’ve had honey before, and once I tried cow’s milk, it was delicious. She was lactating a tremendous amount for her baby, and my family took a quart for ourselves. We’re accustomed to a lot of food you don’t have around here. But you can find some things I love, like cashew cheeses, cashew ice creams, or coconut-based ice creams. Do you like Indian food? It’s so good. Indian food has so many nice spices; the Indian food I eat has no animal products at all. There are a few good Indian places near 28th Street.”

“I’ve been a pescatarian for a few years now; I learned heart disease was the number one killer in the U.S., and animal fats are a huge part. A healthier diet could help me keep my weight down. I do break down and have a hamburger once in a while,” I said.

“Heart disease kills almost 700,000 people a year in the U.S.. Most of those deaths could be avoided by decreasing animal fats; it’s acutely unhealthy for humans.”

“I recently heard a woman over a 110 from Jamaica. Was her name, Daisy or Iris? Said she thinks she’s lived so long because she doesn’t eat chicken and pigs,” Mary said.

“There are those that staunchly deny a link between animal fats and heart disease.”

“You’ve gotta be kidding me; there are people that deny the relationship?” I responded.

“That reminds me of the doctors that used to recommend a specific brand of cigarette. Soooo insane!” Mary explained.

I recalled a Jack Benny show where doctors actually promoted smoking-specific brands like Lucky Strike.

“You can find anyone with any credential to support anything; it’s just the Ethical Bell Curve in action,” Wolfzang responded.

“Hmm, *‘How to Lie With Statistics*,’” I said with a grin.

“Regarding our research exploration, examining components, qualities, and fundamentals necessary to make large-scale behavioral changes with slight effort. Moralizing is to be avoided at all costs; you can’t reach someone when you resonate one's Feelings of Inferiority. Even though guilt and shame are both widely used here to control others, they are quite conflictive to the human mind and lead to too many unexpected, often unhealthy, side-effects.”

“I think I get what you’re saying, that is, making someone feel bad backfires. The walls go up; they stop listening. It is not an effective instrument long-term to change behavior, especially when an embraced belief is a strong societal norm." Mary said, then paused for a moment and finished by saying, "and it's all related to your fascinating work."

"It's a difficult line to walk. Describing the necessity of being Universally Ethical to continuously operate the Tool questions one's embraced beliefs. When you store an idea in the Embraced Belief Cloud Network, the idea becomes more than just any idea. Endless energy is expended to creatively protect its existence. The idea blends in and is normalized as part of a typical life."

"Like you said, frustration not reasoning follows when someone examines an idea you store there."

We left the lavish mansion. Using a code, Wolfzang locked the enormous iron doors, and after a ten-minute walk, we arrived at Des Legumes, a crowded, vibrant vegan restaurant on the upper east side. The type that was so sophisticated that you ordered at a register, clearly overpaid; then only if you're lucky, found a seat. After all, the owners are so secure with who they are that how or when you eat the food you paid a premium for is none of their concern. We all ordered vegetable pot pies, salads, and house-made ginger sodas. Everything came in recycled cardboard containers. We were one of the fortunate and found a table.

"OCS utterly accept that indigenous people, or even those living under certain conditions, needed to eat animals to survive. It was indeed a very practical part of survival for early… primitives. But now, for the vast majority, there are so many options. If humans desire to make exponential scientific advances, they must question all current practices; questioning all accepted norms is part of being able to operate the platform — to be sustainable."

"I'm having a hard time seeing how eating meat has anything to do with scientific advancement," I explained.

"To be a continuous operator of the Tool, you have to be Universally Ethical. You can't just be ethical as it pertains to the human perspective, you can't simply pretend. Eating other very emotional sentients is a clue that the race acts emotionally upon their own — self-interest. Those behaviors pervade and contaminate all parts of science and technology. All the way to the astronomically important discovery and innovation processes. There is a direct relationship between a deeper reflective nature and how seamlessly and inextricably operators can perform intensive, prolonged examinations during the discovery process."

"Hmm, in other words, the behavior itself is a clue that the race is acting emotionally, not Universally Ethically, and that suggests we have a limited ability to work effectively to do the big stuff — time travel."

I thought of the beautiful animal pictures on the wall. "I can see the relevance you put on mastering the principles, the emotional reflexive nature of what OCSs consider the Embraced Belief Cloud Network. Without a deeper understanding of how it drives human behavior, how can you study alterations in large-scale human behavior?"

"I think I get what you're saying. If we're guided by our emotions and make endless decisions based on what's good for ourselves is correct, what stops those inventing and exploring from working in a team and caring about what's good for themselves? Therefore, our science gets contaminated by those that should be neutral, objective, not controlled by the biggest narcissist in the group."

"Quite — you're both making the connections that are essential to understand our systems. It's an acceptance of suffering needlessly inflicted upon your fellow sentients; this deeper connection here is often untenable. But besides that, this misconception of what it means to be ethical infiltrates every aspect of society; there are so many related counterproductive interactions that someone on the same train might consider nuances, typical, acceptable human interactions, but when added together, make a race that will destroy itself and not have the opportunity to evolve."

"Huh, it's a symptom of us being able to embrace self-interested fictitious explanations rather than have a firm grasp on what it is to be — Universally Ethical, and as you said, it is essential to have high scores in all three bell curves to operate the Vac-Plat," Mary explained.

Looking at a large photograph on the wall of a pig surrounded by daisies and smelling them, Wolfzang continued, "You know their brains; the dynamics of their minds are very similar to yours. These beings that you rename for food, pork, sausage, deli meat… words and phrases are used to hide the likelihood of connecting actions to the actual inhumanity of the killing. Like saying 'processed the meat,' instead of inhumanly and often cruelly executed, to dehumanize them, so the actions don't make you feel *sad*, thereby, asking '*why*' — hurting the profitability of the — operation."

"Like you were saying, we don't like to be made to feel bad; we'll tune you out immediately. The defenses will spring right up. Just to think I used to eat them; I'd sooner eat an evil person." Mary responded with a grin; she was known for making jokes about eating people that were evil instead of innocent animals.

Wolfzang smiled and responded, "I suspect, under current market conditions, you'd best regulate that practice extremely well before the term evil person is misused to include those that disagree and are political dissidents."

"How do you think their minds are like ours?" Mary asked.

"Animal brains are very similar. If another Tool building sentient contrasted yours to any mammal's brain, they would see far more similarities than differences. Watch these vulnerable sentients asleep, dreaming. That state of dreaming is so innocent, so playful, and so related to their own Genetically Important Drives in their brainstems. Just like you, the use of escapes is happening when they dream. They are truly your brothers and sisters on the evolutionary tree."

Sitting quietly for a moment, on some level, uneasy. I had — misgivings thinking I might be persuaded out of ever having a hamburger again. I had so many good times in New Paltz, after a long day studying for useless college courses, late at night eating burgers and drinking margaritas. Maybe I was close to bridging the connection he was attempting to make, but I felt something — somehow put off with the conversation. Yes — I felt a little annoyed.

"OK… you've been trying to teach us to express it when we feel—well, frustrated. Why am I feeling uneasy?" Thinking quietly for a moment, they both seemed to go silent and allowed me a moment to reflect on what was bothering me. "I think because I enjoyed a good burger and fries at the New Paltz College Bar, I had some great times! Just thinking about it makes my mouth water." I responded, trying to get my feelings out without allowing myself to appear irritated.

"Perfect, you're listening to the emotional part of your mind without letting it direct you, you're not attempting to support your emotions with logic, you're allowing yourself to feel frustrated but not succumbing to the frustration… you're — objectively reflecting on your emotions, it's among the hardest things to do. This is all essential, and I must say excellent work. It might all seem trivial, but quite conversely, it's huge."

"Hmm, from your vantage point, is it that Dan's not forcing a storyline to fit the emotion and attempting to make it pretty or socially acceptable?" Mary asked.

Looking at me, he replied, "You are truly feeling it and then pragmatically, objectively attempting to analyze it. *That* is essential for what we're doing!"

As he spoke, two women moved their seats closer to us; the place was packed, a few newcomers looked closely at the amount of food on our plates, likely speculating if we were amongst the next to leave, calculating to themselves how much longer we'd be hoarding the chairs we sat in. I quickly concluded the food was not worth these continuous subtle contentious encounters. This business owner approved and green lit a consumer struggle for limited resources. She or he must have made those on the receiving end euphoric by increasing profitability and decreasing integrity. But in the New York City trendy foodie scene when it was "in," seating became competitive.

Wolfzang, not skipping a beat, returned to our unconventionally traversed perception project. "The mind is trained to redirect the emotionally felt frustration. If frustration is overblown or directed at the wrong person, it can lead to death of the person demonstrating the frustration." He explained, then drank some of his ginger soda and continued, "I can't blame you at all. I can see that it must be annoying to hear someone say why your delicious hamburgers connected with emotionally good times are anything but *great*. But stick with me. Whether you eat hamburgers is not what I'm attempting to bring to your attention. It's grasping the concept that universal ethical behavior matters to the continued existence and prosperity of the human race. To your children and your children's children."

I wanted to understand what he was attempting to say. I loved getting paid for this side gig research project and wanted to continue working with him. So, I attempted to deeply comprehend the OCS's very distinct perspective. "The OCSs pragmatic belief in philosophy is that there *is* Universal Ethics, and if we had a better understanding of *it,* wielded it correctly, like OCS, we could be more innovative, seamlessly work in unison for exceptionally longer, more intensive periods of time. Thus, making unfathomable progress, rather than spinning what's ethical, arguing what defines it around and around like a circus show," I said.

"Exactly, just shadows on a cave wall. I'm impressed. Moments like this show me why I love working with you two; you are accurately connecting the pieces, comprehending a different culture, and reflecting upon your own current cultural beliefs."

"That's why I enjoy working with him too," looking at me, Mary said with a flirtatious smile, putting her hand on my knee; as always, she was capable of having great sex appeal with a side of charisma. "Cows, chickens, ducks, goats, sheep, and pigs are so beautiful. They're so trusting and vulnerable. I'd love to have a pig as a pet," she explained.

"One guy I worked with had a pig as a pet. He was a councilman in Peekskill; the pig walked around the house like the family dog, such a smart animal. He said pigs are more trainable than dogs and proved it. The pig did a little dance upon request; he knew the difference between left and right. Such a friendly animal. He always wanted to nuzzle everyone; he was exceptional!"

"Since there are such strong emotional attachments to cats and dogs, killing them for meat doesn't happen here, they resonate your Yearning for Emotional Closeness, but for the highly emotional, highly intelligent pig, here in the U.S., they are killed 300,000 times a day and 10 times that across the world," he responded, gazing at the menu above the registers; then paused for a moment. "They have powerful emotions, just like the human animal. Did you know — mother pigs hum to their babies?"

"That's… incredible! Hum to their babies to calm them down; I didn't know that. That's positively beautiful," Mary responded.

Have you ever read *The Jungle*? By Upton Sinclair? He asked.

"I never did. My sister did. I know she talked about it. Something about people falling into vats of food and then eating them?" I said.

"It was written in the early 1900s it's still quite insightful. Some changes have occurred in some parts of the world. They try—try to stun the poor pigs prior to killing them, here anyway, but it's not always successful because of the masses being killed; all factory work has errors and malfunctions. Even stunning, the poor being isn't regulated in all parts of the world. Beyond that, one doesn't realize how much it messes with the minds of the people killing the pigs; some of these pigs try to nuzzle them, try to be affectionate even after very cruel conditions they're under, but the primitive's jobs are to hit them to get them out of the cages to kill, cut their throats, beat them, to stun them. The repetition of factory work can't be dismissed. The impact on the deeper mind is enormous, dismissed as part of the job, repressed — never discussed. The intense killing is treated like it's just not a thing that should affect a *normal* mind. But you can't just walk away from that… job without significant weaknesses."

"That would be animal cruelty otherwise, and they'd be locked up, I hope," I explained, feeling overwhelmed by what he was explaining.

"I've never thought about it, although, actually, come to think about it, Mark Zuckerberg said you should "kill your own food." Maybe that's his point. Without being preachy, maybe, he thinks if people actually saw this shit, they wouldn't want to eat meat ever… again?" Mary questioned.

"Hmm, that could be it; we were both wondering why he said it. Honestly, it sounded a little out of touch, sadistic," I responded.

"Growing up, how about those commercials for hotdogs with the kindly grandfather voice saying how they only use the *best* meat? Wow, once you connect how truly alike, we are, you're right. Things get weird; you erase and put different words in *the* book. Once you feel we're made of the same stuff, have the same emotions, similar brains, backbones, innocently dream, similar anatomy, I mean, we're just not taught to think about it that way," Mary said, looking like she was pondering.

"Do you think those that have a pig heart or kidney think any different? We're using their parts maybe we shouldn't be eating them?" I said with a grin.

Out of his pocket, he pulled out two pieces of paper folded into four, unfolded them, and handed a copy to each of us; without hesitation, we read quietly.

"It was a long, narrow room with a gallery along it for visitors. At the head, there was a great iron wheel, about twenty feet in circumference, with rings here and there along its edge. Upon both sides of this wheel, there was a narrow space, into which came the hogs at the end of their journey; in the midst of them stood a great burly Negro, bare-armed and bare-chested. He was resting for the moment, for the wheel had stopped while men were cleaning up. In a minute or two, however, it began slowly to revolve, and then the men upon each side of it sprang to work. They had chains which they fastened about the leg of the nearest hog, and the other end of the chain they hooked into one of the rings upon the wheel. So, as the wheel turned, a hog was suddenly jerked off his feet and borne aloft.

At the same instant, the car was assailed by a most terrifying shriek; the visitors started in alarm, the women turned pale and shrank back. The shriek was followed by another, louder and yet more agonizing — for once started upon that journey, the hog never came back; at the top of the wheel he was shunted off upon a trolley, and went sailing down the room. And meantime another was swung up, and then another, and another, until there was a double line of them, each dangling by a foot and kicking in frenzy — and squealing. The uproar was appalling, perilous to the eardrums; one feared there was too much sound for the room to hold — that the walls must give way or the ceiling crack. There were high squeals and low squeals, grunts, and wails of agony; there would come a momentary lull, and then a fresh outburst, louder than ever, surging up to a deafening climax. It was too much for some of the visitors — the men would look at each other, laughing nervously, and the women would stand with hands clenched, and the blood rushing to their faces, and the tears starting in their eyes.

Meantime, heedless of all these things, the men upon the floor were going about their work. Neither squeals of hogs nor tears of visitors made any difference to them; one by one they hooked up the hogs, and one by one with a swift stroke they slit their throats. There was a long line of hogs, with squeals and lifeblood ebbing away together; until at last each started again, and vanished with a splash into a huge vat of boiling water.

It was all so very businesslike that one watched it fascinated. It was porkmaking by machinery, porkmaking by applied mathematics. And yet somehow the most matter-of-fact person could not help thinking of the hogs; they were so innocent, they came so very trustingly; and they were so very human in their protests — and so perfectly within their rights! They had done nothing to deserve it; and it was adding insult to injury, as the thing was done here, swinging them up in this cold-blooded, impersonal way, without a pretense of apology, without the homage of a tear. Now and then a visitor wept, to be sure; but this slaughtering machine ran on, visitors or no visitors. It was like some horrible crime committed in a dungeon, all unseen and unheeded, buried out of sight and of memory.

One could not stand and watch very long without becoming philosophical, without beginning to deal in symbols and similes, and to hear the hog squeal of the universe. Was it permitted to believe that there was nowhere upon the earth, or above the earth, a heaven for hogs, where they were requited for all this suffering? Each one of these hogs was a separate creature. Some were white hogs, some were black; some were brown, some were spotted; some were old, some young; some were long and lean, some were monstrous. And each of them had an individuality of his own, a will of his own, a hope and a heart's desire; each was full of self-confidence, of self-importance, and a sense of dignity. And trusting and strong in faith he had gone about his business, the while a black shadow hung over him and a horrid Fate waited in his pathway. Now suddenly it had swooped upon him, and had seized him by the leg. Relentless, remorseless, it was; all his protests, his screams, were nothing to it — it did its cruel will with him, as if his wishes, his feelings, had simply no existence at all; it cut his throat and watched him gasp out his life. And now was one to believe that there was nowhere a god of hogs, to whom this hog personality was precious, to whom these hog squeals and agonies had a meaning? Who would take this hog into his arms and comfort him, reward him for his work well done, and show him the meaning of his sacrifice? Perhaps some glimpse of all this was in the thoughts of our humble-minded Jurgis, as he turned to go on with the rest of the party, and muttered: "Dieve — but I'm glad I'm not a hog!"

Mary's face became pale. "This is true, isn't it… it's STILL happening? All day long, all over the world? For over a hundred years, all day, every day? Millions of beautiful pigs a day in the world? If you're right and these creatures share our ability to feel emotions to feel love, I can see why other aliens that are forced to fit the criteria of being Universally Ethical to invent and operate their own Vac-Plat, why they don't care to visit us… we suck! This huge number every day? It's well-kept behind the scenes. You never happen upon a pig getting killed; you never have to even think about this, like Upton Sinclair said, 'buried out of sight and of memory.'"

"This carries a strong emotional charge; the discussion needs to be a delicate balance. As Dan astutely disclosed, it's hard not to put up the walls when you hear things that challenge embraced beliefs. That was only a discussion about a simple hamburger. That wasn't challenging, an unquestioned societal norm. You are both incentivized by our endeavor to challenge your preexisting beliefs and keep an open mind. Now, imagine if you weren't partaking in my academic experiment to analyze your reflexive responses. You might just say, 'This is nuts' and then rationalize it by saying things like 'everyone eats meat,' or 'if I don't eat meat, it'll just go to waste — if I don't eat meat, it's not going to change anything.'"

"That's so weird. I did think those things… in the past."

"I get it; there's something else here. It's not about the pigs, the ducks, or the cows. It's an essential ingredient in the operation of the Vac-Plat. For reasons we don't yet entirely yet understand, without this mindset, the platform malfunctions," Mary said.

"Yes! Precisely!"

"So, *that's* interesting. It's actually about our inability to see it as unethical, connecting these behaviors, and not being influenced by societal norms. That's what keeps us from creating the Tool? I still can't believe the numbers are so high."

"I'll be right back. I'm going to go use the bathroom," Mary said.

"Love you," I said, knowing that Mary was struggling with the thoughts of so many trusting pigs being mistreated. She stood up, squeezed through the room of countless hungry patrons jammed closely together, standing in line, hovering over those sitting, waiting on the line that was now stretching to the front door. I realized holding an empty seat wouldn't be comfortable to maintain, so I quickly placed my backpack on it.

"I'd like to do an AFE, our first immersive observation outside of Manhattan in New Jersey. I know it's challenging, but continue to examine from multiple perspectives the divergence of our cultural beliefs. When we're there, you may have to go along with an important storyline. Camouflage. Quite minor, like you're both my kids or something. If you ever feel uncomfortable at all, you need to promise to tell me. We can rearrange the fieldwork easily."

"OK, is this when you have us knock over a bank and drive a getaway car? Is this it? Is this the big ONE that we've been groomed to do?" I said with a smile.

"That would be needlessly complicated — if those were my intentions. I could simply pay someone a couple of thousand bucks for that kind of support," he said with a smile, then continued more seriously, "I assure you, the work that's being done is exactly as I've explained — my interest is of a very specific behaviorally based academic nature. Is this Thursday morning OK for you both?"

I paused for a moment. I knew we had no classes; I was teaching a spreadsheet program in an adult computer class that night. Mary was tutoring a couple of kids that evening. So I replied, "I'm sure we could do it next Thursday morning."

Mary returned from the bathroom and said, "It's so funny. I checked the bathroom cabinets. They had bathroom cleaners and soaps made by companies that test on animals. Places like this kill me; they promote their expensive chichi vegan food, put on a good show, and then don't even buy products in the bathroom that *don't* test on animals."

“That is a fascinating observation; it makes you feel like their hearts aren’t truly into it,” I said.

We got out of our seats, which were immediately claimed by the next group before we even left the table.

Wolfzang walked us to Grand Central, and five minutes later, we were on the train to Beacon, anticipating our upcoming AFE.

That night I received an email that was entitled the *Cambridge Declaration on Consciousness,* “when you have completed the journals, please add this to the back as part of ‘Reference Materials,’” he wrote. He also added the address for our observation.

Child Care Center

Thursday morning, after picking up coffee and tea, then taking over an hour-and-a-half ride down the New York State Thruway, we found ourselves parked outside of a Jersey City community center.

"That was an exhausting drive," Mary said, being sympathetic since I drove. She was right; speeding, being tailgated, and getting cut off was conventional driving when heading toward the city on a weekday morning.

This particular community center was minutes from New York City. We immediately noticed many middle-class families quickly dropping young children, toddlers, and babies off for daycare. Some parents might have been mistaken for upper class with luxury their cars. Still, it was immediately evident, by the disheveled, messy woman taking the children, the filthy unrelated clutter of old manila files, old scattered computer monitors, vintage computer towers, and wires scattered visibly through the front windows that no one with real money would send their kids here. I speculated they were all likely leased vehicles; used to impress other family members and coworkers.

"What could this be about? That was a long drive to see a daycare center. There are hundreds closer to us. But I guess we're getting paid… we've gotta show we're committed to the research," Mary said.

"So far, it's all been effortless to get paid to travel and attempt to understand a uniquely uncommon perspective from his *institute* — easy! It's simply surprising such a group exists. But you're right, to continue to see what that hologram was about, maybe this will help us understand it all."

We watched as parents would push a button next to the door, a painfully loud buzzer would ring, reminding me of *Silence of the Lambs*, then an older woman would appear and reappear. A clear victim of overwork and poor diet choices. Though it was quite a distance, I could see her gasping, difficulty breathing. Sometimes she'd carry a coffee, sometimes a doughnut. Something hit me as unfortunate but part of the fabric of what we perceived as normal. Maybe this wasn't what my fellow ‘primitives’ were meant to do. Watching beautiful youngsters rushed in by their very diligent, very time-obsessed fathers and mothers, these poor men and women were trading these very fleeting moments with these babies and toddlers for something other, something they perceived as essential to their existence. Maybe just scraping by paying for rent and affording to eat. Yet, somehow I felt these adorable children would only be like this, in these magical little bodies, with this extreme innocence for what would seem like seconds in the not-too-distant future.

Mary and I found ourselves repeating, “What could this have to do with the perception experiment? Or even the Vac-Plat?”

Wolfzang saw us from across the parking lot and walked over. “Let’s go in; I’ve explained to the workers we’re here to see my grandson Otter in his classroom and that you're his aunt and uncle.”

“Is this for real? Is he actually your grandson?” I asked while setting up my recorder.

“No, no, this is just one of our own here for a day and a half to help with a few experiments. We do start off young doing our AFEs,” he said with a smile. “So, after, I thought we could talk about what’s here,” he calmly explained.

“This endeavor of your group, isn’t it a little weird to use kids for these experiments? What was that kid they used for classical conditioning experiments in the 1920s? They’d scare the kid each time they presented a white rat.”

“Little Albert!”

“We’re pragmatists that love field explorations. It’s kinda like putting a baseball jersey on a kid here. We simply make sure there’s no impact on his exponentially developing mind.”

It was clear, once again, our reality, our embraced beliefs, were about to be examined. We were acquiring a taste for the OCSs vocabulary and perspectives. I became aware at a soon-to-be upcoming moment I’d fall upon an unexpected assimilation of a surprisingly unusual perspective of my surroundings.

Quietly we watched a mid-twenties, exceedingly well-dressed flawless mother drop off her adorable, pigtailed little toddler. “My friend Kelly said when she dropped her son off at daycare when he was two, she went to work and cried the whole day,” Mary said.

“Could it be that our emotional mind is aware we’re lying to ourselves? Somehow, Kelly knew it wasn’t correct. What we do here? Giving her child to a smiling, underpaid stranger, with no connections, no deep commitment to their success, to be entrusted with them — all day,” I responded.

“I remember even listening to her repeat over and over what a wonderful group of daycare providers worked there and how she didn’t have to worry, so of course, I told her, ‘That’s how everyone does it these days. I’m sure he’ll be fine,’ just trying to make her feel better.”

“I’ll have to agree with you. It is all quite common, perpetuated as the norm, and left unquestioned. All I ask is that you act like I’m your eccentric father. You’ll know when to jump in. We’re only going in for a few minutes. It’ll be a cinch; later, there will be plenty to write about,” Wolfzang said sheepishly.

“We can do that,” I happily replied.

After buzzing the door, then having the frumpy woman, this time carrying a new, barely eaten chocolate doughnut with rainbow sprinkles, slowly open the door, greeting us with, “Y—UP!” We entered this very dank-looking hallway, the lights loudly humming above us; a vintage greenish-blue paint on the walls gave the appearance they hadn’t been painted for over forty years. The women were all unhealthy; most looked like anachronisms, donning clothing stylish from when the walls were painted; most of them were not as disheveled as the one that had just opened the door, but each significantly overweight.

“Here is my other son- and daughter-in-law. They’ll be picking Otter up now and then. We wanted to see the place and see how my grandson is doing,” Wolfzang said to a different middle-aged woman.

Looking a little overwhelmed, yet uninterested in Wolfzang, she responded, “We’ll that’s — unusual. I’ll have to escort you in for a moment. I'm very busy with the kids, so if you wanna stop back another time, it'd be MUCH better."

"Yes, my dear, I just want to see his classroom for three minutes; his parents did tell you we were coming?"

"Yes — but we're much too busy for THIS — anyway, he just started coming here yesterday," she said without emotion.

"Yes, two or three minutes, and we will be out of your hair," he said.

We entered a room with four babies, some toddlers, and two unfriendly women. Both had bags under their eyes and clearly struggled with dietary challenges. Watching a few of the toddlers crying, two other babies swinging in electric sway swingers, going unnaturally fast side-to-side, neither worker seemed particularly concerned with the despondent babies or us.

Wolfzang approached one woman, "Does this facility pay you well, my dear? Do those babies usually cry so much?" he asked unassumingly.

With a strange surprised grin, "Um, no, just better than minimum wage. Why? We're taught to let them cry. Otherwise… they're going to think they're always going to control us, YA know, let em cry it out. It's the right way to go! The 'cry it out' method was invented by Dr. Spock and is scientifically proven to work," she said, sounding extremely self-assured about her chosen scientific philosophy.

Wolfzang looked over at me; I acknowledged his hint and jumped in, "You'll have to excuse my eccentric father. He often asks intrusive questions. He cares deeply about how others are making ends meet."

The pretty little girl with pigtails we saw being dropped off was in the room. She sat on the ground and cried, "Mommy… I want my mommy, mommy!" The woman walking around her simply ignored the crying. We soon realized from their perspective the sobbing girl was to be ignored due to her "bad behavior." She needed to be taught her place in this mechanized relationship between her and these unhappy, abysmally paid caretakers that would tell her what to do, not the other way around. It was painful to see her go from being a perfectly satisfied, joyful little being and to now completely stressed and purposefully ignored.

Wolfzang pulled out a beautiful teddy bear from his jacket pocket. Once again demonstrating his magician-like propensity, there was no puffiness in his jacket, no bulge to conceal this stuffed little bear. The exceptional quality of the stuffy was outstanding and unquestionably handmade. But what was most inconceivable was that on the back of its beautifully knitted sweater, someone had knitted the words "Anne's Teddy."

"This is for you, Anne… we all love you! Don't let this place hurt you!" Wolfzang said calmly and directly while kneeling down and handing it to her as the workers' backs were turned and their focus was on other — duties. The new beautiful bear and Wolfzang's words seemed to calm the little girl. Mary gazed at the sight with an unbreakable stare.

"I think that was already enough today. In this short time, you've gotten an excellent three-dimensional sample; you've actually observed volumes. Let's see what we can surmise. We'll go to a diner close by and try to wash the negative energy of… this *place* — away." We accompanied him out the door, got into our own cars, and followed him. Today he was driving a BMW of some sort that seemed to be a more current mode of transportation than the much older classic vehicle he had previously shown up in; the driving continued to be — demanding. One needs to prepare themselves mentally before driving in Jersey City during rush hour. Simply turning into the diner's parking lot and crossing two lanes of traffic that were speeding at us was unnerving. Somehow these Jersey drivers went from stopped to breaking the sound barrier.

We entered the diner. Without a word, a waitress pointed out a booth while placing three menus on the table, followed immediately by three glasses of water, giving us a nod and a smile.

Wolfzang took off his jacket and placed it on the side of him. We hung our jackets on a post next to the booth, sat, and placed the recorder on the table. He immediately began, "Long ago, we realized to develop the most powerful operators of the Vac-Plat, those that make insanely brilliant discoveries, we needed to consider the development of the cloud-like network of billions of neurons, mainly in the neocortex. So, we began to focus on how to create the strongest possible cloud network, how to make this specific network as dense and resilient as neurologically possible, how to raise offspring that are capable of continuous four-dimensional thinking and maximum scores in the three bell curves."

“As you’ve said, these are the attributes operators need for the Vac-Plat, so it doesn’t like blow up or something?” I asked comically.

“Instead of a scary army of goose-stepping soldiers, OCSs are rearing a society of highly intelligent, multifaceted geniuses?”

“Yes, what followed for us was a complete reevaluation, a paradigm shift of what we thought to be normal, perceived as normal in so many past societies. If we wanted to raise our offspring to score what’s considered genius in all three bell curves, we had to completely reconstruct so many embraced systems.”

Wolfzang took a sip of his water, paused, and continued. “After attempting a non-dogmatic, completely independent analytically-objective view of what was successful to obtain our goals, that is, we needed to better define what makes a strong network cloud mainly in the neocortex — the Primary Cloud, our findings were more than… fascinating. They’ve changed *us*, as a society, even our simple mundane, mediocre interactions. You would find our approaches to child-rearing to be distinct; yours and ours are utterly disparate systems.”

“So, all the way down to everyday interaction?” Mary asked.

“Your *group* sort of thinks of yourselves as a society, not just an institute; that’s interesting. I mean, there are colleges in the U.S. with tens of thousands of students, but it’s even larger; you have a youth program? It’s more of a society that its citizens consider an innovation platform and not so much an institute?” I asked somewhat rhetorically, thinking out loud.

“I’d say that sounds accurate.”

“Now that’s astonishing. Your entire group is based upon the utilization of the Tool; even the nuances of child development are thought to be of extreme, absolute importance. All to get the most effective *operators*, as you call them?” Mary said.

“Exactly, the development of this network of billions of neurons, mainly in the neocortex, is the most important thing of all… *of all*!” He said with a smile. “Without the correct approach, our societal fabric would begin to crumble. Each and every developing child needs to receive this extremely nurturing developmental period; not fabricated, not seemingly, not a veneer, a real deep connective developmental period. After we developed systems that correctly aligned themselves with the creation of an exceptionally durable and flexible Primary Cloud, we nearly never observe *any* Expected Toxic Outcomes. ETOs are the things that the Tool is designed to neutralize."

"Since that's the case, I see why you take the matter so… seriously," Mary said.

Suddenly, I realized that they still had Otter at that gross daycare. In the car, we realized that Wolfzang never even pointed him out. "Aren't you worried about Otter?" I asked.

"He was only there for a brief period yesterday; he'll be out of there by 11:00 am today, never to return. We've got him under close surveillance. We've prepared it, so he's been sleeping for most of his time there."

The waitress approached wearing a blue and white checkered apron on which a name tag read "Dorothy." Yes, possibly by her own design, she looked like Dorothy from the *Wizard of Oz*, but with a sunflower tattoo on her arm. "So—do you know what you'd like?" She asked in a pleasant voice.

"Two coffees and one tea. Is it too early to order three garden salads?"

"Nope, can *do*!" She smiled, turned, and went through the double doors of the kitchen.

"Stress weakens the Primary Cloud. Kids that cry all the time are putting a great deal of stress on their developing minds. The emotional drives of the brainstem and limbic system will resonate, overpower and weaken the Primary Cloud. The infinitely powerful Yearning for Emotional Closeness will not be appropriately responded to. These uninterested, disconnected caretakers will ignore, even scorn, the children when they should be supplying affection, calmness, kindness — love. What they're doing there will weaken the all-important developing network cloud, not strengthen it. Over time, this can have some long-term significant side-effects."

"They all looked… miserable; the kids and the women."

"So, like, how? What types of side-effects?" Mary asked.

“There are many; if you imagine the Genetically Important Drives within the brainstem radiating through the Primary Cloud Network, one of the most important jobs of the cloud-like network is to conceal and console the emotional drives. The Genetically Important Drives within the brainstem and limbic system that evolved mega-annum ago to get primitives to survive long enough to have offspring. If this cloud network of billions of neurons, we call the Primary Cloud, the essential filter, isn’t capable of dealing with the passing emotions or if some of the cloud network is overstressed and develops poorly. That is, if there are weaknesses within the cloud, there are related side effects.” He said, sipping some water, then continued, “Well, one minor example might be the exaggerated Need to Control Others or control the environment. We all have some degree of Need to Control the Environment; although, if one's childhood was traumatic — after one embraces an idea into the Embraced Belief Cloud Network, the mind will fight to keep a controlled environment, fight to save the storyline they’ve embraced as fact.”

“There are two cloud networks composed of billions of neurons? Mainly in the neocortex?” I asked.

“Yes, one, the Primary Cloud network has several necessary responsibilities. It’s the filter responsible for addressing the resonating emotional Genetically Important Drives, it’s where thinking about thinking and executive functioning occurs, dealing with the *other humans*, and then it interacts with the — the Embraced Belief Cloud Network. One might consider the Embraced Belief Cloud Network the smaller network. These networks of billions of neurons dynamically interact and are inextricably interwoven with each other.”

“I think I get the dynamic interaction,” Mary said.

“Not me, but maybe… there are two network clouds mainly in the neocortex, the Embraced Belief Cloud Network and the Primary Cloud, but separately there’s the Genetically Important Drives?” I said with hesitance.

“Yes, the Genetically Important Drives are in the brainstem and limbic system and are where emotions are generated.”

“You say what you’re calling the Primary Cloud is a cloud-like network that's the go-between, the one that is dealing with our brainstems emotions, simultaneously dealing with our Embraced Belief Cloud Network, yet cares how the world sees us?" Mary responded.

"OK," I said.

"The OCSs use the term Primary Cloud instead of Ego because… as you said, we have too many preconceived associations with the heavily, perhaps overused term… Ego? That is, the OCSs working definition of the word Ego has significantly changed after reexamination, reconstruction; they now call it the 'Primary Cloud?'" Mary asked.

"True, for us, horseless carriage evolved to L-sport for land transport. As I once said, there are plenty of succinct differences, noticeable vocabulary differences that would occur over a period of time in an objective, pragmatic society."

"Don't psychoanalysis or the Freudian types find the term particularly annoying, you know, replacing stuff?"

"Well, the word 'Ego' is thrown around *so* willy-nilly here by every certified expert. The confused impressions of the term are astounding at times. But ironic if a group that is supposed to be about analysis and reflection finds being questioned and challenged annoying. The intricate complexities, the unrelated principles that we've discovered, therefore warranted such a — terminology review."

"I think we steered you away from what you were saying — about weakening this Primary Cloud."

"Yes, an out-of-control or dysfunctional childhood weakens an area allowing the Need to Control the Environment or Need to Control Others to overcome the Primary Cloud, so *when* that person embraces an idea, they can't cope with changing the embraced belief."

"WOW, I get it. I've known people with crazed political ideas — just nutsy. Some were in the Green Party, some were Republicans, left-wing or right-wing, but they were simply intense, nearly conspiratorial ideas. They functioned so normally every day, did their jobs, and were actually kind of nice. Otherwise, when it came to certain — beliefs, they were just… off. This guy Robbie thought the democrats were all conspiring together to become communists, and Sara, who was in the Green Party, believed all genetically modified foods were going to kill everyone."

"I've seen it too — in religious zealots. I mean the ones that won't let you have your own opinion or no opinion. When I worked at a summer camp, there was a woman there who just wouldn't stop; if you disagreed with her that Jesus is the only true God, she despised you like you had red horns and a tail. Relentlessly quoting all sections of the bible. When I couldn't respond, it was as if I should be convicted of a criminal act; the whole summer, I avoided her like the plague," Mary said.

"Yes, well, they've embraced these beliefs and will often show venom if you don't agree with them. Their Primary Cloud is overwhelmed by the Need to Control the Environment and the Need to Control Others. Then also supported by Feelings of Inferiority and the Narcissistic Drive. They believe if you were their friend, you must agree with every detail, and yes, this all comes from a very unstable, often traumatic childhood," Wolfzang responded.

"I can immediately see how that could enervate any group trying to innovate or discover, to have those types interwoven with what needs to be an objective experiment," I responded.

"Precisely. These poor primitives can be exceptionally intelligent, very capable in so many ways, but just have a weakening in the cloud because of the suffering or trauma in childhood; makes writing in pencil in their book too difficult."

"Wasn't Hitler beaten into a coma by his father? Talk about an unstable traumatic childhood. Then the unhinged rigid embraced beliefs that followed. Talk about someone that needed control of the world," I said.

"Very good, you're thinking — interdisciplinary, you're pulling from multiple domains of historical knowledge, fibers of discovery come from every direction."

I noticed Mary looking out the window. We both watched two men in pinstripe business suits get out of a spotless red Porsche. They showed a much different reaction to Wolfzang's car than we had; it must have been a recognizably fancy model to those in the know. Both men circled the vehicle, glanced inside. After looking at the car, the two men turned around and entered the diner, taking seats at the other end against a window. Returning to the conversation, "For the journals, how would you suggest that this experience is valuable to get a better understanding of the Tool?" Mary asked.

"Impressive… what a succinct question. You're wondering why *I'd* bring you here — exactly. Let's look at it this way, within the brainstem and limbic system, one of the two most powerful Genetically Important Drives is the Yearning for Emotional Closeness. This powerful drive helps to cultivate health, that is, the resilience and density of the Primary Cloud. If the experiences are mainly positive, the child has time to learn through peaceful exploration. If the beginning experiential interactions with others are toxic, detached, or punishing, the little one avoids others or demonstrates less enthusiasm for investigating the world around her or him."

"Hmm… that is, if the caretaker is nurturing interesting new things, the child relates their own emotional feelings of joy with learning. They examine and explore without hesitation, *not* expending the quickly evaporating brain time and power to avoid punishment — a concrete, remedial but time-consuming activity?" Mary said.

"Huh! That's quite a point."

"Quite right, calmness, positive affirmations, and love is the fuel that allows accidents during exploration to occur without inducing stress. *If* the child gets punished by an unstable caretaker frequently or unexpectedly during exploration or feels someone might withdraw from fulfilling their Yearning for Emotional Closeness they will have less time strengthening the quickly developing Primary Cloud; spending time and energy avoiding pain."

"I see," I said, thinking for a moment. "Yeah, there's more here! To understand your work or a society's larger behaviors. It's much more important to fully understand and profoundly care about this quickly developing part of the mind rather than just pretend it's going to grow strong no matter what conditions the child's mind is under," I said.

"If around the wrong *caretakers*, the child begins to avoid things that feel emotionally distressing, things that overwhelm them by impacting their Yearning for Emotional Closeness, no matter what the convoluted scientific reasoning to do it to them… or maybe the child is actually being punished by those that rely on punishment to change behavior.

Instead of pursuing and developing interests, building upon exponentially growing connections that become the seeds of future complex connections, the child attempts to solve the often unsolvable; dealing with probability, erratic emotional caretaker's behavior; some simply emotionally withdraw. *Here*, endless innocent little ones are trained to have critical abusive self-talk that cripples future prospects for themselves and so many others."

"Hmm, your point is — painful. So many little ones here put all that crucial, never to return, indispensable developmental time into dealing with the dysfunctional nature of those around them. But then forevermore are left with weaknesses," Mary responded.

"The mind is like a beautiful flower. All the conditions must be right at the moment when it will spontaneously grow. All things in the natural world grow organically on a cyclical wave on an upward axis. They must not miss connections that so much will later be built upon."

"That's incredible. These *essential moments* in time when the mind is growing exponentially, wasted, wasted forever."

"What is this society of yours like? With this approach, these focused fundamental beliefs?" Mary asked, wide-eyed.

"Well, since we realize our resources need to be allocated in the mind's development to our young, we are exceptionally nurturing, calm, loving, playful, silly, and even goofy by your standards. We have learned to be very attuned to following their interests rather than limiting them."

"I remember what you're saying. As kids, we needed to follow directions and be 'functional to fit in.'"

"I know, my father always said, 'kids are meant to be seen and not heard,' he pretended to be joking, but he really meant it," I said.

The waitress returned with the drinks, "You wouldn't believe this, but most of our salad is bad. I guess someone left it out too long. Would you like something else?" She asked.

"We're probably fine — do you have any other vegan options?" Wolfzang asked.

“We do! We have a super-duper vegan burger; it’s my favorite. I talked them into making it here!” She replied.

“Would you folks like a vegan burger on me?” Wolfzang asked.

“Sounds great,” I said.

“Yeah, great!” Mary said.

“I’ll let him know,” she replied and then walked to the kitchen.

Wolfzang continued, “What you would find the most amazing is how we treat each other. Can you remember seeing — family members that truly have a deep love for each other? You could immediately sense nothing could break the bonds, that they’re genuinely there to support each other without underlying motives?”

“I’ve always hoped the two of us exuded that type of energy, but besides, I have seen it from a distance. Things were so broken growing up that I undoubtedly dreamed of that kind of commitment — love. That’s not to say we haven’t struggled with growing, being married; we both kept so many of our family’s traits when we first got together, we like to say we’re growing up together,” Mary said.

“I think you’re both refreshingly honest and upbeat. The OCSs all act that way to each other. Maybe that’s why I feel very comfortable with the two of you.”

“That’s batty? How can the OCSs? What did Aarav say? Tens of thousands of people, and you say, act like an unusually affectionate and adoring married couple?” I asked.

“It's done, and there is nothing — well, romantic or physical about it. It’s a true genuine compassion and consideration toward each other. But what’s important to realize is that here it seems unnecessary, completely unrelated to science, technology, discovery, innovation, but that is why primitives fail.”

I thought about an article I once read about how Carl Sagan's parents were unusually loving toward each other. I wondered to myself if there was some relationship between that and his countless enlightened keen insights. His robust Primary Cloud, as Wolfzang might put it. Watching the cars go by, I then thought of all the road rage I’d seen. There is so much poison people are so easily willing to dish out to each other, quite the opposite of his description.

"It's true when I think of a genius scientist, I never think of lightheartedness or compassion. I think of factual and even a cold, a highly focused person wearing a white jacket, wearing glasses," Mary responded.

"Exactly. That perception is a misconception, a two-dimensional understanding of what is essential for productivity, innovation, and discovery."

I couldn't help to think of Einstein's lightheartedness and his well-known silliness.

"Without being there, seeing it, feeling it, primitives can't grasp the power a group has that has that degree of trust, dedication, consideration toward each other, the strong bonds become an unstoppable force, laser-focused at discovering, inventing."

"You're all not like swingers or something?" I asked, only half-joking, yet thinking this was the moment it all falls apart. After all, so much about the OCSs was contrary to us — here.

"No, no, my wife and I are both very committed to each other; it's a monogamous relationship," Wolfzang responded.

"It sounds like the OCSs genuinely do care deeply for each other!" Mary said.

"Very much so. It's a powerfully deep, uncompetitive brotherly and sisterly love. There's a complete interest of raising each other's ability to have the highest possible scores in all three bell curves, the derivative of which are unimaginable bounties for *all*."

The waitress returned with the burgers. "These are my favorite. They're actually made from beets, vegan bread crumbs, brown rice, lentils, thyme, dry mustard, onion, garlic, and almond butter. Are you all vegans? Here's a little of my own vegan cheese for the side. I sell vegan cheeses at some of the farmer's markets in the city… trying to make a go of it!" She said in her very vibrant Dorothy voice.

In this very unremarkable-looking diner, these burgers were anything but average. A red burger, the onions, tomatoes, arugula, spinach, ketchup, vegan cheese all came together in one bite. Dorothy suddenly wasn't a waitress to me but a vibrant genius-artist slash entrepreneur, passionate about all things vegan. I could see the city was on the verge of some serious vegan cultural shifting, and she would be one of the beautifully hearted, good witches.

"We're sort of attempting to be!" Mary said with a smile, then biting into the burger with an "Mmm! Unbelievable!"

Wolfzang tasted the cheese, "This cheese is *amazing*!" He said with great exuberance.

"Here's my card and the locations it's being sold." She replied. The card read, "Aunt Dot's Vegan Cheeses."

"We're in the city all the time; we'll get some soon!" Mary replied.

"It's the best! Let me know if there's anything else I can get for you," she said with a glowing smile. I could tell Dorothy was going to make a successful business person; she had a mission and loved her work.

Wolfzang returned to the subject at hand, "the understanding of the genetically important drive, Yearning for Emotional Closeness is all tangled up in your society. Many parents believe, 'I get that, you get this,' parents here are notorious for using 'love' as a commodity when no such thing should ever… ever happen. Many parents end up having their own interests at heart."

"I can see that. These discussions about parents and love can be charged with emotions. It's not like talking about math, science or discoveries, innovation, and aliens. The walls go forcibly up when talking about this stuff. It can immediately touch a nerve; I'd even put up a few iron walls," I explained.

We all took a few moments savoring our beet burger. I knew I'd have overlooked it *if* I wasn't being prompted to challenge my perception and try something new. After the first bite, I couldn't stop; it was delectable. The combination was divine, a word I reserve for very few foods.

"Acting deeply thoughtful, connected, and compassionate is an essential ingredient. Most here would see these essential qualities as completely unnecessary and unrelated to discovery and innovation. They may view fierce competition as the most productive way to create, innovate, and discover. Many would tag expressions from the very strong drive, Yearning for Emotional Closeness as needy or overly affectionate. But *that* is where our two cultures diverge significantly. Under the correct conditions, with the strongest Primary Clouds, and the best scores in all three bell curves, humans can achieve this bond on an unbelievable scale. The… the *thing* is, if I told you, with a complete understanding, grasp of the implication, and complete desire of developing this type of bond on an extremely large scale in society, the race becomes a race of multiverse time travelers. *But*, without the correct desire and understanding, you simply destroy yourselves," he said. We all sat silently as Wolfzang drank some water. "So, *if* primitives were directly given *that* exact — option, would they achieve the mandatory result? Or would certain ones amongst you just be incapable? Persuade others that it's a theoretical construct founded upon 'fuzzy thinking.' I suspect you'd see them continuously negate the thought as absurd, using persuasive sciency explanations simply because they're unwilling or, in many cases, completely unsure where to even begin developing such a dynamic."

"Wow, a combination of behaviors I've seen, all propelled by this drive in our brainstem and limbic system, these observable sustainable behaviors that show themselves under certain conditions within our population have that much of an importance to our future, and if we can't make it flourish by a certain point, we destroy ourselves? — *crazy*," Mary responded in a moment of clarity.

"Wow! Mary! But I see it too, the product, the prize we desire, curing disease, saving the planet, time travel. We think it's achieved by intellectual competition and toil, competing to get into the room, competing when we get into room. The entire process magnifying the wrong behaviors, and we're missing the ingredient that needs to be put into the mixture. We even treat the necessary ingredient like it's unnecessary, or even — weak, rationalizing against it, why we don't need it."

Having another bite of my burger and taking a sip of water, looking out the window and then toward the kitchen, I continued, "I think I get it; I always perceived future humans as well, like Spock in *Star Trek*, sort of a very analytical cold, smart and fixated on the facts. But you're saying it's not like that at all; for the human race to evolve to multiverse travelers, we need to embrace how this deeply rooted Genetically Important Drive in our brainstem and limbic system, this 'Yearning for Emotional Closeness,' how it actually functions, its principles and mechanics and then harness its power for the benefit of discovery and innovation?"

"Now, I'm impressed!" Mary said with a smile.

"Well, you know it helps to be writing the journals. I get to listen and re-listen to our conversations, so some of this stuff is kind of sticking."

"Exactly! What you said," Wolfzang responded, then paused for a moment, sipped some coffee, and continued, "As you know, our founders came to believe that only a few out of every large sample population of primitives were the right fit, so they cherry-picked the ones that had an array of specific mental attributes. After a sound foundation of like-minded, they focused on developing a hardy, dynamic Primary Cloud for all. The OCSs have since built upward, matured, and solidified their understandings and *thrived* — in a very multi-universal sense.

"Whoa!"

"Yeah — Whoa!"

The background music playing from a speaker above became louder, the song *Chasing Cars* came on. Dorothy must have been a fan because the volume got louder.

"Forget what we're told,

Before we get too old,

Show me a garden that's bursting into life!"

Mary must have also connected to the lyrics.

"It's all quite beautiful these beliefs of your… people, the OCS. You're giving us a highly refined, intricately developed, unique explanation of the possibility of a better world. I never imagined that would happen. I feel we're leaving our embraced beliefs behind. For us, this is becoming more than a sociological experiment," Mary said.

I felt what she was saying on a deep level. "You are... you're helping us attain a more dynamic Embraced Belief Cloud Network, aren't you?" I added.

The song continued,

"All that I am,

All that I ever was,

Is here in your perfect eyes; they're all I can see!"

I looked into Mary's blue eyes and thought about this beautiful cloud of flickering stars and sparkling connections in her mind. I imagined it in vivid detail, the energy, the twinkling of billions of synapses. It was as if I was traveling through her pupils as black tunnels, and I could see a glittering galaxy of billions of stars, all within a cloud of gas. Then, I saw beyond the cloud into the distance. I imagined her as a beautiful two-year-old. I could see her smiling and laughing. She was wearing a little dress. So innocent at two, not knowing her soon-to-be struggles that would pain her and carry with her into the future. But there in my vision, so pure, unhurt — trusting. Such an unbelievably beautiful glowing little girl radiating kindness to all the world. I glanced out the window and played off a tear, itching my nose while disposing of it.

It was there in that mediocre-looking diner, in that average booth somewhere in congested New Jersey of all places, I began to conceptualize what he was bringing to my attention. During one of our first meetings, he had said he saw the two-year-olds in all of us. But it wasn't as it sounded. I realized it wasn't just a meaningless platitude or inferring that we were nothing but a bunch of silly, know-nothing toddlers; there was great compassion in his words. This was what the OCS actually feel for *us*. Was this trip today designed to bridge our limited views? This indescribable enlightening connection that I could, with some support, have spontaneously drawn? Was it all pre-planned, pre-engineered? How could he have accomplished — *this*?

The two businessmen got out of their booth and were preparing to leave when they walked over to our table. “Hello, I’m Flavio; this is Marco. We couldn’t help to notice your — splendid car outside. We both work for *the* well-known Ritolli Brokerage House; we can promise double-digit returns on *your* money. That is *your* car outside—right?” Flavio asked, moving his hands unnaturally to help emphasize his words, directing his question more toward the senior member of our party.

“I’m afraid it’s my friend's car. He’s from old money, you know, captains of industry, that sort of thing. I’d be happy to give him a card if you have one?” Wolfzang asked.

“What’s your friend's name? Maybe I know him,” Flavio asked, now clearly being intrusive.

“I’m sorry. He’s asked that I don’t pass his name around, but I’ll see he gets your card.”

“OK — *thanks*!” He responded, apparently having no more legitimate angles or ideas to get to the money that Wolfzang was keeping from him. The two men handed him their cards and capitulated, said “goodbye!” walked out of the door, and did another lap around Wolfzang’s car, but with less enthusiasm.

“AFEs are both art and skill. Picking a vehicle, clothing, shoes, carrying something unusual; it can attract undue attention and then complicate the focus at hand. Yet, every unique and varied experience makes you better prepared for the future, and by now, I have had a vast array of uniquely useful experiences to draw upon,” he said with a smile.

He took another bite of his beet burger, waited a moment, then continued, “OCSs being objective pragmatists, we began to fully realize that a weakened Primary Cloud leads individuals to cause Expected Toxic Outcomes on the Vac-Plat. ETO's, being by far the greatest hinderance to all exponential discovery and innovation. These ETO's can be extremely subtle and one may easily assume they are natural, unimportant. As I mentioned these *things*, these naturally occurring behaviors are what the platform is designed to observe, identify and never underestimate. Therefore, everything, absolutely everything that could weaken the cloud during the human animals' developmental period *matters*."

Mary, leaning her face on one palm, looking a little depressed and contemplative, responded, "For a short time, I worked at a daycare right after high school. It was appalling; the other girls were so petty. They all talked trash about each other, and the place was terribly run. It was just a bunch of young girls who simply didn't care, just wanted the paycheck. The owner was such a narcissist. She was like 80; she'd come in once a day to see the place. Her make-up, hair, clothes, and shoes were always perfected. Talk about setting the stage for being disconnected. She didn't care about the kids; they were just income generators, but parents sent their kids there because the place looked *fancy*. Everyone knew to put on a nice face. She had a professional website, colorful brochures, gave a competitive price, was friendly, and rented a bus that sent the kids on day trips, but it was all for pazazz. There was NO love, no calmness, no nurturing in the whole place. The kids were scolded for the dumbest things. If a kid wasn't potty trained or pooped in their pants, the little kid would get screamed at. The two women that oversaw the place were always rigid and coarse with the kids; they didn't even like kids. It's so sad when you think about it; I'm so grateful I only worked there a couple of months!"

Thinking for a moment about our field observation, I explained, "I get it; they've embraced the cry-it-out method not because it's right, but because it makes life easier, it's less work. Then they defend the emotionally embraced belief with logic and reason."

"When she said 'it's been scientifically proven,' I'm sure she's said the same thing to the poor parents as if she's objectively investigated the matter; now they probably do it at home," Mary said.

"But, those that have a higher intelligence act just as self-assured and are better equipped to persuade those around them with their embraced beliefs using an entire arsenal of in vogue buzz terms such as 'evidence-based practice, clinical data proves' or 'empirically proven studies,'" Wolfzang responded.

Mary sat in deep thought and then said, "How long do you think they let those poor kids cry for? I would have never let that happen with the kids I watched."

Looking at us with concern," They let the sensitive ones cry for hours, very sadly… hours if they have to. Do you know what that does to a developing mind? Over time it weakens the little one."

Feeling a bit saddened by the practice, I responded simply, "That is painful to think about."

"Those poor kids and those poor parents. I know the parents want the best for their babies… their little ones; I wish they could see what you're showing us," Mary said, sounding glum.

"What you've said in the past about how market forces have taken over, do you think, sadly, the cry it out method is simply the most cost-effective for them? They'd have to employ more staff if they wanted to hug, cradle, provide love to the crying little ones, but since this belief is telling them if they respond, it'll just make them cry more later, they are incentivized to buy into it letting those tiny new beings cry ceaselessly?" I asked.

"Exactly. They are heavily reinforced to embrace the belief and then support the belief with tidbits of supporting information they happen upon throughout time. You know *confirmation bias* is a potent force for those that aren't attempting to objectively examine."

Dorothy returned, "How's everything?"

"Amazing," Wolfzang responded. "That's great that you're focusing on such vibrant locations in the city; lots of great ideas are lost by starting off in a sluggish community that can't support such a substantive idea; Starbucks started on Pike Place, a high-volume vibrant location, then they were able to experiment with ideas and had the capital to fail with their continuous well-calculated speculations."

“Hmm, I never thought of it that way; I guess I just want to succeed,” she responded.

“I’m sure you will, but from my experience, you’ve gotta love your failures. So many successes will only happen if you have plenty of bang ups. Try to have as many as you can. You have to fail first to succeed big. If you succeed on your first try, you're vulnerable to large failures due to undeserved over-confidence. The business you’ve chosen can thoughtfully decrease the desire for animal products. I honestly wouldn’t share my thoughts with you if you were in another business.”

“I can see that… about failing. I had a little store in a strongly conservative town with cheap storefronts and poor foot traffic. I thought people would find me, but it was quite dismal. The locals even made fun of the vegan cheese rather than help support the idea; I’m *so* happy I got out of there, but I learned a lot about business and people. Even though I broke even on that one, well lost a little, really — I guess. You’re right! Thinking about it now, I still found it to be quite valuable.” Dorothy responded, taking our plates away, then asked, “Coffee refill?”

“Those kinds of experiences are more valuable than getting an MBA from so many professors that have limited experience trying ideas out in real-time. You see things quite clearly; you’ll do fantastic; keep going!” Wolfzang said with a smile.

“I agree. I’ve been recently noticing some of my MBA professors have only had unending successes; they’ve never even once suggested they’d made any wrong moves. But they sure can tell you what everyone else is doing wrong.

“Unnatural growth.”

“I dated a guy like that one time. I know the type. His mother made his bed and washed his dishes until he got a Ph.D., then he got a great job, began to believe he was indeed the guy behind the desk with the answers, and never had a clue how rough life is. He really thought his opinions were unequivocally *correct*,” Dorothy said with a smile.

“Wow, I think you’re one of us!” Mary responded.

Wolfzang continued as Dorothy walked back to the kitchen, “You have to understand, these childcare workers are significantly overworked for the number of children they have to — monitor. They work to conform them, so they need as little direct attention as possible. Their goal is to keep them quiet, have them not look to them for nurturing; they are training them to unquestionably follow directives."

"Incredible!…. So cold, so sad, you can almost imagine where one can end up later in life if that's what's expected of them."

"They're being trained to march in line," Mary responded.

"But, to some degree, they're young; they have to learn to follow some directions?" I wondered out loud.

"The child that receives gentle nurturing around every corner develops an extremely dense, robust, resilient Primary Cloud. They follow complex directions exceptionally well and are geniuses at problem-solving. The mind isn't circulating in every direction dealing with their emotions, which can overwhelm them." He paused for a long moment, picked at a few remaining scraps of beet burger. "Though! There is something even more significant… What we find to be of the utmost importance to all of us. The true reason for exponential future discovery and innovation. That is, our enormous motivation for our laser-like focus on this very early development — the child begins to develop the ability to harness *imagination*. A child can begin to plan and use this most important instrument for discovery and innovation, the nucleus of all great things to come."

"But, it seems too typical. Don't kids just play, pretend naturally? I guess — I can see the importance. It's kinda like when I was a kid, how public television always promoted using imagination," I said, feeling skeptical about the importance of what almost seemed an exhausted-hokey term.

"It's essential… to fully comprehend the fundamentals of our work together; you need to grasp the imminent importance we put on mastering the ability to direct, guide, and harness imagination. I want you to think of today's visit as a glimpse of the period when humans have the earliest signs of the use of this creative complex phenomenon to comprehend the incomprehensible and to freely think four-dimensionally," he said, then went silent for a moment.

"This four-dimensional thing, how would you describe it."

“For us, for this project, it’s like being there with someone, knowing them, who they are, having a three-dimensional understanding of them, but then glimpsing at how they acted and looked as a toddler and imagining how they act and look throughout their existence, all the way to a very old age. One long connected image.”

“Huh, four dimensions applied to humans,” I said, pondering his point.

“Imagination can be a brilliant star that turns into a black hole. If the mind is weakened, it might become guided and controlled by the need for fantasy. Fantasy is an extremely powerful form of escape. Thereafter, the use of imagination during escapes might control them, possibly for their entire life. Escapes are, after all, as essential to the mind as water is to the human body. Imagination is like a beautiful beam of light shooting across space. You can ride it. Or, if you know how, you can harness and direct it to go to places that are simply *unimaginable*.”

“Right — didn’t Einstein have some sort of quote about knowledge and imagination? How did it go?” Mary asked.

“Quite right, brilliant thought!” He said with a smile. His enthusiasm for Mary’s point was palpable. “His best known was ‘I am enough of an artist to draw freely upon my imagination. Imagination is more important than knowledge. Knowledge is limited. *Imagination* encircles the world.’”

Dorothy returned with the coffee, gave us all a pleasant smile, and put the bill on the table. “Take your time; whenever you're ready, let me know if I can get you anything else,” she said.

“I think we’re just great,” Mary responded.

“Thanks, Dorothy, it was fantastic! Just wonderful; you are going to go right to the top!” Wolfzang explained.

“You three are the best!” She responded.

Wolfzang looked out the window for a moment, then said, “There, in those — daycares… the child’s mind is left going in circles trying to solve a way to avoid the pain. They’re left on perpetual high alert. The pendulum speeds up to cope, matching the intensity of their frustrated caretakers, sometimes well concealed subtly frustrated caretakers. But they feel it quite deeply. The pendulum I’ve spoken of, the speed back and forth, is two-dimensional. But now imagine that pendulum hanging ball oscillating, creating an oscillating wave as it swings back and forth. The voltage of the mind, dysfunctional caretakers *unknowingly* train the kids who they are the stewards of to have erratic voltage. This powerful fast-swinging pendulum is extremely absorbing to the mind as they pass through time, through life."

"I think I'm getting what you're saying; if you put a pencil on the swinging ball, it would draw an oscillating wave. Thus it's not just the swing back and forth but the voltage of the swing that counts," I said.

"Hmm, sort of tense internal strife. I'm picturing a person you gotta walk on eggshells around because their pendulum is speeding across, and the voltage of the swing is *so* high."

"And this is emulated by the little ones. It's not a genetic predisposition. These maladjusted skills the child acquires can last a lifetime; what they are exposed to often becomes, *the way*, the way they treat the next generation," Wolfzang explained was quite for a moment then continued. "If I stood 5 feet away and threw a child's ball at you with some effort, no big deal. If I stood 5 feet away and threw a 40-pound cannon ball at you with effort it *would* be a big deal! Same size ball same speed different powers to overwhelm."

"I've never really thought about how this developmental period is essentially a window of opportunity we have for developing a mind within a society, which is the reason for exponential advancement," I said, trying to examine aloud the OCSs' perspective and today's essential experience through Wolfzang's eyes.

"The thing is, it's not just extreme abuse that weakens the Primary Cloud. There is a lot of subtle abuse in the guise of discipline, abuse of withdrawing love, cruel, repeated subtle remarks, so the kid acts perfectly in the eyes of the self-interested subjective caregiver. These things are far more ubiquitous than you might imagine."

Once again, it looked like Wolfzang was using his pointer finger to rub his thumbnail, first horizontally, then vertically. Next, he went into his jacket pocket and pulled out his tablet that was far too big to have been in it; yet another magic trick.

YouTube appeared with a young 20-something mother, dressed like she was ready to go dancing, video shooting all around her very colorful, exceedingly fashionable furnished home.

Speaking extremely quickly, the mother began, “My 6-month-old won’t go to sleep at night, so I put him in this sway swing, hang these floating balloons near him, then I wrap him tightly in these blankets, — isn’t he cute? *Isn’t he* cute! Look at his *cute* nose; then I put this giant TV loud, I turn the swing dial to full speed, and finally, put a *formula* bottle in his mouth. Done and done!”

“Oh my *god*!” Mary said with a gasp. “This *is* a joke? *Right*?”

“This is not a joke. This is a real parent? Right?” I asked.

“Quite, the baby needs to be held and *loved*,” Wolfzang said and went on, “He needs love, calmness, feeling his mother's very natural rhythms, her heartbeat against him, his family calmly singing to him, not this — spectacle. She states her beliefs with such self-assuredness without the least bit of hesitation or objective reflection or attempts to understand a more complete picture of the baby's mind that yearns for natural love and human warmth. Millions of years of evolution, the baby needs something, and this *video* is not it.”

Every moment of growth is a cherished moment by OCS, not an inconvenience. We feel endlessly lucky to take part in every second of this ‘window of opportunity.’ In the nature vs. nurture argument, we see environmental forces as having a vastly greater impact than is believed in current technologically advancing cultures. We are all born with possible weaknesses that can be compounded by those around us. We don’t see those that develop a mood disorder or other conditions as having a genetic issue, just adversely impacted by the world during important moments of growth.

“I’ve known two families that adopted children from overseas, one little girl from a Chinese orphanage. She had her legs tied together, so she couldn’t move too quickly. One boy from a Russian orphanage was left strapped in a chair all day before he was adopted by loving parents. The little girl had a host of anger issues. When the boy was adopted, he looked like he had autism, the way he would rock back and forth to soothe himself when he’d cry,” Mary said.

Taking in a deep breath, "Total travesties," he said, shaking his head.

"Do you need anything?" Dorothy asked.

"We're great!" Mary responded.

I fell into deep thought and realized how a short time ago, I thought we were at the pinnacle of child development, believing we did it better than anyone ever throughout human history. But, after this brief review of our embraced beliefs and a glimpse of what *could be*, I drew a new opinion. We were perpetuating in-vogue beliefs about child development created by those that sounded incredibly self-confident.

"So — are you both able to sneak away for three or four days for another AFE? The meeting itself is actually quite short. As always, I'll reimburse you for the travel and time, but I require some concise journals for our study regarding a particular individual. It's important to me to get an intricate account of *your* current perceptions all the while contrasting what you now perceive the OCSs viewpoints *might* be."

"How three-dimensional as you've said."

"Sounds complicated… but fascinating. Sort of an exponential level of reflection?" I said with hesitation.

"Precisely! But quite valuable for the research we're doing. It involves someone I'm working with down in South Carolina. I'll discuss the logistics with you as the time gets closer in about a month."

"Great, this has been immensely interesting. We almost feel like journalists trying to get a better understanding of your… societies societal perspectives, your own embraced beliefs," I responded with a wry smile.

"Every field observation is significant. They'll all be interwoven when we're done and paint a complete picture of the OCS."

"It does — it feels just like being an independent journalist. It's the most fun we've ever had *working*," Mary responded.

"Alright, so we'll set it up. Let's head out."

"Can we leave a tip?" I asked.

“Oh, no, trust me, the OCS fully fund my research. Never worry about such matters,” he said and then left a 50 percent tip on the table.

We put our jackets on, said the last goodbye to Dorothy, walked out the door, said goodbye to Wolfzang, and headed back up the Thruway.

“This is all so — *nuts*; he’s right, you know; we are primitives. That was a terrible sight today. I would have bought into it, the entire thing, if we had a kid and worked in the city. We’re always pressured with time, just like those poor parents who send the kids *there*.” Mary said.

I was quiet for a moment and reflected on our Analytical Field Exploration. “How does he have all this stuff in his pocket? That freaking bear with the girl’s name on it? The other OCS that are observing the daycare must have set that up and realized the girl was being mistreated or something. I always feel a bit nutty after our visits.”

“Right, remember that guy dressed in gray on Block Island? Each visit leaves you a little — off,” Mary responded.

“Each time we meet him, we see something we once believed true slightly differently.”

A few days later, I received an email from Wolfzang in which he explained he was busy with several AFEs and it would be sometime next month before we traveled down south, but gave a full description. It appeared to be a fourteen-hour ride and a couple of overnights. Apparently, we would have plenty of free time to enjoy the scenery and do some hiking at state parks without him, all for another brief but potent observation. To us, it seemed a bit expensive for someone to finance, but after seeing the mansion on the Upper East Side, the BMW, it was clear money was abundantly available for his research. In another email, we scheduled a short walk in the city for the upcoming weekend.”

Lower Manhattan

Purchased coffee and chai tea with almond milk from an upbeat barista at Bank Square, then boarded the train and headed down the Hudson. We eagerly anticipated our upcoming visit with our down-to-earth, astute, psychologically adroit benefactor, sociological mentor, and possible time traveler. He mentioned in his email because of his schedule; it would only be a short walk. After, on our own, we planned to explore the parts of the city that we'd so far ignored; today, we decided upon a walk across the Brooklyn Bridge.

Wolfzang was at the top of the platform when we arrived at Grand Central; I immediately prepped the recorder. Today he dressed in casual New York cosmopolitan attire; sleeker pants seemed all the rage. I, on the other hand, always seemed to be about ten years behind the styles in Manhattan. I would be more up-to-date with the fashions of Seattle. Mary had once realized the best way to determine if our fashion was dated was to walk by the Empire State Building. Those that were dressed like New Yorkers were overlooked by the aggressive red shirt, red hat, observatory ticket sellers, but those like me that had fashion challenges were always a target for an intense sales pitch, sometimes multiple pitches on the block between 33rd and 34th Street, on 5th avenue.

As we walked through Grand Central, a sizable poster for Albert Einstein School of Medicine hung overhead.

As we all glanced at the photo of Einstein, Wolfzang began, "As you understand, the how of his discoveries have been a fervent focus for the OCS. Early OCSs realized that once we had a correct profile of him psychologically and a correct mental framework for the human animal, we could powerfully improve our own speed of discovery and innovation. Yet, at first, we too, had to upskill and learn to ignore all the speculative hero worship. Some here had concluded his success had a neurological genesis. His inferior parietal lobe was 15 percent wider. But we know it's all shadows on the wall, rather basic over-analysis. You stare at anything long enough trying to find something by those desirous of success, and you make rather interesting, quite convincing connections."

I recalled I once heard Einstein didn't know the speed of sound and had to look it up. I always thought that was strange that humanity's best physicist couldn't just rattle that number off the top of his head.

Taking notice of three homeless men sitting together, he paused for a moment. One guy smiled and nodded at Wolfzang, and he smiled back. Yet the man took no notice of the two of us; I wondered if he was one of the OCSs doing an Analytical Field Exploration. But, before I could ask, Wolfzang continued, "We refer to his discoveries as his derivatives. You must be careful, so much about him is legend. His quotes are a great place to start to try to understand him. Many of his quotes and ideas have been widely disseminated over the years. You can get the essence of what he said. But I wouldn't be surprised if most of the quotes you'll hear are only the gist of what he meant."

"Hmm… O… K? Sounds like the telephone game."

"So he was working upon a distinct set of fundamentals, but how?" Mary asked.

"Imagine a society that bases its understanding of everything on a sun god, then ask a venerated priest why you two act as you do; you'll get a complete fable about a sunbeam controlling you. Here, you've embraced that the very soft science of psychology has IT ALL under control, but there is endless speculation, wrongly embraced in vogue beliefs pontificated by overly self-assured certified therapists that are more often only *half-right*. Half of the speculations are just as inaccurate as a sunbeam controlling you."

"They're just flipping a coin but directing clients with professional certainty. If questioned, they can simply point to the framed certificate on the wall."

"As you said, if we knew what we were doing, the big things like homelessness, slavery, suicide, and starvation would have been overcome. We just rebrand and juggle around our failures for a prettier picture, to feel we've advanced," I said.

“Riding the oscillating wave with a slightly upward slanted axis for both technology and hard science discoveries, but a much flatter axis for all the soft sciences. Yet, OCSs believe a 75-degree axis is attainable for *both* with the correct foundational understandings.”

“Wow!”

“One must be skeptical, optimistic, and highly ethical to be an operator of the Vac-Plat. To harness the power of the mind, we need to not only understand but master how the mind reflexively attempts to deal with stressors and pressures. Fully understand the everyday dynamics of the mind.”

“Optimistic people are just nicer to be around. I want to be around them! I can see how they add to productivity. Although, I’ve met fake nice people that are just waiting to take something or trap others with toxic games,” Mary explained.

“Just knowing unethical primitives can hide behind well-wishing friendship masks and are plentiful here is essential for a healthier life. Honest, upbeat optimism intertwined with objective analytical review intensely fosters the necessary group cohesiveness we strive for. This sort of awareness was part of Einstein's psychological profile, which was paramount to his and — our success. Einstein said, ‘Stay away from negative people. They have a problem for every solution.’ He scored well in all three bell curves. His optimism, ability to use escapes, he himself chose. These seemingly simple factors made him uniquely situated to make magnificent discoveries,” he said, then paused. "Many here are taught to be their own worst enemies.”

“I get that,” I said.

“The pressure to succeed, produce, conform is extreme. Parents put a tremendous amount of pressure on their children to be perfect. Since each of us has our own two-year-old within us that never leaves us, we must be kind, nurturing to that two-year-old within. Much like we would be to any other two-year-old child. By being extremely critical of your own self, and inwardly lashing at yourself to be perfect, you are privately abusing your own two-year-old. Here the abusive self-talk is widespread. It’s quite tragic and impedes all growth.”

“A few years ago, I talked with a therapist that suggested the enormous importance of watching your inner self-talk. It takes practice to rewire the way you treat yourself. When I finally took notice, I could see how hard I was on myself throughout childhood — even cruel,” Mary said.

“Do you think one of your parents taught you to be critical?” Wolfzang asked.

“You’ve got it! I was always an adult with all the responsibilities, never a child in her eyes,” Mary replied.

“Quite a responsibility for a little girl. Often the walls go up; the defenses protect those that were supposed to protect you but taught you to abuse yourself through your inner dialog. It’s a skill of digging out the truth, deciphering, listening very closely, recognizing, and objectively examining the way one was trained to treat themselves. Some might never recall or recognize what really happened in an entire lifetime, being trained from a very young age. Many parents mistakenly believe it helps drive the child to deal with the very tough world or to help them have a productive, successful future; productivity shouldn’t be accomplished that way. Cruel self-talk is the basis for many human mental and physical conditions.”

“I think I’m getting it, it’s not that humans are not intelligent enough to do great things, but part of the reason is the way we were trained to interact with our own emotional selves; we’ve embraced the wrong ways to treat our very own two-year-olds, which makes us fundamentally dysfunctional, especially to operate the Tool,” I said.

“I see the connections you’re attempting to have us draw. Amazing — the daycare, those kids, and us. It’s interconnected for a society that wants to make exponential scientific discoveries. Your point is if it’s the actually developing child or the child still within us resonating from our brainstem and limbic system, we have to know how to relate to overcome seemingly unsolvable enigmatic difficulties in science. We’re the caretakers for our own two-year-olds, and we’re also the bitty mean old ladies ignoring or scolding our own Anne, hurting her by purposely ignoring her, not holding her, loving her when she’s in pain.”

“*Perfect*, quite analogous and impressively deduced. You’re drawing the correct conclusions from the AFE. If one is optimistic and kind to themselves, they will more often try something novel, use their imagination to experiment, and explore the uncontrollable. They may support their own selves in creative thinking rather than beating themselves up and losing a world-changing idea. You know, as the nice man from Ulm once said, 'I stay with a problem longer,' he did it with kinder self-talk." He said, messing up his hair, then continued, "If the individual fails at something, it can just be part of a journey they'll learn from. While someone that was trained to be crueler may be reflexively critical of themselves and vulnerable to all the whims and speculations of their bang-up when dealing with a self-interested narcissistic coworker, classmate, supervisor, parent or professor."

"Hmm, you mean they take those that disparage them seriously after an attempt that fails?"

"I seem to know a few very intelligent people that have done little. I'm often amazed at the reasons they come up with for not trying something adventurous… Thinking about them, I bet they have immensely critical self-talk," I responded.

"It could be a symptom of several factors; often, critical self-talk has a lot to do with it. If an individual doesn't do something repeatedly, then their Genetically Important Drive, Feelings of Inferiority is reflexively resonated. Frequently, the person unknowingly defaults upon that powerful Genetically Important Drive, Feelings of Inferiority. Then reflexively, emotionally, *often incorrectly*, he or she believes the task *can't* be done. Self-doubting thoughts like, 'if it's easy, I would have done it already,' — from a visceral gut level."

"So you're saying; you don't do, you don't do, you don't do, then emotionally you viscerally feel you can't do it? *It* can't be done?" I said.

"Quite right, the genetically important drive, Feelings of Inferiority, kicks in, and all of a sudden, your mind goes to work on why logically you can't do it. Once again, the embraced emotional belief is well supported by logic. But those that are more prone to be optimistic and nicer to their two-year-old may never fully embrace the *can't do;* likely going ahead trying *it* and not having the negative self-talk that compounds and resonates with their genetically important drive, Feelings of Inferiority."

"I see. There was more to Einstein than just a high IQ," I responded.

"There's a fitting quote from the Roman philosopher Seneca, 'It is not because things are difficult that we do not dare, it is because we do not dare that they are difficult,'" Wolfzang said.

"Oh, so maybe it's part of our Embraced Beliefs Cloud Network, again an emotional feeling supported by our *logic*."

"'All of humanity's problems stem from man's inability to sit quietly in a room alone,' said the French philosopher Blaise Pascal. I suspect that *here*, most primitives wouldn't benefit from sitting quietly alone in a room because they've been trained to be too critical of themselves, even the high IQ types. We must be trained to objectively observe our own thoughts and correctly identify them, and be adroitly skilled at identifying when they are subjective or harsh," Wolfzang said with a smile.

We continued to walk through our metropolis. It was a beautiful sunny day; things seemed buzzing with life. I continued to ponder his points. "But wait — what do you mean he 'chose his own escapes?'" I asked.

"That, my friend, is a hugely important question. It would be akin to asking what is behaviorism. Or what is psychodynamics? Certainly worth a bit of time to explore."

"Escapes? hmm, I have a feeling it's not as benign as we make it out to be?" Mary said, sounding perplexed.

"It's an enormous driver of human behavior but goes completely unrecognized because it is so seamlessly interwoven with behavior. But once intricately understood, it becomes part of the answer, a powerful predictor of human behavior, essential for our research."

"I suspect that without these deeper understandings, these distinctions, a uniquely complex explanation of human behavior, one could not produce a Tool that could silence emotionally produced behaviors. Making us better than what we are?" I asked.

"Escapes are described within the OCS Mental Model as a stream with water-like properties. Without understanding escapes, its principles, attributes, and how the human mind uses it to function, we could never have done so much. Escapes are as important to the human mind as water is to the human body. I can't impress the importance of a complete understanding of ***it*** upon you enough."

As we walked down 5th Avenue, we both remained silent. We were attempting to contemplate this component of a model he had not yet fully described. Yet, we weren't pushing him, allowing him to methodically determine when the time was right. We were now wrestling with the elements he held as fundamental to the functioning of the Vac-Plat.

"Einstein's escapes were mainly intellectual pursuits. Yet, he had others. He played the violin, sailed a boat, and drank iced coffee. Escapes decompress stressors and pressures. The mind goes to them without conscious thought. Once you learn to control your own escapes, to know when you're using them, you have a much more powerful mind."

"Like how? Could I levitate." I asked jokingly.

"No, no, you can tap into the full power of your mind. To be another Einstein, one must tap into escapes. Many do it unknowingly, but the control occurs when you fully understand, harness, and direct. If you use them as a prescription to overcome life's stressors and pressures, you build an incomprehensibly valuable perpetual motion machine feeding on free energy in the mind."

"It sort of reminds me of what Taoists call Wu Wei or maybe techy people call 'the zone,'" I responded.

"There are certainly elements of each belief, but to study it, to control them, you must master what it is, without dogmas. Once you genuinely know what it is, how the mind functions with escapes, you may never understand how humans survive without the understanding."

"Let me have it. I want this *superpower*," I replied.

“I can see how you’d liken it to a superpower. If you went to India and watched the Fakir performances and witnessed how they put themselves into a trance, slow down their heartrates, the incredible endurance of pain from body piercings, the clear impact on the mind from spinning during their whirling dervishes you’d witness some impressive performances of *this* essential dynamic of the mind. Some sit in postures for days at a time. It’s a focal point for the mind, the act itself is an escape. Once you understand the characteristics and applications of escapes, how they are essential to the mind you might begin to imagine what *can be* if you controlled what has been only recognized as unimportant, trivial, or there by tourists *a sideshow*. I could imagine how I’d be much less effective, even ineffective, if I didn’t know this *stuff*. So we’ll continue to teach you about the OCSs understanding; you will need time to objectively observe, grasp, and examine it all around you and get messy with how it exists in the natural world. If you’re available, we’ll meet for breakfast next weekend here in the city and continue the conversation then.”

“Oh — man! You gotta go? At least we’ll continue next week,” Mary said with disappointment in her voice.

“Vaarwel!” He said, made a right onto 12th street, and walked into a densely packed bookstore. We continued south toward the Brooklyn Bridge.

“If he was in such a rush to leave, why would he have walked into a bookstore?” I said.

“I know. You would think he had to rush off to a train or something. But, whatever, we’ll see him next weekend.”

Kachaz's Bagel, Escapes

We received a call from Wolfzang midweek and were given the location of a cafe in lower Manhattan. He suggested we could stay in the city overnight at a hotel the OCSs overbooked and had already paid for. The hotel on Crosby Street was the tallest in the area and only a few blocks from the cafe. I told Mary about the email, and her immediate response was, “Wow, this is the best job *ever*!”

That Saturday morning was like so many others, Bank Square Cafe, a coffee for me, a chai tea latte with almond milk for Mary; then we got on the Hudson Line to the city.

“Why don’t we just come out and say we think he’s from a different time and place?” I said, sipping my coffee and looking out the windows at the Hudson.

“He’s curiously smart, even for a professor. I feel excited about wherever all this is going. *If* this is simply just part of a perception experiment or something *much* bigger. When he *thinks* we’re ready, he’ll tell us more. Though, how can we convince him we’re ready to know *now*?”

“He seems to think it has something to do with over-stressing our minds, maybe, finding out the reality we believe is different than what we perceive,” I said.

“True, he seems to be quite concerned with stressing us out, a weakening of *this* primary network cloud, as he calls it.”

"It's perplexing. Could it be that he's experiencing some sort of age transformation, cycling through different life stages? Aging, then undergoing a process or using a substance that resets him to a younger age? We know the OCSs aren’t driven by material possessions. It's like a wealthy individual who doesn't attach value to expensive cars and simply uses them for practical purposes. As soon as one car accumulates high mileage, they replace it with a new luxury vehicle. I don't mean to say that he disregards his body; he's *quite* health-conscious, but maybe the fixation on youth and appearances, which is prevalent here, doesn't hold the same significance for him. He perceives healthy eating and exercise as acts of self-kindness rather than a means to impress or compete with others."

“It’s incredible how thoroughly he believes there are two people in us, someone that can be logical and then a two-year-old, and how it’s all about being nice to the emotional two-year-old. I can see it. He’s not vain. He’s just compassionate and nurturing to his two-year-old and his physical body. I can see his point, why he believes we have to be Universally Ethical; there’s more to it, to be compassionate to other sentients like other animals, just by default, you become compassionate where it counts for productivity — Whoa!” Mary explained, surprising herself with this revelation while looking out the window at the Hudson, sipping her chai.

“Wow, that’s a cool thought.” I said, then went silent for a moment, thinking, then continued, “Also, if there’s this deep connection with his wife, how is she included in this — cycle? Maybe, they sort of grow old together over and over again? It would align with the high level of importance they hold for this Genetically Important Drive in the brainstem and limbic system, that drive he calls the Yearning for Emotional Closeness.”

“Do they grow old, enjoy the experience, then have a process that resets their youth together? Hmm…. Since he so strongly believes it’s all about real-world experiences, to get the most realistic experience, the complete field experience, maybe, he doesn’t wear a disguise? He embraces all authentic experiences, even the bad ones, as possibly learning something hugely unexpected. That Greek saying… Amor fati. Love thy fate,” Mary said calmly.

“This age thing is one of those things that unless we completely immersed ourselves in his society, we wouldn’t be able to fully comprehend. Why something that seems alterable with their advanced technological abilities isn’t being changed indefinitely? So we wouldn’t notice? Why he chooses to leave this clue, this paradox? Sticking out in clear view,” I said, then going silent for a moment, “unless… he wants that clue and others to stick out to help us assimilate!” I said.

“Weird — so, maybe he wanted us to have this conversation, something obvious to figure out, slowly at a speed that wouldn’t throw our Primary Cloud off balance by our emotional drives overpowering it? Maybe… if primitives feel the control of figuring something out themselves, then enormous earthquakes in our world perceptions don't break down? He gets the long-term response he's attempting to achieve."

"Hmm, crazy! You've got brains behind those stunning good looks," I said, touching her leg. Maybe I was being corny, but it was true. "I bet you're right. Leaving that aside for a moment, he was in his 80s when we first met him, no matter how our brains try to — readjust reality. Say he had around that time come up with this project, this Analytical Field Exploration, writing a journal and planting the seeds of the Vac-Plat," I responded.

"Yes, but maybe he's also slowing down his aging; if so, we don't know how much time is actually passing between our visits. It could be decades?" Mary said, pondering.

"What you're saying is that we're only seeing him once every couple of decades since he has many game boards on the Vac-Plat, with interwoven, intersecting fibers. Every moment, every meeting with us, has been somewhat choreographed, but we just assume it's another day. It makes me wonder if there is a team of OCS or at least significant AI assistance watching and reviewing everything that is happening in his AFE. Continuously listening to our conversations with our black square."

"Weird… OK, this is gotta be all nutso! Maybe we're simply reading too far into it? But would he need a team if, for him, time is elongated? He could just take all the time needed and revisit this game board as he comes upon new information elsewhere. It feels a little — scary."

"Yeah, this is all pure speculation, but — I think we both agree that he is purposefully attempting to assimilate us and not scare us. It's amazing how these Genetically Important Drives exist, like the Need to Control the Environment; they're the reason for us to act emotionally and are the reason for our probability planet. If nothing else, he has proven to me we primitives are emotionally and incentive-driven."

The address he provided led us to the bagel shop in downtown Manhattan, between or maybe within Chinatown and Little Italy. The bagel cafe was right next to a strange old gun shop; according to a sign, it was the "oldest gun shop in New York." Likely the only gun shop left in the heart of the city. The shop was so out of place we had to *look* and walked in; it appeared more like a clothing shop than a gun shop, with no guns at all. There were some targets, a few ammunition boxes, holsters, and gun-related paraphernalia. We quickly cured our inquisitive minds and walked out and into the bagel shop. Kachaz's was a lively 70s-style bagel cafe. Streisand's music playing and smells in the air suggested they had perfected the art of New York City bagel making.

Far in the back, we could see our dynamically aging friend sitting with two extra chairs.

"Hey!" He called out, giving us a wave.

Wolfzang looked like a man approaching 60, maybe 2 or 3 years younger than last time. Feeling giddy and excited to see him, I became forward, "*Ok*, you look younger than ever! We know you have the ability to travel in time. You're not vain; OCSs live for innovation and discovery; this isn't about looks; you have some way of resetting your age. Your technology is vastly superior to anything we understand — you don't want to freak us out either." I blurted out, with the waitress standing near enough to hear me, aware she was watching, I realized this place was far too crowded to press those sorts of accusations if we intended to stay and not be perceived as complete certifiable nut jobs, no matter how lighthearted I intended to make my voice. I then added a "Ha-huhhh," to cleverly throw off any onlooker. Well, admittedly, I just looked loony. We began taking a seat, and I placed my microphone on the table.

"You look… G-r-e-a-t." Mary said as we sat, sounding like she was seeing a friend that had dyed her hair some frightful color.

In a low voice, he responded. "I've never denied it. I'm just trying to slowly adjust you to my… novel information, but you know that too. If anything freaks people out, it's messing with someone's… reality, but don't let me remind you this is a perception sociological experiment we're performing," he said with a smile.

Looking at Mary, "Thanks for the — compliment, don't worry, there's nothing nefarious within this AFE. We're just walking on a journey without sprinting and giving you both a heart attack. I admit our technology is far beyond what you're familiar with; that alone is quite unnerving to most. Let's jump into why we're meeting here, the metaphorical stream in the OCSs mental model, where we left off."

“Escapes?” Mary asked.

“That’s exciting. We know an understanding of the stream will help us better understand the Tool,” I explained.

“True.... Adhering to the principles that underpin the Vac-Plat and the OCSs, as always, I’ll describe it with clarity, directness, and simplicity.”

“That reminds me of a *Buffett* quote, ‘There seems to be some perverse human characteristic that likes to make easy things difficult.’” I responded, once again attempting to think interdisciplinary as he had previously propagated.

“It’s all very true, on the Vac-Plat for all discoveries, we always leave very understandable journals, never needlessly complicated, always succinct as possible, so anyone of us can take the time to fully understand the discoveries, how and why they were made, it’s all part of being an OCS, and established within our Fundamental Doc.”

“You mean you don’t hide the secret formula until you’re paid for a shiny certificate of completion?” Mary said with a grin.

“Whoa, that’s right — remember that first email you sent us? You said how important it was for us to explain why we came up with our conclusions; we’re doing it... taking part in the Vac-Plat, weird!”

“Yes, OCSs are all Vac-Plat nearly all the time. Don’t let it surprise you,” he said, then paused for a moment. “Without a definitive understanding of how escapes work, this metaphorical stream, humans cannot understand the OCSs mental model and thereby never work out the details of the Tool.”

Our waitress approached the table, a brown-haired girl in her 20s. I immediately assumed she was an NYU student; she just sort of looked the part. Maybe it was the many NYU flags we passed on Broadway. But she was quite fitting for this vibrant cafe. “Hey! Do you know what you would like?” She asked, sounding extremely upbeat.

Looking at the menu, we ordered sesame bagels, vegan cream cheese, coffee for Wolfzang and myself, and tea for Mary.

“Great choice; the sesame bagels are *my* favorite!” she said jovially and scurried away.

"So — again, this essential component. Metaphorically, humans are fishlike. They swim within but never notice since it's part of life. Put another way, this is a major component of the OCS Mental Model and to, my work, and to this perception research work."

"Hmm," I said, a bit befuddled.

"Escapes… humans are emotionally, incentive and escape-driven animals." He said, then paused and looked at the entire cafe as if he was looking for something or someone; then continued, "Since behaviorism is one ingredient in human behavior, let's start with Skinner. BF Skinner had a 'man with a hammer syndrome.' Everything was a nail, and he thought everyone that didn't agree with him was a fool. Because of his success, sycophants surrounded him, and he was entirely sure rewards and punishment could completely explain human behavior. He certainly had some good insights about human behavior but walked too far down a path never to return."

"I've saw his old interviews in Psych classes. He seemed — a bit self-confident, unquestionably correct. When challenged, he was quite dismissive. Strangely his demeanor impacted me, and I remember agreeing with him. Thinking he *must* be right," I replied.

"Sadly, quite common indeed for venerated academics, just like any other primitive with any other embraced belief. Behaviorism is a two-dimensional explanation for human behavior; it needs a three-dimensional model. And for hubris… it has no place in scientific exploration. On the Vac-Plat, it's an Expected Toxic Outcome; recognized and quickly nullified."

"Would you like more coffee, Wolf?" The waitress asked.

"That would be great," he responded. She poured the coffee and then quickly attended to another customer that needed a refill. The seats were tightly packed, and people were quickly filling in the gaps.

"Wow, you two know each other?" Mary asked.

"You know me — I have a tendency of asking a lot of questions. Her name is Cindy."

"So, escapes, they're different than both emotions and incentives?" I asked, having a deep desire to try to etch out an understanding about this cog within the OCSs mental model that was essential to understanding Wolfzang's work in a definitive, more complete way.

"Human behaviors are a symptom of what's going on in the mind. Yet, the region or sub-field in psychology of Behaviorism focuses on the human animals' responses to rewards and punishment. The charts and data they can create are fantastic and quite convincing — *but* unfortunately, limited in scope and even accuracy. Like so many other charts, it'll tell you volumes about those that generated the data being communicated. A more complete picture that could be used to forecast human behavior would include other necessary elements."

"Like these Genetically Important Drives in the brainstem and limbic system, the Primary Cloud, this thing you refer to as escapes?"

"Yes. Escapes cool off genetically important emotional drives within the brainstem and limbic system. This perpetual dynamic occurring within the human mind needs to be understood for all its intricacies. Otherwise, you are simply truncating the data and showing pretty charts."

"Cooled off?" Mary asked.

"When the mind experiences day-to-day stressors and pressures, they are reflexively calmed by escapes."

"I get it, that's pretty basic, so, we get stressed out, then we exercise, eat, play a video game? That calms us down," I said.

"Yes, very good, but the enormity of escapes, the intricacies, principles, and characteristics of the process hasn't been accepted *here*; when it comes to behavior. So… it's vastly larger than it sounds. It's so ubiquitous with living that *here* the details have not been correctly identified. Those here influencing psychological beliefs with a theory that becomes widely embraced are not always interested in the correct answer and end up defending the wrong yet, highly lucrative answers. Money is a powerful persuader of truth."

Our smiling waitress delivered the bounty. There's nothing quite as good as a New York City bagel; I've been told it's the water that makes it so delish. Dense, packed with sesame seeds, firmly pressed. The vegan vegetable cream cheese an ideal companion; the coffee also far above ordinary. We paused to eat. I stared over at the backs of a few of the customers in the bustling cafe, sitting on the old stools at the bar.

"Without a mastery of this essential component, escapes, you will never fully understand your own mind or other's surprising behaviors. It's a bedrock of all other understandings and systems we utilize."

"This — stream in the OCSs mental model sounds like one pillar everything else rests on?" Mary responded.

"True. Escapes are all about absorbing the mind—all for the unconscious need to reduce stressors and pressures that impact our Genetically Important Drives. We're either using some degree of escape or living entirely in the moment, like running away from a wolf. Running away from a wolf is one of those moments in life that you never forget because you're *all-in…* the moment."

I recalled a Civil War documentary, "Hmm, I remember learning about Robert E. Lee saying on his deathbed, "Strike the tents!" Like you said, because at that moment long before in his life, he was fully immersed in the moment. He was running away from a wolf," I replied.

"Nice interdisciplinary point," Mary said with a smile.

"True, superb! Or, Stonewall Jackson's last words, "Let us cross over the river and rest under the shade of the trees. "As each of their Primary Network Clouds were breaking down, they had that very vivid memory because, at that moment in his life, he was utterly absorbed by the moment. It's like eternally being there. That's why childhood abuse and trauma is so *terrible* and formative," Wolfzang said.

"I can see the difficulty science currently has. We're truncating our behaviors, focusing on things that don't matter, and not seeing the entire picture and all the moving parts; if we don't understand our own minds. If we don't identify our flaws and neutralize them, we will always contaminate our science with the things we have unknowingly evolved to do," Mary responded.

"Precisely Mary. As an individual's stressors and pressures increase, the mind reflexively redirects itself. This is a simple concept, but because primitives are hard-wired a certain way, it goes largely unnoticed, just accepted as the natural state of being."

"So, if we don't understand the actual fundamentals of human behavior, if we fixate on the wrong details, data that is unessential, we will be trapped circulating on our probability planet?" I responded.

"You can stare at and speculate the relevance of data forever and a day. Without a solid objectively correct fundamental picture of what's driving behavior, you are likely to over-analyze or misinterpret what's occurring."

"So for this component of the mental model, what you're saying is if we get stressed out, our mind automatically redirects itself to something else? Something calming?" Mary stated while looking at a large, yellowing, worn-out picture of Barbara Streisand hanging over another table.

"Not necessarily calming, as you know it, but fulfilling specific criteria to reduce stressors and pressures."

"Weird, so it's not calming, but it reduces stressors and pressures? I think I lost you," Mary said.

Taking a napkin and a pink and white pen with the cafe's name, he began to draw what looked to be a tall glass of water with water overflowing and splashing out. Then, he made an arrow pointing to the overflowing water.

"You just hit upon it; that's one of the things that makes it so elusive; one can imagine a glass of water. The water in the glass represents life's stressors and pressures, all adding together. We say stressors and pressures because some things are clearly stressful, but even those things that are fast-paced and demanding could be pressures on the mind. Say a birthday might be enjoyable for someone but full of irritating demands —*pressures*," Wolfzang explained.

"So, like a holiday that you might think is fun, but you've got limited time to get everything done. You want everything to be perfect, all the gifts and food. You fear others' negative responses," I affirmed.

Wolfzang nodded, then pointing to the overflowing water, continued, "If that glass of water overflows, the overflow that I've drawn an arrow to, represents countless compulsive symptoms, including mental difficulties such as repetitive thoughts, desire to eat, or physical problems such as physical pain, migraines, stomach problems, back pain, desire to drink, desire for drugs. The overflowing water is the compulsive, reflexive thoughts and behaviors one may experience. When someone is experiencing a symptom, they must look at their emotional state, their environment, their own pendulum, and the emotional pace of those around them. Thoughts must be on the stressors and pressures in the glass. That is, do not — do not, look at the symptoms. Thinking and focusing on the symptom only increases the symptoms; look at what's in the glass or why the glass fills so quickly."

"Overflowing water are symptoms. The stressors and pressures are within the glass adding up — Hmm," Mary said.

"But, when you said 'increase symptoms,' how?" I asked.

"Escapes are all about absorbing the mind's attention. When the mind realizes something absorbs its attention, then it's a successful escape. If, for example, eating does the trick, then one becomes addicted to eating to decrease resonating Genetically Important Drives. But life is stressful, so the mind becomes more and more reliant upon particular escapes to absorb the attention. More and more food needs to be used, eventually quite compulsively, quite reflexively — all to decompress from perceived stressors and pressures."

"Wow, I used to get these terrible stomach problems, but then I realized they were stress-induced, then they went away," Mary said.

"Yes, these — symptoms keep businesses in business; there is little profitability in what I'm telling you. If what I'm explaining was embraced, it would create financial chaos here."

"I can see what you're saying. With my stomach problems, so many people gave me advice. There are a million suggestions on the internet, and everyone seems so sure, especially when they're selling a product or service. So, I eventually got a colonoscopy, and only after *that* the doctor said it was likely stress. Why didn't he just say it was likely stress in the first place? He never even mentioned it before the colonoscopy. *Whatever*… my insurance paid for it." Mary replied.

"Fascinating, in many ways, the mind cares little how it redirects itself away from stressors and pressures, only that it gets redirected from stressors and pressures *to* something, and that 'something' varies. What absorbs the mind, whose mind, how, and why, that *is* a fascinating study. Some people are profoundly pained inside; they've been traumatized, under nurtured, abused, their mind is spinning, and needs a strong way to absorb their mind and decrease the water in the glass — the stressors and pressures," Wolfzang expressed, paused and watched a man leave his bar stool.

"Do you remember how I said general laws of science have great parallels to understanding human behavior? If one tries to quantify aspects of behavior with numbers, it makes it two-dimensional. Water, the natural behavior of water, those attributes serve a useful explanation of escapes, the fast-moving dynamics of this one essential component within the OCS Mental Model."

"I see, rather than numbers, the natural characteristics of water represent the quickly moving behavior of escapes rather than a graph or number chart. It gives a better three-dimensional explanation. That's amazing. We embraced the belief that only numbers can represent the multiverse and all things scientific. Otherwise, it's pseudosciences or fuzzy thinking, but you say we're truncating the most accurate paralleled description."

"Me too! I'm finally getting why you once said general laws of science have significant importance to comprehending human behavior," Mary said.

"Precisely."

Sipping his coffee, Wolfzang paused, then continued, "One of our founders, MonkeyTzu, a name given after, not during his lifetime, worked with hundreds of children with autism for over 15 years. He was fully immersed in the interactions, not just performing safe applauded in vogue office speculations. After observing the repetitive behaviors that were usually linked with the condition, he soon believed related, similar behaviors were occurring for particular psycho-dynamic fundamental reasons. After several years of continuous interactive observations in a multitude of family settings, he hypothesized that moderate to severe autism was due to a weakening in the network cloud of billions of neurons located mainly in the neocortex. What we call the Primary Cloud was somehow less capable. As you're now understanding, the need for escapes are interrelated to the Genetically Important Drives of the brainstem and limbic system. Escapes reflexively calm… soothe the resonating Genetically Important Drives. A key component to understanding the behaviors of autism was defining the attributes of escapes. To truly observe the interrelationship of escapes and the Genetically Important Drives an individual must develop a deeper understanding of the individual with autism. Understand what their home life is truly like. He had to truly connect with those that had autism. This led to a window into the Genetically Important Drives of the brainstem and limbic system. The children he worked with didn't care if their escapes were socially acceptable because that was a function within the Primary Cloud. Yet like everyone else they needed to absorb the mind's attention if the Genetically Important Drives were resonated."

"Need anything, Wolf?" The waitress asked.

"No, my dear, we're great!"

"In the field, that is, when he listened and attempted to connect to each family, he saw things uninterrupted as it naturally happened in their homes. He witnessed family dynamics as they really were, not as he assumed."

"Working with a large random sample of families must have been difficult, especially if what you've been saying about nearly seventy percent of us being more self-interested," Mary said.

"OCSs are much more attuned to how intensive the field can be. Rest and relaxation, long balanced reflection, and symbolic activities after an AFE are essential. Especially if you're attempting to assimilate yourself in another's environment."

"Wow! I knew a kid with autism. He always lined up plastic ducks. Huh, now that I think about it, he was resonating his Need to Control the Environment, wasn't he? Putting his eyes level to the little toy ducks. Organizing them in a perfect line. I see it now; people with autism are resonating these drives; that's why there are so many similarities! They are the same as us; they need to use escapes, incredible!" Mary explained.

"Yes, you've got it, Mary. It didn't take you long to put it together," Wolfzang responded.

"Yeah, I remember too. The family was quite middle class but spent a fortune to go to some highly venerated doctor that was an ivy-league minted guru. Charging a huge amount for certifications and the magic formula to cure autism. He looked like a saint to parents, acted unquestionably sure, yet raked in enormous profits. After they spent the money, they thought the son had improved, yet he looked the same; I couldn't tell them… that, though."

"Yet, those around the *good* doctor think themselves and him at the cutting edge of science."

"Exactly!"

"How often did MonkeyTzu visit families?" I asked.

"He would go into the homes for one hour 2 times per week, sometimes for several years, to work with one to five-year-olds," paused and said, "Like Marcus Aurelius said, 'nothing has such power to broaden the mind as the ability to investigate systematically and truly all that comes under thy observation in life.'"

"I think I get what you're saying; since a person with autism's cloud-like network, mainly in the neocortex, is weakened, they often do not care what they use as an escape, even if society deems it awkward. If you know what the Genetically Important Drives of the brainstem and limbic system are, you can see them responding to them?" I asked, reviewing his point.

"Yes, precisely, a person with severe autism doesn't care to be socially acceptable due to the weakening of the network cloud mainly in the neocortex, where thinking about thinking and executive functioning is occurring, they'll outwardly show a strong socially unacceptable repetitive behavior. It's his or her use of an escape to deal with the Genetically Important Drives, reinforced over time, that then becomes compulsive and reflexive."

"Each behavior is a symptom and shows you somehow they are resonating their Genetically Important Drives, deeply rooted in the brainstem and limbic system," Mary said.

"Very good — but don't you sometimes use escapes just for *fun*, like chewing gum? Listening to music? Watching a movie? Eating ice cream? These things will, in a very natural time-passing way, just lower the water in the glass." Wolfzang explained.

"I think I see. Each behavior is a symptom and shows you somehow they are resonating their Genetically Important Drives deeply rooted in the brainstem and limbic system, or accumulated stressors and pressures."

"Ohh, each behavior is a symptom and shows they are resonating their Genetically Important Drives deeply rooted in the brainstem and limbic system" I paused for a moment in deep thought. "*Or*, something just because it's familiar, calming — soothing." I said in amazement.

"That's incredible!" Mary responded.

"But there are some complexities to this glass of water metaphor. If anything has become related, a trigger, AKA a paired stimulus, that resonates these deeply rooted Genetically Important Drives. Then, just a glimpse or something that reflexively reminds the individual of the stressor or pressure, the redirection occurs, the use of escapes is triggered, the behavior occurs. It all ends up being immediate and reflexive."

"You mean if something is paired to the stimulus… I remember psych 101, so a stimulus can be paired with resonating the Genetically Important Drives? I get it — Wow! So in a Pavlovian way, the bell rings, we salivate, a bell rings, and my Genetically Important Drives resonate, and I then, without thought, turn to the escapes that I know calms them — SO cool!" Mary said, sounding quite excited.

"Wow, classical conditioning is part of the mix. I get why behaviors in autism are so elusive. The stimulus could be anything at all, anything once tied to the stressor or pressure. It could be quite personal to the individual?" I asked, sounding excited; the great coffee helped, but I felt I completely understood; I could see why OCSs lived for discoveries;

grasping a fascinating new concept gives the same high as winning at a slot machine.

"Yes, precisely, classical conditioning. The person gets exposed to a trigger, with or without conscious thought, recalls a stimulus linked to a stressor or pressure, so the mind reflexively redirects the attention to an escape to calm the mind. Because humans are such complicated animals, these connections can be many, many connections deep; someone might see a shoe that reminded them of a shoe they wore when they worked with a cruel demanding boss and then felt like listening to music, or someone can't figure out a computer hardware problem might feel a hunger pain, or, it might simply be a time of the day that's related to a resonating Genetically Important Drive."

A robust baker dressed all in white quickly opened the double doors from the kitchen and walked by, bringing several baskets of fresh flat bagels aka flaggels to the front display case. The smells of which filled the air as he passed.

"Since there is a weakening of the cloud-like network mainly in the neocortex for people with autism, a person with severe autism cannot as easily conceal when these deeply rooted emotional drives are impacted — But, but, we are all the same, hard-wired the same way. We simply conceal our resonating emotional drives better; we are unknowingly guided toward escapes that are more socially appropriate. Our cloud-like network of billions of neurons, mainly in the neocortex, is resilient and dense enough to conceal the resonating drives and not be overpowered by them. Although, those with autism, we are seeing the Genetically Important Drives interacting with humans' absolute need to use escapes."

"Like you had said, 'escapes are as important to the human mind as water is to the human body.'"

"So the spectrum of autism goes from mild when the cloud is just slightly weakened to severe when the cloud network is — not functioning?" Mary asked.

"Yes, you've got it; those *here* will someday realize how severe autism and somnambulism, which is sleepwalking parallel, are both indicative of absence of a fully functioning Primary Cloud."

"So once we understand sleepwalking, we can cure autism?" Mary said.

"True…" he said with some trepidation.

"I can see it. We're all the same," Mary said.

"We're all just a bunch of emotionally driven beings dealing with stimuli in our environment that are resonating our genetically important emotional drives. Wow, it brings classical conditioning to a whole new level. Crazy — We're more than just driven by emotions and incentives. I see it on a different level," I said.

Looking toward the front doors and in deep thought, Mary said, "I knew a guy with high-functioning Autism. He had no patience for anyone. He would be utterly fixated on his engineering job when he was under stress at home with a very abusive wife; he would consume himself with the job, utterly fixate and escape into his work. Yet, he would remarkably produce during those times; he even received several engineering patents."

"When I think of the word 'escapes,' I think of a hobby, reading, playing a video game, watching sports, all good stuff, but this is much more complex?" I asked.

"Escapes are all those things, but to understand the true function of the mind, it's the closest existing term, but even that term needs some — fine-tuning, as it applies to the OCS Mental Model," Wolfzang explained as he reached for his pen and a napkin.

He wrote on the napkin:

Characteristics of Escapes: 1. Absorb the mind to varying degrees. 2. Must be predictable. 3. Take time. 4. If you don't choose an escape, the mind will find one for you. 5. Escapes are neutral but, they can be harmful.

"These characteristics of escapes are essential for a complete understanding of our research, our *journals*."

"They can be harmful; that sounds odd — concerning?" I asked.

“Hmm? That sounds anti-intuitive, but I guess it would be like my stomach problems. Other things that absorb someone’s mind like over-eating, drugs, alcohol?” Mary replied.

“Didn’t some doctor want you to take medicine for it?”

“That’s right; I’m glad I never did,” Mary responded.

“Yes, this is anti-intuitive, like you said, quite anti-intuitive. Why would something that developed over millions of years be harmful to the human animal? It all comes down to what has proved genetically important. Simply, it is more important that we have physical pain, desire for drugs, want to eat rather than demonstrate frustration — aggressiveness outwardly, which has limited the life expectancy of countless earlier ancestors.”

“So, bad shit happened to those that let out their raw emotions, got pissed off, showed anger. For, humans to survive in a society they had to conceal — repress these powerful emotional drives,” Mary said.

He paused for a moment, took a sip of his coffee, and then said, “Yes, bad *shit*, like being killed. You must learn to attune yourself to your own symptoms when you get a migraine, when you are driven to eat, the act of worrying, when you feel the urge to listen to music, when you desire to exercise; learn to recognize these things and then train yourself to identify which Genetically Important Drive or drives are being resonated. What’s filling the glass full of water? Or why your glass of water fills quickly from a trigger?”

“Huh, the act of worrying.”

“Some have dug out the hole. They become quite skilled at worrying, their imagination and creativity can be astounding. One must realize the reflexive nature of worrying, the absorbing nature of the act. It does indeed fit all the characteristics necessary to fit an escape.”

“So every time I want to exercise, I’m resonating these drives?”

“No, no, not necessarily. You might have trained your body to enjoy the hit of endorphins you’ll get and help you lower the water in the glass in a consistent manner. A sort of daily stimulant. Sometimes you're simply conditioned to desire escapes as a prescription to lower your own existing stressors and pressures. Much like if you become conditioned to take a certain medication, you have a deep desire to use it as scheduled, as trained.

“Whoa! So you mean we’ll see the escapes, see the symptoms before we even know what’s bothering us?” Mary responded.

“Precisely. You might feel frustrated, but then again, you may have many more times when you observe yourself grabbing a pizza first.”

He looked at a couple being seated not too far from us, a couple with a strong British accent. “Flaggels, what’s a *flaggel*?” The man asked his wife while looking at the menu. Mary and I smiled at each other.

“Most fascinating to us, within the dynamics of the mind, the deeper part of the mind knows things before the Primary Cloud in the neocortex. The little one has difficulty getting the point across, but that is a ‘gut feeling.’”

“Hmm.”

“Escapes surround you, are interwoven with your every day; they work so seamlessly you don’t even realize you are reflexively drawn to them.”

“It’s almost boggling that they can be harmful in a larger sense, but we still use them?” I asked.

“Yes… I can see that to be a struggle; why would your mind want to lead you down an unhealthy path? But, it’s the immediacy. It shows the genetic importance of redirecting the mind away from demonstrating frustration in social situations. Your mind cares that something is absorbing to it, that something lowers the water level, not that it could kill you in the long run.”

“So escapes exist to absorb the mind to some degree, to decrease stressors and pressures? Stressors and pressures are all things that resonate or are linked to resonating your emotional drives,” I said rhetorically, having both elbows on the table and one hand on my face gazing at the drawing.

“Great — the mind must focus on something to help decrease its stressors and pressures. Cigarettes are a good example. Nicotine itself is a mood alterer,” he said, then pointed to the picture he had drawn of the water in the glass. "If it lowers the water level, if a drug stimulates the mood, it works. If another type of drug alters perception, absorbs attention by altering perception, it works. If compulsively eating absorbs the attention and acts as a depressant as food digests and calms the individual down, lowering the water level, it works. If bodily pain absorbs the attention, it works. If cutting yourself absorbs the attention, it works. If repeating something compulsively absorbs your attention, it works. It doesn't have to be a complete absorption of attention, just a small portion. If focusing on something academic absorbs your attention, it works," he said, sounding redundant but nonetheless powerfully making his point.

"I see. The behavior, as you've said, is a symptom of what's going on with your emotions; it's the ability of the symptom to absorb your attention," I responded.

"Escapes are imperative; someone stops smoking, and then they gain weight. You put someone in solitary confinement; they hallucinate due to a lack of escapes and a quickly moving pendulum. If you don't choose an escape, the mind will find one for you. The stronger the drives resonate along with weaknesses within the Primary Cloud due to trauma, the more difficulty one has *coping*."

"That's fascinating, so whatever the behavior, a hobby, reading, exercise, compulsive eating, drugs, a migraine, all have to do with absorbing your attention away from these resonating Genetically Important Drives?" Mary asked.

"Exactly. Exercise might be a healthy absorption of the mind, lowering the glass of water level, while compulsive eating or painful repetitive thoughts are an unhealthy absorption of the mind."

"The poor people addicted to crack or meth, they've probably had traumatic events that have weakened their Primary Cloud and have driven them to require something that so intensely absorbs their mind?" Mary asked.

"Good point. One may begin to ask how, or more poignantly, *who*? — caused the weakening of the Primary Cloud. If the wrong person has access to the child, a terrible weakness can occur unless they later get the proper support, are willing to objectively reflect upon their own emotions, or are capable since many put up powerful walls to defend against recalling the painful events, they'll likely remain in a weakened state. If significantly weakened, they can be overpowered by their emotional drives, which can send them into a spin where they need something of extreme power to absorb their attention; and in walks the stronger, more destructive mood-altering attention absorbers."

"Fascinating…. So we are all struggling with the same dynamics of the mind, but let's say some of us have had messed up childhoods. We're always beating ourselves up. We might be prone to say migraines?" I said.

"That's quite correct. Someone might be resonating their drives. They may have taken on a real helper, goodist, or martyr role in life, always attempting to be perfect and good, which is infuriating in many ways to their own two-year-old since she or he is so regularly overlooked for the benefit of another, often less deserving; it causes great emotional strife."

"Wow, that was me as a kid and into my 20s with my family. I was such a helper monkey. That was my role. That is what they expected of me." Silent for a moment, Mary continued, "I can see how varied escapes can be. Anything that absorbs the mind can be an escape, stomach aches, migraines, repetitive thoughts, exercise, academic information, a job, all designed to absorb the mind's attention," Mary responded.

"Some extremely talented primitives have had horrible childhoods, their inner-selves are painfully wounded, things are never resolved, these pains and struggle with their emotions last a lifetime since they never enlightened about the correct methods for recovery. The energy expended on escapes are enormous, all to combat the resonating emotional drives, then maybe they find art or an occupation and use it as their escape, their way to reduce the overwhelming suffering. Van Gogh is only one of the endless possible examples."

"So, some geniuses are geniuses because they are coping with their stressors and pressures, the water shooting out of the glass. I get it. This stream in the model is so powerful. They find an escape and expend endless energy absorbed in and focusing upon it to calm their Genetically Important Drives," I responded.

“You're getting it. Some geniuses are powerfully driven to use their escapes to deal with intensely reoccurring, resonating emotional drives. They become a slave to their escapes, always painting, always working, and always dealing with the overflowing glass of water. Along with being reinforced by the avoidance of the stressor or pressure, the success and progress generated by the escape becomes the reinforcement, and what a powerful dopamine hit,” Wolfzang explained.

Shading in the overflowing water from his glass diagram, he continued. “Some that are wounded by life may have a quickly rising cup of water, seemingly benign things set them off, modest demands, simple interactions, small losses of control, harmless teasing which is perceived as attacks on their importance. All causes them great stressors and pressures because of painful associations to their dysfunctional childhood, thereby, the mind is reflexively drawn to the very thing that has been substantiated, that will absorb it.”

“I would imagine, when a workaholic is stressed out in life, his mind reflexively thinks about his work?” I responded.

“Yes! The ceaseless balancing act of those that are unwitting escape addicts. Which are more common here than you might ever suspect. Take the work away, give the person a long weekend or a period without that work, and they may have physical pains, get a migraine, have anxiety. An equally intense focus that absorbs the mind. Yet, that person would likely be fine to go away on an exciting trip. The trip would absorb their attention.” he responded, then took a sip of his coffee. “Please excuse me for a moment,” he said, got up, and went into a bathroom next to the cash register. Mary and I sat quietly and listened to the song *Making Love Out of Nothing at All*, by Air Supply as we continued to eat our bagels.

He returned from the bathroom and continued, “Now imagine if you could harness that hard-wired ability to focus and enjoy the focus, the thing that made Einstein the genius he was. If you fully understand the OCS model, if you fully understand the processes involved, it is quite possible.”

“It was the use of escapes that made Einstein so smart? He simply tapped into it?” Mary asked.

"Very good. And every time he felt like he made progress, had a slight success in a new or different understanding, he got the cheese, a nice hit of dopamine, reinforcing each small success. His uncle taught him how to use math as an escape. The connection with his uncle resonated his Yearning for Emotional Closeness. His uncle was able to help him dig out the hole for the water to run to, for the lake of water to form. The same way, parents here train their children how to use a particular escape, sports, jobs, or hobbies. When viewed as an escape, it's easy to imagine how a career gets passed down through generations."

"Huh, as you said, the Ethical Bell Curve, he was kind to himself, so the mistakes were no big deal. They didn't resonate with his Feelings of Inferiority that could overpower his Primary Cloud," I added.

"You're building the correct profile, kind self-talk, the piloting of his own escapes dedicated to discovery and innovation, as Einstein said, 'It's not that I'm so smart, it's just that I stay with a problem longer.' We don't believe he was superior to anyone else or beyond reproach. He had his own set of — challenges and weaknesses he needed to address, including developing a richer, more frequent, deeper connection with his own children. I do highly recommend you investigate and study his quotes. They are a window into his… mental processes." He paused for a moment then continued, "Do you remember what I'd said about David Hume the 18th century philosopher?"

"Sure, you'd said how he believed we have emotions then use our *logic* to support those emotions."

"Well, it's important to note that Einstein circa 1928 had said something like he would never have dared to overthrow the science of Newton if he had not read Hume."

"Huh! There's a relationship between them… *Amazing*."

We stared at the glass of water he so easily drew for us.

"You are quite an artist," Mary said.

"I've drawn it many times since I was quite young."

It became clear this simple drawing was a hugely important part of the OCSs cultural perspectives. It impacted his entire society and their governmental and economic systems. His AFEs were all built upon what they believed to be driving human behavior. To him, this axiomatic dynamic, these emotional drives, and the response to them were incorporated into every aspect of life. Yet, somehow, by becoming universally compassionate sentients, their complex, intricate understandings and systems were continuously perpetuated and strengthened.

“Out of the six, the two most powerful Genetically Important Drives are Yearning for Emotional Closeness and Resentment of Demands. Resentment of Demands is vital to completely grasp.”

“Demands, but we all got 'em; I mean, pay me well enough I’ll do nutty stuff.”

“MonkeyTzu realized if he gave someone with autism a direct demand, they would appear to not understand, but he began to recognize the individual would expend tremendous energy to avoid the demand. They’d strategize how to not perform the command. Showing fascinating problem-solving skills often well above what their IQ scores demonstrated.”

Mary finishing her bagel, putting the last small piece back on the plate, said jokingly, “Dan hates it when I put too many demands on him but is driven by love.”

He paused and smiled. “Your job now is to see the dynamics all around you. Certain conditions are quite remarkable. Take stuttering, for example. Think of the glass of water. The overflow of water is again the symptom, the reflexive compulsive behavior. For the person who stutters and focuses on the production of speech, the mind is absorbed into the production of each word. Through conditioning, the stuttering becomes worse and worse, more and more reflexive, compulsive, all because it absorbs the mind during periods of stressors and pressures, or what the individual has connected to stressors and pressures. You can imagine the self-sustaining, incessant, infinite loop of how anxious stuttering must make someone; when their mind is absorbed into the production of words, it’s quite an excruciating cycle. The mind becomes reflexively absorbed by the word production rather than the true cause, the water level in the glass, the triggers related to stressors and pressures that immediately raise the water level to overflow from the glass.”

"Wow, what a pain in the ass that must be! Everyone knows how public speaking makes people anxious. I could see how someone could feel anxious if they're afraid of stuttering and have the demand of talking to others. *Now* I can see what you mean. How escapes can be harmful in a larger scope," Mary responded.

"If you read your current academic papers regarding stuttering, you'd find a high percentage of them acknowledge there is an anxiety component related to the phenomena."

"It's still hard to imagine that the mind perceives the demonstration of frustration more deadly than putting up with such an attention-consuming anxiety-inflicting condition. Why it's not just better to get frustrated?" I said.

"This is the way the mind has been organized. Eons have passed, and humans survive better when they are redirected rather than expressing their anger in groups. So, when they become outwardly frustrated, they get into fights, they challenge powerful narcissists that see them as disposable, they do something rash, and they die. Genetically, those that were redirected to think about something — unrelated, survived and passed on their genes."

Mary and I sat quietly for a moment.

"Hmm, one might die if they ran around showing how they honestly felt with the bottled-up stress. So, escapes absorb the heat from the mind, and they do it without conscious thought, and the mind can connect these stressors and pressures to triggers that raise our glasses' water level instantly."

"Quite right — so what are your society's more acceptable escapes? These things that absorb the mind's attention?" Wolfzang asked.

"Sure, things that absorb your attention — I'd say movies, shopping, music, sports, food, exercise, video games, painting, collecting," Mary responded.

"Sex," I said jokingly. "Ok — so these Genetically Important Drives of the brainstem and limbic system? There are six of them, what are they all again?" I asked.

On a napkin, he wrote:

Resentment of Demands (Very strong)

LOVE aka, Yearning for Emotional Closeness (Very strong)

Control of Environment

Control of Others

Feelings of Inferiority

Narcissistic Drive

"You'll see hints of these genetically important behavioral drives in your current mental disorders. Terms and labels *the* psychological committees have voted and approved as now unquestionably forever accurate." He said with a smile. "Disorders that have been rigidly hyper-categorized, separated, and compartmentalized instead of seeing the fundamental interrelationships between each; the inextricably intertwined existence of each. For example, someone with borderline personality disorder greatly fears abandonment, that is, the overpowering of the Primary Cloud by the resonance of Yearning for Emotional Closeness, the Need to Control Others, Feelings of Inferiority, and the Narcissistic Drive. At some point, the child's mind was weakened. Now, these emotional drives overpower the mind," he explained.

"Huh, Narcissistic Drive? Why not just Narcissism, the other Genetically Important Drives don't have 'drive' after them?"

"Very good observation, you've noticed something of significance. If you look at a patch of wild flowers things are growing in every direction. There might be caterpillars, bees, beetles all interacting with the plants growing in every direction. It's all profoundly beautiful. This would be the natural world. The human mind wants to format and truncate. It emotionally feels good to Control the Environment. The word Narcissism doesn't get the point across, nor does the word Narcissistic. To pragmatically make the point, we like not force fitting all the terms to look *the same*. So we prefer Narcissistic Drive."

He took his tablet out of his jogger's backpack hanging on the back of his chair; a cartoon began that showed two cave people and an enormous boulder.

"All of the Genetically Important Drives of the brainstem and limbic system exist because of millions of years of evolution. They all have had infinitely positive genetic consequences; otherwise, they would have faded out of existence," he explained, paused for a moment, then continued, "If — if you go back 2400 years ago to the Greeks, you'll find the same emotional responses, if you go back 4000 years ago to the Sumerians, same thing, same Genetically Important Drives dictating their behaviors, but these hugely important genetically important behavioral drives located in the brainstem and limbic system go much further than that and have had plenty of time to show their importance. If you go back 3.5 million years to Australopithecus Afarensis, known as, Lucy, she'd have the same genetically important behavioral drives, but her neocortex wouldn't be as well developed. You'd be able to see these emotional drives more clearly. Her behavioral responses would be more obvious due to a less robust, less dense Primary Cloud. Escapes were a thing just less prominent; groups were smaller. The more continuous struggle to stay alive kept her in the moment. Escapes evolved to redirect the mind due to the huge genetic value of living in larger more complex groups. For Lucy, the Genetically Important Drives *could* run the show and get positive genetic returns."

I would guess that Don Martin had made the animation of the cavemen on the screen. A title appeared: *Feelings of Inferiority*. The two cave people observe the boulder; one says, "I can do it!" and tries to jump on top of the boulder and falls off, much like an 80s video game, "The End!" Appeared across the screen, followed by a gravestone.

Being a little unclear where this was going, we both gave a nervous chuckle. "Uh-huh?"

The other cave person looks at the boulder, looks down, and says, "I *can't* do that, NO WAY!." POP, POP, POP, POP lots of little cave babies holding clubs, "THE WINNER!"

Mary laughed and said, "I get it! Resonating Feelings of Inferiority isn't always bad!"

I smiled and said, "That's — pretty funny!"

"That was the same video I was shown when I was a little kid learning about the Genetically Important Drives of the brainstem and limbic system; it's a real classic," he explained, pausing for a moment, then continued, "To perform the required analysis on oneself, one must learn to step away from themselves… step out of themselves, observe their physical and mental responses to the world around them. To care deeply about the part of the mind responsible for thinking about thinking which must be resilient enough to handle intensely objective complex reflection and never be offended by those that question one's own embraced beliefs, yet recognize when they're confronting someone that is… biased and subjective, possibly protecting their own embraced beliefs by attacking yours."

"Wow six, *six* different emotional drives that have wreaked havoc on human's throughout history."

"So there are the prominent six essential when understanding human behavior. It *is* incredible to think that groups of neurons in the brainstem and limbic system are hardwired to produce very particular behavioral outcomes. But that is an exploration for the future. It goes very deep, there are minor Genetically Important Drives beyond the six. Like the fear of water, which one would see if your Primary Cloud breaks down. You can see this when someone gets rabies and becomes hydrophobic."

"What you're saying is that when you get rabies, your Primary Cloud breaks down, and then you become phobic of water?" I asked.

"Well, yes, the planet is largely water; it would make sense to be hard-wired to be fearful of water, to have a Genetically Important Drive deep within the brainstem and limbic system to help you get out of the water if your executive functioning severely weakens quickly and your gasping, drowning. But that rarely impacts human behavior. It's a minor Genetically Important Drive within the brainstem and limbic system."

"Huh, but for this study we're just interested in the six?"

"That's right," Wolfzang said with a smile.

Our waitress walked by and acknowledged us with her upbeat, pleasant nod and smile.

"Watch Cindy with the blonde girl that just walked in."

We saw the blonde girl enter before Cindy noticed her; she was about 15 feet away from Cindy. Cindy acted normally and said, "Hi! How are you?" in her cheerful voice, then turned around and bit her fingernails.

"That girl used to work here with Cindy. The girl is a pathological liar, a complete narcissist; she even tried to get Cindy in trouble with the boss to curry favor. She was an absolute nightmare, and Cindy is prone to being a bit of a caretaker. But did you notice what happened?"

"Yes, she started biting her nails when she turned around," Mary responded.

"Exactly, that is the escape behavior; she didn't even realize she did it; it was reflexive and immediately helped in absorbing part of her attention away from her resonating drives," Wolfzang responded.

"Wow, I'm sure she wasn't even aware of it," I said.

"Again, with classical conditioning, aka Pavlovian conditions, the bell rings, and the drives resonate. Cindy came close to quitting the job just to get away from her. Luckily, the other girl found the right job, boss, well, sugar daddy to take advantage of and didn't need to target poor Cindy anymore — but she still likes the bagels here," Wolfzang explained with a chuckle.

"That's incredible. So all of these little behaviors we do, biting lips, biting nails, tics, repetitive thoughts, drinking? It's all the same stuff? We're all hard-wired the same way, with variations being nearly unlimited?" I asked.

"You've got it; it's typically about absorbing the mind, redirecting the mind; these escapes are conditioned and, over time, become extremely strong. The mind recognizes they are useful for absorbing attention, they are reinforced over and over, then something like nail-biting becomes reflexive and compulsive, the poor girl's fingers actually get bloody at times," Wolfzang responded.

"How do we rid ourselves of the more vile escapes we've unknowingly acquired?" Mary asked.

"Well, the first step is to understand and know what's going on, acceptance of the processes at work; it is, after all, the human mind's defense mechanism. The more you need it, the more frustrated a person will become hearing about the OCS Mental Model. The recovery process includes reflecting on the why, then you start to reward yourself for using new, healthier escapes," Wolfzang explained.

"But — they are changeable?" Mary responded.

"Yes, quite possible, and it's quite doable. We're trained from childhood to control the process and direct our escapes. When you understand it, the power is quite astonishing what you can accomplish with the directed focus," Wolfzang explained.

Mary and I both seemed to let out some air. "Whoa, that is good news," I said.

"How long? How long will it take to change these things?" Mary asked.

"Mostly, in just a few weeks, if you have the right techniques, knowing how to use symbolism to communicate with your inner mind and skillfully use rewarding alternative healthy escapes to absorb the mind's attention."

"Wow, just a few weeks," Mary responded.

"Traumatic childhoods, traumatic events, take little more work. They make the escapes have a higher voltage and are more easily triggered. The Primary Cloud is still coping with painful events, especially if you believe in forgiveness, to us, a euphemism for repression. But yes, again, quite doable; you have to understand the mind as we do and not buy into the dogmas trained here. Also — many friends, family, and co-workers enable the use of unhealthy habits."

"That's insane! We're all like Arrav; those around us are pulling us back into some sort of poverty of the mind, enabling our progress," I said.

"Well, yes, humans are sentients capable of reflection, Therefore, there is the possibility of free will. To choose your own escape, you must be consistent and make it fun. You're dealing with escapes that have water-like attributes. From my own experience, it's like you're digging out a lake for water to run into. The water runs to the easiest, most available lowest point. If you want to change your escape to exercise, you must connect positive emotions to it. When you begin the process, early conditioning is slow. In the beginning, give yourself plenty of rewards. Make sure you engineer dopamine hits to condition the activity. Make it fun and exceptionally important — it must be easily available. Adding other escapes, such as music while you're doing it, giving yourself a fairytale-like fantasy story for the use to promote it to your own inner mind," Wolfzang explained.

"Huh, OCSs would never berate yourself for not exercising or failing a diet. Acting like a punishing drill sergeant. I'm starting to see you'd see that act as detrimental to long-term success. No… You'd suspect your systems were failing and work on the engineering of those systems to condition the *escape*."

"Wow, that's insightful," I said, pondering Mary's understanding. "So you use multiple escapes at the same time? Or reinforce an escape with the use of another. Expected hits of dopamine. Use inspiring symbolic storylines to promote it?" I asked.

"Escapes are the prescription you *must* master. You become acquainted with the dosages and how to combine them, how to motivate your own little self," Wolfzang said.

Smiling at Cindy for a moment, Wolfzang said, "You are undeniably great with people. You will do exceptionally well in life with your adroit people skills; identifying and knowing how to handle high-conflict people is one of the best skills you can have in life in this hugely populated city. Anyone would be lucky to work with you."

"What a thoughtful thing to say," Cindy responded, as a slight rosiness showed on her face. She pivoted and walked toward the register.

"Again, if escapes are a huge reason for human behavior but it is not fully understood and therefore calamitously overlooked by primitives, it affects every part of society, including scientific progress. If the Vac-Plat is all about understanding human behavior and neutralizing things that humans can do to avoid shooting themselves in the foot, it is an essential understanding."

"Wow, OCSs believe escapes are *that* big of a deal, that big of a driver of human behavior? That important to understanding the mind?" Mary said.

"Stephen Hawking lived unexpectedly long with ALS. He lived so long because he perceived the world optimistically. This world perception helped him retain low stressors and pressures; simultaneously, he immersed himself in powerfully absorbing academic escapes for long periods every day. When escapes are intensely used, and stressors and pressures are low, the mind-body does its optimum for cell repair and growth."

"That's so funny. I remember learning about the oldest documented living woman; what was her name?"

"Jeanne Calment," Wolfzang responded.

"That's it. Supposedly, her family owned a store, which helped her financially live a life of low stress, and then she had a bunch of physical hobbies — escapes, like bike riding, swimming, and mountaineering. She lived until she was 122."

"Huh! It's *so* interesting. Never in my Psych classes did they talk about anything other than rewards, punishment, or chemicals in the mind driving human behavior. How could it not be impacting human behavior when you recognize how escapes are ubiquitous within everyday life? — We clearly all need it?" Mary said.

"Professionals in the fields related to human behavior have been trained, they have embraced beliefs and now will only build upon that training, repeating what they forevermore agree with."

"Hmm… Like any other embraced belief, you can't contradict them head-on. You must slowly, gracefully, thoughtfully describe a novel idea that might seem — from a different time."

"After all, as you've said, the Embraced Belief Cloud Network with its billions of neurons treats academic theories like all other beliefs, whether economic, religious, political, or in this case, psychological. Most will simply dislike you for confronting an embraced belief, not objectively examining a clearly developed novel idea for validity," Mary said, smiling.

“We’ve covered a lot of essential info so far; why don’t the two of you check into your hotel? I’ll meet back up with you around 1:00 on our benches at Washington Square Park.” Wolfzang said, reaching for his wallet and then going over to Cindy, who was near the cash register. We both said goodbye to our exceptionally goodist waitress and walked out the door onto the now-crowded sidewalk, then walked over to the hotel around the corner on Crosby Street.

At first glance, the elegance was remarkable. As we walked through the metal arches, hanging ivy, hanging lights, it was clear the designers knew how to enchant. We checked in with a formal, business-appropriate receptionist and received a key card for a room on one of the highest floors. It wasn’t hard to feel wealthy for a moment as we walked through the door to our room. The windows were from floor to ceiling; the views were exceptional, a corner room with views north and west. The room was bright white and azure blue, contrasting and quite striking.

“Like he said, OCSs have relentlessly studied and mastered prescribing their own rest and relaxation to recover from intensive AFEs; it’s essential for their purposes — I think they’re systematically rewarding themselves for the hard work they’re willing to put into their discovery and innovation, and this — room, they don’t use it to show off, impress or gain an upper hand on others; they use it for quiet, calm, reflection,” I said, checking out the glass shower with its own window looking over the building tops of lower Manhattan.

“I’d love to live here! It’s all about the experience to them; they can care less about owning stuff. Why don’t you put the recorder into your backpack and put the backpack into the bathroom?” Mary said, falling back onto the luxurious soft bed and oversized pillows. Where I soon followed, and we took a little time for our very own — imaginative, relaxing escape.

After which, we briefly fell asleep. Our next visit was getting close, so we both took refreshingly powerful hot showers overlooking the city. The heavy steam and the smell of the hotel’s luxurious, unfamiliar, unique soap made the shower an absorbing experience.

“This was so reinvigorating! That stuff about escapes he was covering today, it seems somewhat obvious — yet with detailed essential complexities that are counter-intuitive?” I said.

“Yeah, I know almost like the mind doesn’t want you to know, and that’s what sent humans — well, primitives into a tailspin living on, as he says, ‘this probability planet.’”

“I guess when you add it all together. Most of all, like he says, 67% of us are easily convinced of the wrong answers because the answer benefits ourselves emotionally. *Then* to use escapes reflexively during periods of stressors and pressures. Like he said, if you don’t pick your own escapes, an escape will pick you. Yet another irrational act that we’d fight to defend. It becomes clearer why our large-scale perpetual outcomes are sometimes a little *better* or a little *worse*, but in the end — chance.”

“I’ll meet you in the hallway,” I said, waiting for Mary to finish getting ready.

“Yup!”

I walked out into the hallway, started looking through the large windows near the elevators, and heard our hotel room door shut. Mary was going to make a left toward the elevators, so I hid behind the corner. I jumped out like a little kid and said, “BOOO!” BUT… it wasn’t Mary. It was some guy in a business suit. “AHHHHHHH!” he screamed.

“I’m… SO SORRY! I thought you were my wife!” I said, feeling insanely embarrassed, like a goofy little kid.

“OH, oh — it’s… alright!” The man calmly replied, smiled almost appreciatively, and walked casually by.

I immediately realized I was so lucky I didn’t get reflexively punched in the face. He was unusually easygoing — down to earth. I honestly wouldn’t have blamed the guy at all if I ended up with a black eye. I speculated he was an OCS staying in the hotel. He wasn’t angry or frustrated about my tomfoolery, just comically surprised. I told Mary what had happened, and she couldn’t stop laughing; she laughed for blocks.

It wasn't long before we got to Washington Square Park; sitting on our familiar benches was Wolfzang facing north toward the fountain. Today they had grand pianos scattered throughout the park, played by seasoned pianists. Though, the pieces I did not quite recognize.

"I've enjoyed staying there in the past. Aren't the views fantastic?"

"Well, I have a story to tell you!" I reiterated the hilarity to Wolfzang, and we all laughed for another fifteen minutes, barely able to focus. "The place was *incredible*; we're so lucky your… group overbooked. Let us know if you ever overbook *anything* else; we can be the OCSs bottom feeders from now on," Mary said grinning.

"Where were we? What else do you need to know for you to get a complete grasp of the OCSs understanding of the essential water glass? Oh, yes — when you resonate your Genetically Important Drives, your dreams are built around them. You feel inferior, you feel out of control, your mind builds a dream around the genetic drive that had some serious action that day."

"So dreams are escapes?" Mary asked.

"Dreams are an extension of escapes when you sleep. Escapes are so essential to the human mind that when you go to sleep, you can't stop using them. They are simply a different form of escape. Without escapes, the mind simply doesn't function correctly. And as I said, the mind will create its own escapes if put into a place without any."

"About the dream thing, I think I get it, so I resonate my Genetically Important Drives, then later at night, my escapes build a storyline around that day's energetically resonating drive?" Mary explained.

"You've got it, so say you're dealing with a complete narcissist one day. You pull up to a small town, then walk into this library you've never been to before and immediately notice the library is organized strangely. This librarian holds extremely rigid liberal views, but all the views are intertwined with highly biased beliefs against men. She considers herself a progressive with feminist ideals. But clearly, if you spoke with her, you'd find an extremely hostile individual that thinks herself exceptionally enlightened. This librarian has taken it upon herself after seizing control of the place 25 years ago to organize it in her own peculiar way. She can't be fired since she's the sister of someone important in town, but she's an absolute nightmare to deal with, and everyone knows it. So, to find the books you need, you become her servant, and she likes that; she is indeed a narcissist. She relishes holding power over others, remedial as it might appear to anyone else, making each patron conform to her very narrow view of how she is the queen of *this* domain. She charged absurd late fees on any late media that isn't a book, which in her view, 'shouldn't be in a library anyway.' Unquestionably, you will find a very wounded little girl in her, and, undoubtedly, something painfully unresolved. She terrorizes anyone that reminds her of someone that once hurt her, and there are countless perpetrators. If she doesn't like you, watch out; you might never get the book you're there for, and if she can, she'll attempt to wound you to help herself feel more in control."

"Man, tell me where this *is*? I want to stay out of that town altogether," I said.

He smiled, "This is simply a thought experiment, but on your probability planet — *it* exists. Small town politics can be quite… *challenging*."

"Go on, so what about this tyrant and her books?" Mary asked.

"So, you walk in and are forced to ask her, 'Where can I find the science fiction section?' She replies, 'It's posted right in front of you!' You immediately feel like you did as a kid, facing an oppressive bully. You feel lost and a little out of control, so you press on, 'I'm sorry, where is it in front of me?' 'Keep looking! I can't believe you don't understand what I'm saying!' she replies. You've offended her; her highly efficient novel system isn't as effective as she believes it is. You start to wonder if you should just run away, but you positively want the book; you took a special trip over to get the book only this library carries. So, you respond, 'I, unfortunately, don't know… I'm sorry,' she responds quite condescendingly, '400s to the right.' When you find the book and return to check it out, you try to make limited conversation because you realize she isn't balanced, and then she makes a comment, 'Good luck, reading it — *it's* a *big* book.' You continue to ignore her; you know she's insinuating that you have some sort of comprehension issue in her disparaging way, but she has effectively resonated your Feelings of Inferiority, and you feel a little out of control. Hours pass, much later at night; you have a dream that is manufactured around the resonating of your Feelings of Inferiority and the Need to Control the Environment."

"That particular bird seems to be ubiquitous! The type can be found at the DMV, the post office, and in customer service. I've encountered individuals like her in various guises, sometimes as a man, eagerly exerting the limited authority they possess over others."

"Right, those types magnify the nothing power they have into something ridiculous. You're stuck thinking about them long after trying to understand it — them," Mary responded.

"I know — people like that send your mind into a loop."

"The mind absorbs others' cruel comments. We feel the subtle comments. They resonate our Genetically Important Drives sometimes without our awareness, like it or not. The more you are unaware of the mind's dynamics, the more control it has over you. When you have a high conflict person, they can resonate your Genetically Important Drives of the brainstem and limbic system, sometimes quite powerfully — skillfully," he said, waiting for a moment and once again rubbing his thumbnail.

"Let me shift gears a little, just for the sake of argumentation, regarding what you said earlier today; I'd like you to assume entirely without me utterly proving it to you that I can travel through time and space, that there are indeed vast multiple timelines that the OCS have unlimited access to."

"Wow, but you will not prove it to us?" I said.

"This is a perception experiment. So, let me continue with your line of reasoning. I'm here for observation and hands-on interactions for research purposes. I'm not here to physically move everyone around. I'm here to learn the most effective way to alter a timeline without making it traumatic or even noticeable for the many millions of inhabitants involved."

"'When you do things right, no one will think you did anything at all;' wasn't that line in a *Futurama* episode?" Mary said.

Wolfzang, impressed by Mary's levity, smiled.

Wolfzang was like one of the grand piano players in the park today. I couldn't identify the song he was playing, but there was something mesmerizing about his words. It all sounded unexpectedly soothing, graceful as if the multiverse, not him, had said these things acting in its most honest state. I recognized that he, the virtuoso, had a complete mastery of how long to hold each key and when to slow or speed up the notes.

As we sat there looking at the fountains, I thought about what he said months ago. How general rules of science parallel other scientific phenomena but can be a more exacting description than the use of numbers or numeric data. Simultaneously, I grappled with his point that numbers, amounts, and quantities are not science, just an attempt to communicate the phenomenon. In a prolonged moment of clarity, I contemplated this belief that the general properties of water shared essential characteristics of the OCS understanding of escapes. As he had mentioned, these general rules of science that he recognized as meaningful were a three-dimensional description of the phenomenon rather than a two-dimensional numerical quantity, which may, at times, be ambiguous or truncated.

I gazed at the water shooting out of the fountain into the sky; I imagined a giant glass of water with all the stressors and pressures acting as water filling the glass each day of our existence. The water shooting up out of the glass being all of our compulsive, reflexive, uncontrollable symptoms, headaches, stomachaches, excessive eating, fixations, an irresistible need to drink alcohol, gambling, shopping, obsessive thoughts, ruminating on worry, or even the desire for fun stuff like listening to music, doing art, or playing video games. I glanced at a homeless man, a girl wearing an 80s-style fluorescent red and yellow shirt, and a couple of kids eating ice cream cones, and thought how each of us human animals were experiencing this dynamic occurring in the mind, this mental phenomenon. I wrestled with the idea that he believed it was essential to understand this process to achieve the healthiest, most remarkable existence. "Clearly, how else could an entire society be like him, unbiased, radiating good health and optimism, and down to the bone bred for discovery and innovation?" I thought to myself. Reflecting on my past, I could remember so many times I reflexively was drawn toward eating, watching movies, running, or just fueling needless circular argumentation. I began to embrace his working description of escapes as quite reasonable. If this was indeed completely accurate, I wondered how we got through our entire lives, never accepting the processes or observing ourselves. How our brains wanted the process to remain an enigma, to continue the momentary advantage of not showing frustration. We were unwittingly led to use unhealthy escapes, which added to us remaining — primitive. For those of us with trauma, weaknesses, and triggers, those glasses would fill right to the top, and we would turn right to the bad stuff to cope.

"The water thing, how it's used to describe escapes, it makes sense — I see it now! You've been bringing us to these benches facing this fountain, watching the water shooting up. The people are all walking around it, naturally doing what they do — being oh so… human. That point you made; using numeric values and data can end up truncating essential information or be used deceptively by someone with underlying motivations. The seemingly trivial point, I thought then, you made about perception relative to the observer — your point was vastly more insightful, wasn't it? Your point was that there are essentially important… general laws of science that are aligned with human behavior. The general properties of water mirror or parallel the principles of escapes. When you said, 'escapes are as important to the human mind as water is to the human body. The glass of water fills itself with stressors and pressures; then the overflow is compulsive, reflexive behaviors.'"

"And… you mentioned THAT you should look at the stressors and pressures in the glass or why the water raises so rapidly, not the symptoms, the overflowing water. You also explained that escapes cool the resonating Genetically Important Drives within the brainstem and limbic system. Sort of like a cool stream flowing over the heated emotional drives," Mary added.

"Yet, you can tap into the escapes like an enormous, fast-moving, unstoppable majestic river. But also — to create an escape, you have to strategically and systematically dig out the hole for the lake for the water to run to by conditioning and making the escape extremely available so the water easily runs to the right place. The attributes of water and not numbers is — essential and astounding."

"Wait, I see it, what Dan was saying… It's not a fountain. It's a symbolic metaphor for the powerful overflowing water. The fountain surrounded by all these unique characters, unique but the same, all acting on these same fundamentals. You've pointed out the absolute importance of symbolism, symbolic activities, and how it's the necessary language to interact with the brainstem and limbic system. This place was meant for the symbolism! To communicate with our — little ones, you're talking to us, and you're doing things to communicate with our inner 2-year-olds. *Amazing*! The OCSs always see communicating with humans as dealing with two separate beings. We're only taught how to communicate with the one here and often mistreat the other."

"Bravo! You're both progressing splendidly! Why don't the two of you enjoy the city? We'll meet back up tomorrow morning at about 9:00, right here." Wolfzang explained, then handed me yet another white envelope.

Washington Square, Finn

Later that night, Mary and I walked over Manhattan Bridge to the DUMBO area. Many enormous structures in the city leave a dreamlike feeling, leaving a sense that you're only a speck of dust in the universal sense, a reminder that when working collectively, we can accomplish things that would be otherwise insurmountable. Walking along Washington Street under the bridge, we gazed in awe at the enormous piers, columns, and structural triangles. The gigantic sight of aesthetic geometric symmetry prompted contemplations of our perception assignment. It seemed clearer there. Without another timeline to compare our own technological advancements, it was hazy to accept that we were only showing a tiny fraction of our potential to innovate.

It was there I did as we agreed. I wrestled with his views and drew a conclusion. Without an intense desire to objectively reflect on our own abilities. If our hard-wired drives endlessly energized us to believe ourselves the center of the universe, these same drives would naturally defend our emotions and conceal what we were as a whole: innovative bumblers. Thus, the emotionally driven majority just persisted with logic to defend and sustain the existing ineffective systems we applauded, accepted, insisted to retain, and then damned us never to become what we could be.

"Still — this time-traveling thing, it's gotta be an extension of his perception research? Why wouldn't he just give us evidence? Well, besides the hologram?" I said, once again feeling suspicious of Wolfzang's intentions.

"True, he's paying us for our time, he brings up a lot of interesting recondite points, I mean, everything about other's reactions, why they do stuff, even things we feel, you know, really feel deep down — it makes *sense*. Maybe our only choice has been to take this well-financed ride a little further each time. Admit it. We're enjoying this *undertaking*, the places we're visiting, the unexpected but required deep introspections," Mary explained.

"I mean, we're sort of basing everything on his contrasting but intricately developed underlying beliefs about science and human behavior, his ever-progressing youthful appearance — that hologram, the recorders," I said, looking a bit confounded. "Isn't that strange? I mean, we haven't seen a spaceship? Any other OCSs? We never even met Otter?" I said.

After tiring ourselves from the long walk and intensely pondering his insights, we found ourselves sitting quietly in the large white chairs in the hotel room, looking through the huge windows at the city's building tops. I thought of the Well's quote, "Our thoughts ran free of precision in our festive after-dinner atmosphere."

"Could you imagine *what* could be? If this Vac-Plat thing takes root in our timeline, during our lifetime?" Mary said.

"Even if we are part of the founders *here* and don't know it yet, that's good enough for me. It's some sort of ultimate level of existence and compassion they're striving for."

"I get it. If we're doing this to change *everything*, to make a kinder, more beautiful world, then it's not about us; they don't even give the real names of their founders. These OCSs disdain idol worship, but I can already see the unbelievable benefits of not being what we are."

"Right! Nullifying our reptilian brains to become something… better, something stunningly *magnificent*," I replied.

"This hyper-awareness he places on symbolism, such a different view. Another thing we just accept as the water we swim in. I can see we've gotta attune ourselves to the world around us, see *when* and *how* our inner selves might be guided. Fully attentive when someone or some group might be attempting to influence our inner mind, and then be highly suspicious, even *insulted*. I see it, political, religious leaders, top dogs, corporate execs of all sorts, throughout history have used symbolism, symbolic theater that resonates our emotional drives to control the herd."

"They're always suspicious as to why others might desire to do that, not look past it. Continuously thinking about the two parts of the mind and the essential communication. When I think back how so many times I've been oblivious, influenced by others and their clearly pre-engineered desire — to guide me."

"Like the time I got that speeding ticket in Esopus. Do you remember when I went to court? That huge courtroom for such a tiny town? The enormously high ceiling, the windows. What does that cost the taxpayers to heat? The building itself must have cost the town a fortune. Then the theater-like production, the almighty judge sat high above everyone. He even had special lights shining on him to add to his omniscient magnificence. The court secretary sitting below him surrounded by computer monitors. You couldn't see her as she yelled out 'case number 0234 *the people* versus Dan Caracal.' How absurd and clearly designed to resonate one's Feelings of Inferiority. Having to call him "your honor." It was a speed trap. I was doing 8 miles over the speed limit right after the speed limit changed. Yet, it did impact me. The entire ridiculous symbolic theatrical setup was created to make the perp feel — subservient, small, weak — childlike. I just wanted to pay my silly fine and get out, not act out a ridiculous theatrical role of a naughty boy."

"Unaware, but purposely designed for symbolic impact. These powerful designs are everywhere. Imagine if we were taught from a young age to perpetually decipher and be clued into the act. Truly realize when someone was playing on our Genetically Important Drives for their own benefit. Rather than being another primitive blindly led by our resonating emotional drives, we'd laugh at the theatrical productions rather than guided by them."

"If we were in tune, accepted our little selves, and communicated well, much would be done differently. Without acceptance, manipulation is more accessible to those with particular goals in mind," I said, staring down from the window at the dome top of a once-old police station, now redesigned into condos and inhabited by Leonardo DiCaprio.

To most, this would just be a room with a fantastic view, but to the OCS, it's a place to challenge the mind to perceive the city and its inhabitants from a distinct vantage point. For the rest of the night, we forgot about the journals.

The next day, we woke up invigorated and excited to continue our work with Wolfzang. I found myself listening to the recorder and researching things he said. After quickly picking up coffee and tea, we walked over to Washington Square Park. There was Wolfzang once again, sitting on the same park benches facing north toward the fountain.

"You gave us a lot to think about yesterday," I said, fixing the recorder to the inside of my pocket.

“What I’ve explained about behavior is not that much different than what you might already think, but it’s how the details all come together.”

Looking at my phone, I replied, “That’s amazing. This morning, I ran across this quote and thought about what you’d said. Also by Einstein, ‘all of science is nothing more than the refinement of everyday thinking.’”

“Very good! OCS simply harnessed our mind's need to reduce stressors and pressures, then objectively and pragmatically refined, refined, refined our psychodynamic understandings, while assiduously neutralizing our inherent natures.”

“Not us. We’re all about building upon in-vogue, currently accepted beliefs. We thereby blindly build on and applaud existing mistakes — well, beliefs. What did that economics professor say to me, ‘find an existing theory and join the discussion.’ Though most often partially correct ideas interlaced with wrongly embraced beliefs keep the gears spinning.”

“Those on the Vac-Plat aren’t being incentivized to have a voice, join the current heavily applauded discussion, alter other’s perception for self-interest; this fundamental is a necessary ingredient in our *secret sauce.* It’s a hard concept to imagine here; we can *trust* each other's perceptions, discoveries — observations. There aren’t countless benefits to someone to act emotionally driven with the majority, winning by quashing accurate views, and not being pragmatically objective.”

Wolfzang fell silent for a moment, sipped his coffee, and watched a couple, each dressed similarly in jeans and a t-shirt, holding hands and strolling by.

“When I was quite young, I was interested in observing the Primary Cloud in an individual before and after a weakening. The loss or damage to it. After investigating and doing many AFEs — one I still ponder was with a gentleman named Finn, located in 1848.”

“Woah… Woah, slow down, ‘located in 1848?’” I said.

“Yes, that’s right, you’re still digesting my — well, the parameters for our sociological perception experiment,” he said with a smile, “time and space are interwoven to the OCSs we are — after all, located here and now."

"Don't let Dan interrupt you; yes, we're aware… this pertains to the perception exploration, but just in case, this metaphorical story has a deeper meaning or something? We know how you work with many stylistic devices. You know, in case this isn't just some sort of analogy-based thought experiment," Mary said with a chuckle.

Ignoring Mary's obvious hint to prove himself, he continued, "I met him by procuring a position as a laborer with the Rutland & Burlington Railroad. I needed to develop an intimate knowledge of him and the subtle complexities of his personality."

"A three-dimensional understanding of his personality… as you'd say," I replied.

"Yes, precisely," he said. Paused, pulled an unusual blueish berry out of his pocket, and began feeding the pigeons. "He was, indeed, a well-spoken gentleman of the highest quality. Often talking about his childhood and his grandmother in New Hampshire, and a girl — Laura, whom he was in love with from Tarrytown. We developed a connection by the time of his accident in September of 1848. Yet, I knew he was going to get a rod shot through his skull, and that particular day — I didn't show up for work. I couldn't bear to witness that very thoughtful, intelligent, kind man get so badly injured."

"Being such a compassionate person, how could you let it happen?" Mary asked.

"These things have already happened. It was a necessary scientific inquiry. Being there, fully immersed, experiencing his world with all my senses, I was able to fully examine how the incident impacted his network of billions of neurons, mainly in his neocortex, yet left his Genetically Important Drives fully intact. I tried to give him a bit more — happiness in life by connecting to him to some degree before and after IT happened."

"I thought OCSs were — Universally Ethical? Wouldn't you have to save him?"

“We’re pragmatically Universally Ethical. His timeline, like yours, has many organically essential occurrences that I’d rather not muck up. If it’s a healthy enough timeline, we really shouldn’t intervene too much. Thought, environmental factors, humans hardwired nature reheal slight interactions to a predictable timeline. So being low-key is part of the program. Yet I needed to intricately examine close up the finite details I might otherwise miss. An essential but disregarded detail when reading an article, observing, or passively using our metaverse. The gold standard for us is the AFE, a *completely* accurate immersive AFE.”

“I can’t even imagine what you know about us. But, you know it all… don’t you, how it ends?” Mary explained.

Deflecting Mary’s question, Wolfzang continued. “The spike shot up. His mouth was opened at the moment of impact. It traveled under his left cheekbone and left through the top of his skull. Traveling right through the cloud network of billions of neurons mainly in his neocortex — his Primary Cloud.”

“Whoa, what a grizzly scene. Poor guy!”

“So — he survived. It sounds like a lobotomy,” I responded.

“Did you notice any similarities to severe autism? This weakening of the network of billions of neurons, mainly in the neocortex?”

“It was a weakening of his Primary Cloud, but this was via a traumatic brain injury. Some details of the weakening are different since it was such a sudden mechanical occurrence,” he paused, took a sip of his coffee, then continued, “From then on, he was easily frustrated and usually perseverated on THE spike he kept with him; he knew the size, every imperfection on that — *thing*.”

“You deeply cared about Finn; what a difficult thing it must be to have to allow things to just happen,” I said.

“I do struggle with that one. Even if I intervened, there is so much acting on the moment that things often invariably still happen,” he said with a grimace. “All the work I do. Our AFEs are not combat to win a crown. It’s like building a yellow brick road that the other sentients can walk on and follow to the Emerald City. Yet, it’s not necessarily always painless. You can get a bloody nose, scrapes, and experience heartache. There are moments of growth that are hugely painful but necessary. We don't believe in embracing the fictional storyline of being clinically disconnected from the experience. You risk losing hugely crucial, subtle, or accidentally omitted strings that could bring it all together. We never pretend that moments don't impact us, but we experience the moment and grow stronger after… from the recovery process."

"You allow the experience to happen and then know how to effectively recover from it by having a mastery of this particular mental process the OCSs have — embraced?" Mary asked.

"True, how to listen to, communicate with, and nurture your inner mind. Things are painful; there is evil in the world, if you're fully objective and honest with yourself and others, you become — *aware*, and you'll vividly see the world as it *is*, not through a fuzzy lens, and that is infinitely powerful."

"It sounds like the remuneration *or* reward for not using logic to substantiate emotional beliefs as humans have done throughout their existence."

"Our recovery process can be involved, but it's *highly* effective. We need recovery time after intensive AFEs. After Finn, I needed a lot of reflection and a lot of symbolic communication to nurture my inner mind. Though it was long ago, it left me with insights I built upon ever since, the bedrock for so much I do today. I'm endlessly grateful to have known him. He wanted things we all want."

"It almost seems like you not only expect pain during your Analytical Field Explorations, you see it as fundamental to discovery, innovation, and emotional growth?" I asked.

"Quite an essential reason why the OCS have a great love for each other; we are accepting we have all suffered to excel upward. You can't pretend you're not impacted, your little one knows the truth, and it's all about accepting the way things truly impact you. Acceptance and understanding will end the pain generated by the powerfully resonating emotional drives."

"Wow, an entire society that can recover from any and all weakenings!"

“And therefore, no homeless, drug addicts, alcoholics — no narcissists.”

“To me, my fellow OCSs are the most interesting beings in the multiverse. They tell true stories that can dwarf the most captivating movie you’ve ever seen.”

Wolfzang sat quietly for a few moments feeding the pigeons. By now, he was attracting over a dozen. I thought of the Mary Poppins song, “Tuppence A Bag.” I knew we felt appreciation for him just as the squirrels, the pigeons, and little Anna had; somehow, he knew how to elevate others in his presence.

“After — the spike, it was all he focused on. It absorbed his attention; it was his intellectual escape; instead of all the emotional pain he had suffered, he would just think of that *thing*. He knew everything about spikes used for the railroad. After the brain injury, his temperament had changed; he was now easily frustrated and was unable to conceal his emotional drives.”

“Poor Finn,” I said, empathizing for Wolfzang, suspecting this did really happen. “Even after the tragedy, he still needed what we all need, but he no longer cared to make his escape socially appropriate.”

“As you said, escapes exist to redirect the mind and decrease stressors and pressures. They’re essential to the human mind, thus the fixation on the spike — it was how his mind was redirected after the traumatic event? Coped with his resonating Genetically Important Drives.”

“Triggers were everywhere. He suffered an indescribable loss; the water in the glass was often turbulent, *quick* to overflow.”

Two of the dozen pigeons seemed to be the most aggressive at getting the berries which made me think, what were the dynamics in the pigeon world? Those tiny brains, they’re still acting so like those I’d known that needed to win every argument, contorting facts into the endless shades of gray to win.

Five curiously dressed devotees of something or possibly someone wearing bonnets and Phrygian caps, striped button-down shirts, sat on the benches facing east. “You know that… group?” I asked.

“Nope, not at all. I’d love to know what they’re about,” he replied with a smile.

"Sooo, not to offend you," I said with hesitation. "OCSs are definitely not a cult?" I asked.

"The thing is, so many unassuming types Yearning for Emotional Closeness get sucked into cults because the cult leader knows how to skillfully resonate and target another's emotional drives," Wolfzang said.

"Yeah, as you said, clearly those manipulative types are interwoven into our fabric. When I was 19, I was lifeguarding at a golf course. One older guy was so friendly, acted so interested in me, the whole time, he was just trying to get me into a pyramid scheme," I responded.

"From the OCSs conception, we desired all OCSs to be objective, skeptical, and aware that 66.66% of all primitives are strongly self-interested, and 33.33% of those have significant ethical challenges. Whereas a cult leader wants his followers to blindly follow, spinning logic and reason into fuzziness. We wanted everyone to observe and understand the mind and fully understand why people blindly follow others."

"Hmm, sort of an anti-cult group with cult-like attributes, an inverse cult group?" I said, attempting to decipher his point, laughing after I said it and getting a laugh from Mary.

"33.33, 33.33, 33.33, I might be skeptical that OCS are oversimplifying the Ethical Bell Curve," Mary said.

"Several factors make it not so — *elementary*; one might suggest the bell curve here is shifted because the average primitive acts upon self-interest, not Universal Ethics, yet you all fall upon your own normalized bell curve since primitives are driven by emotions, incentives, and escapes. 66.66 percent will use logic to benefit themselves, using logic subjectively not all but most of the time, making the larger unregulated behavioral products — chance. Since we see the Ethical Bell Curve as a species wide phenomenon, some countries may have embraced more corrupt beliefs, some countries may have better systems to watch out for those that are purely self-interested."

I thought of an African country I had recently read about. A place where they let some business guy preaching God sell a gasoline tonic to cure AIDS to impoverished village folk.

"Hmm, as you've said, a race that scores high in all three bell curves is the only type of sentient that can create and continuously operate the Tool," Mary said, sipping her tea.

"I think I get what you're saying; if you contrast the Ethical Bell Curve to the intelligence bell curve, the average person has an average IQ of 100, but our average ethical quotient of 100 would be someone that is still more likely to use logic to defend their own emotional beliefs. Here, it's not until you reach a genius ethical quotient do you see someone using logic to decipher their emotionally embraced beliefs."

"In Statistics of Psych, my professor talked about the IQ bell curve, never the Emotional Quotient or the possibility of the Ethical Quotient. In college, this IQ bell curve thing seemed so — well, mildly important, but I guess if you base the fundamentals of your work on three intertwined but different bell curves and see us as living on a probability planet, *it's* worth revisiting."

"I can see the difficulty. It's easy to test someone for an IQ, but the Ethical Quotient, how could it be done? Do you ask a direct question, "Would you hurt a sentient that is defenseless? Who would you steal from? How often do you lie to get your wants and needs met? Do you want to destroy those you can't control?" Mary said.

Smiling at her silly sadistic query, I replied, "I get it; it's clear how any breathing person would answer. That's why the Ethical Quotient has been exceedingly elusive."

"If a flourishing society focused its near-limitless resources into the development of its citizens to score exceptionally high in all three bell curves, with the absolute end goal of being optimum Vac-Plat operators, I could only imagine what could be accomplished?" Mary explained.

"It's much more than emotions, emotional awareness, compassion to all living things — this deep intensive focus is how to make exponential technological and scientific progress."

"One might control bugs, make animated holograms, control their aging process — multiverse travel?"

"You're getting a vivid picture; it's a paradigm shift for altering large-scale behaviors. We go from living by probability, being dysfunctional, to being compassionate and extremely effective. The human race can thereby become pragmatic objective reflective sentients that resonate with the multiverse."

"Amazing! The multiverse opens its arms up and finally embraces — *us*."

"One can't design the Vac-Plat without a complete acceptance of the Ethical Bell Curve and how it's interconnected to our own well-being. Your current scientific and discovery methods and your experimental methods have to protect against endless contamination by countless primitives involved before the experiment, during the experiment, and after the experiment. Nearly all attempts at innovation, discovery, and experimentation get corrupted by those involved. Once a sentient reorganizes, can accept themselves for what they truly are and root out all the underlying reasons for impairing the work, progress exponentially multiplies."

"I see — with the Vac-Plat, you are solving the problems completely and for good. Pre-Vac-Plat, primitives tried to invent excessive, even absurdly complex band-aids to fix what humans do relentlessly, naturally, things our reptilian ancestors passed to us, which many of us can't even *admit* we do, what you've called Expected Toxic Outcomes."

"Quite correct!"

I continued with my line of reasoning, "Once we become Universally Ethical objective beings, our tools will reflect what we are?"

"Precisely. Give a pen to an unethical sentient, and that being might use it to enslave, cheat, mistreat others. Give a pen to a Universally Ethical sentient, and that being will attempt to further their complete understandings, make lasting connections with those they are unfamiliar with, and make useful discoveries valuable to all compassionate living beings."

"Fascinating!"

"That is *fascinating*!"

I stared for a few moments at the rising and falling water in the center of the fountain. "So, these highly ethical types do they look down on everyone else? You know sort of the self-righteous types. You can never be good enough, so they always feel better than you. I've known plenty of pious types that are just *miserable* to be around."

"I could see how you might come to that conclusion knowing who you know. But, to know the people I know in a three-dimensional way you'd have to understand how they react to their Genetically Important Drives. If they felt better than you, they'd recognize their Narcissistic Drive resonating. If they felt superior to *any* other living being they'd quickly realize how unhealthy that viewpoint is. Feeling superior to others is truly an emotionally driven belief, it might *feel* right, but it leads to *terrible* places," Wolfzang explained.

"Wow! When I envision a society of people like *that*, that are ethical and down-to-earth, it must be — well, utopia," Mary responded.

"It makes us look like a bunch of hate-filled misguided Neanderthals."

"Neanderthals weren't any more hate-filled than current humans. They were just less capable of concealing their emotional drives in a group. Though on that point, highly intelligent primitives with low ethical quotients can be extremely persuasive and leave even the most ethical individual questioning objective views. Here, the amount of time and other wasted resources combating this deflection, redirection, and confusion is enormous."

"Generations must chase their own tails because they are being redirected by convincing or intoxicating self-interested primitives."

"Decades, or sometimes, *centuries* pass with compelling, persuasive, yet destructive leadership in charge," Wolfzang explained. Paused for a moment, "There's a neat little device, a toy; I'd like to show you a bit uptown. You're heading back that way anyway? Let's take a walk together," he explained, and with that, we followed our guide up the northeast pathway of the park and onto the city sidewalk.

“Hmm,” Mary said, still pondering his point. “From a science and technological standpoint, they damage our prospects for their own self-interested gain. Perpetuate the probability planet,” Mary explained.

“It creates a systemic problem for growth. If you look deep enough into the minds of tyrants, dictators, and oppressors, you will find a very weak, wounded inner self. We simply recognized the enormous implications of this weakened human could have on a large society and then set our sights accordingly. The sort inhabits all professions, are in all walks of life-impacting other persuadable primitives to act more — well, like them.”

“Hmm — just like a disease, destructive behaviors spread.”

“So, if OCSs see everyone as a two-year-old child, you become more capable of identifying those that are acting purely emotionally, rather than buying the false narrative for their actions,” Mary explained.

As we walked along 5th Avenue on this busy city street, I pondered deeply. I couldn’t help but to wrongly guess where my fellow side walkers were on the Ethical Bell Curve; was a seemingly benign older man wearing a business jacket a sadistic jerk just waiting to entrap others in his web? Was he hiding a manipulative, controlling, callous nature? Even at that moment, I knew there was something biased, a bit unhealthy about this type of speculation, but when the guessing begins, and dozens are passing by, these uncontrolled thoughts flow in and out.

“I remember how my grandmother once said, ‘People in New York City couldn’t say hello to everyone they pass on the sidewalk because there simply isn’t enough time.’ As a kid, she sounded so self-assured, it sounded so logical, but now, being much less idealistic, I see how naively idealistic that was. If one out of twenty-five of us is a sociopath, since you pass hundreds on the streets in a day, I suspect you want to avoid those you haven’t already filtered out,” I said.

“Don’t be afraid of an interaction. Just always have an exit strategy planned, accept you might deal with a high conflict, unwell individual. You might want to become invisible at any moment,” Wolfzang responded. We came upon the Iron Building. He pointed to a large building in the distance. “There’s the Math Emporium,” he explained. A couple of hundred feet later, we walked into a bright, colorful foyer and a large entrance to the gift shop to the left. We then began to examine the math-related oddities for sale. He guided us to a particular corner of the gift shop and picked up one of the many toys on the shelf.

"Like many phenomena, one may think, 'neat, a weird science abnormality,' but the abnormalities are where the truth about the world is hiding. Anomalies are more often abnormalities because your view of the multiverse is incorrect, not because something is just strange or different."

"Whoa, that's deep. I get it. You pull the loose string, and the entire world unravels in a way you never imagined?" Mary responded.

"The unusual and unique are perceived vastly differently to the OCSs. If someone happened to be born with something unique, it's embraced as beautiful, individual, not something to be concealed, altered, or improved. Conformity is not our thing."

"*That* perception makes me feel like a *mindless* marching soldier. What a refreshing way to view differences," Mary said.

I stared at the toy; I simply saw a plastic kids' toy with hundreds of metal beads, reminiscent of a flipping hourglass with a bunch of pegs that the beads would pass through. It sort of reminded me of the *Price is Right* Plinko machine.

"This! — This is Pascal's Triangle! This is a Galton Board!" He said with fervor as if he was pulling a sheet off of a very important product and presenting it to a large audience.

He flipped the little board over, and the hundreds of beads rushed around the pegs and fell to the bottom. There at the bottom was his beloved bell curve.

He said, "Name three typical occupations,"

I responded, "Dentist, doctor, computer programmer."

"Perfect examples, all three of those occupations include a broad scope of people, all three occupations would have somewhat of a skewed or — shifted bell curve if they took an IQ test, they may have a higher than average IQ. They weren't just born that way, but they learned how to compete, study, repeat to satisfy academic requirements. The doctor and dentist might have a slightly better ability to deal with others to get their own wants and needs met, dealing day-to-day with patients. They also may, at times, be guided by their Narcissistic Drive since they are often surrounded by those resonating *that* emotional drive. Yet, all three have a normal distribution for the ethical quotient."

"I get it. All three bell curves are separate, distinct, interwoven, and affecting each other. Just to think the IQ is all that exists is two-dimensional and leads to incomplete speculations regarding behavior," I said.

"Your point is that you might run into the dentist from the *Little Shop of Horrors*? Someone that will grind down your perfectly fine teeth and tell you to get new teeth, making huge profits from your misfortune. I met a father and daughter dentist like that; after one consultation, they suggested tens of thousands of dollars of work!" Mary explained.

"I remember that. Didn't they have some kooky holistic name like 'Mindful Wisdom Teeth?'"

"Yeah, as you said, they were both really nice, which made them more — believable."

"They'll find lots of cavities, overanalyze, exaggerate, have a fancy office, impressive equipment, appear highly intelligent, all the while benefiting from your trust in them," he responded.

"I watched a documentary on one nationwide dentistry company that pushes their dentists to find a specific number of root canals every week because that's where the margins are — that's scary!" I said.

He paused, then continued, "But what if you said a different occupation, such as a stockbroker or used car salesperson? Certain occupations might have filtering systems during the hiring and retaining process that tests and checks to see how *productive* the individual is in that line of work?"

"I can see that if you're too honest in sales, too compassionate, and feel normal levels of guilt, you might have difficulty achieving your sales goals," I responded.

"True, the Ethical Bell Curve has been quite elusive due to its intricacies. Primitives simply want everything to be fast and two-dimensional. Quantifiable with static numbers. Testing abilities here are simply insufficient. Currently, many primitives would find ethical testing intrusive because how can you trust what others will do with the information they gather? It was essential that people became comfortable with artificial intelligence in their everyday lives before it could be undeniably identified."

"Hmm, it was?" Mary asked.

"It almost sounds like to make the Tool; we needed the component of artificial intelligence not for the reason we thought it would be useful, like for answering questions quickly, or solving intractable problems, the importance was to save us from ourselves. To identify and detect those that were undetectable, deceptive with a smile, acting self-interested, being emotionally and incentive-driven?" I said, feeling I accomplished organizing what he was attempting to convey.

"Excellent, and yet there are further interesting complexities to the ethical quotient. For example, a child might be taught to steal from a faceless corporation and trained to enjoy the rush of stealing by a troubled parent. Things like that have little to no impact on one's ethical quotient. The ethical quotient is simply the ability to be compassionate to all living things — especially yourself."

"I see. So something like dumping toxic material that one knows can harm other living things would hurt your scoring in the ethical quotient, but possessing an illegal drug wouldn't," I paused and thought. "Interesting… That's not the way we're taught good and evil, being a good citizen and all that. Following the laws for the good of everyone. The OCSs understanding takes the entire person into account, upbringing, the circumstance, and how the action is impacting other living things."

"Or, take a place like Nigeria. Millions live in extreme poverty. Some have access to the internet. Just by scamming some silly American out of a couple of hundred bucks, you can feed your entire family for a year. It doesn't take an ethically challenged person to act what appears unethically."

"Who wouldn't do it to feed their family?"

An old homeless man with brown, dirty, worn, heavy clothes snatched our attention. He stood leaning back on the horizontal frame of the large windows, asking a passerby for spare change. As I watched one of New York's less fortunate, it occurred to me that on any given day, several thousand homeless inhabited this city full of great wealth. Reflecting for a moment, I realized we weren't superior in any way to the generations that came before us. That homeless man was the string that Mary and Wolfzang talked about. If all of our currently embraced psychological theories were correct, why couldn't we reach those that clearly needed help? Why did he still exist in his state of mind? Not just medicating those that are homeless, hiding them in a shelter, keeping them off the affluent street corners, but truly reaching them and resolving the difficulties within this Primary Cloud Network, as Wolfzang defined it. Why wasn't it a top priority for us? This one man, standing by this one window at this moment, happened to be present when I was capable of contemplation. It wasn't simply that his brain was biologically malfunctioning; it was that *we* didn't understand how to help our brothers and sisters. Wolfzang was right; we needed to fix ourselves from the bottom up. This man was only a hint, a symptom, that we weren't ready for time travel. He was a reminder that our underlying systems were faulty and that we were not ready to proceed.

Wolfzang noticed my prolonged stare. "The OCS immediately see his two-year-old. We see him as he was as a beautiful, joyful, small child. It's not that hard. Try it."

I could see what he meant; in a two-dimensional way, he seemed scary, unkempt, erratic, completely out there, therefore, possibly dangerous. Yet I pushed myself to attempt his experiment. "I'm imagining him toddling around, not great at walking yet. He's smiling. He's laughing, I can see it — he's full of joy and innocence, he's full of — TRUST. There's adults in the room; they're angry. They're out of control. They're screaming at him, hitting him for the dumbest things. He's just a little kid! The guy is calling him 'stupid, retarded,' and there's a woman, she's just watching, letting *it* happen." I said. My heart sank. Did Wolfzang implant that vivid thought into my mind? Where did it come from?

"Yes — you're starting to see it now; he wasn't made this way. He's stuck. His Primary Cloud was weakened, likely during or throughout development, then over time, due to life's stressors and pressures, things compounded. His emotional drives now overpower him. He can't logically deal with them as someone with a robust or, at the very least, sufficient Primary Cloud can. If he looked as he is, as we see him, he would be a vulnerable two-year-old boy. If those… here could see it, maybe someone would attempt to nurture him calmly, compassionately over a significant period of time, using the correct techniques to communicate with his little one and finding the real trauma that had occurred. We call it Our Rehabilitation Process or ORP. He is not just some bum that refuses to get a job; he's not just some dirty drugged-out guy capable of no good. He's equal to you — to me, to Mary, with a weakening within an important part of the mind, making his being resemble the innocence of a two-year-old child. Many like him roam the city since those here do not understand, can't see."

"Those you work with believe the homeless can be helped completely and forever?"

"Yes — you have simply embraced the wrong fundamental answers about the mind. As Einstein said, 'Problems cannot be solved with the same mindset that created them.'"

Wolfzang, seeing I was in deep thought, allowed me a moment and walked to the other side of the gift shop, then began looking at the many brain teaser puzzles and returned, "Oh — yes, before that unfortunate man, we were talking about the ethical quotient. Possible triggers that demonstrate weaknesses that occurred due to trauma. For example, if someone met a stranger that had physical attributes a childhood abuser, the individual might quickly become hostile toward that person. These are all very specific, short-lived difficulties that are evaluated and recognized for what they are, understood with a complete picture of the person."

"A three-dimensional profile is needed of the person to obtain these dynamic scores on the Ethical Bell Curve," I said rhetorically.

"Interesting, I get what you're saying. *Without* the acceptance and interest of resolving dysfunction with the correct model, using a more accurate explanation for the dynamics within the mind, we couldn't correctly proceed evolutionarily?" Mary stated, sounding particularly insightful.

"One might liken it to accepting the world as a sphere. If a society fights it, insists it's not true, or ignores it, the society remains incapable of many things, mainly navigating around the globe effectively, and after that, they could never put satellites into orbit, launch spaceships, or take all succeeding steps technologically."

"Hmm, but you're saying an incorrect embrace of what's driving human behavior or embraced psychological beliefs due to a society's fundamental dogmas leads to the same technological dead end because without the correct underlying psychological model of how the mind functions, the Tool could never correctly operate?"

"I suspect many primitives have a vested interest or incentives in keeping things the way they are. Why would self-interested primitives want to change things if the system benefits them? Like a pharmaceutical company that wants you to take a lifelong mood alterer rather than solve the issue? Their fiduciary responsibility is to their shareholders to make excellent returns takes precedence over their target market," I explained.

"Or the professors I've falsely applauded so I'd get a good grade — they keep indoctrinating students with inaccurate dogmas that they have a vested interest in perpetuating. If things changed, they would lose their coveted positions," Mary responded.

"True, if you got to know those with a vested interest, you'd see they were exceptionally skilled at making you feel inferior; if you have objective questions on the theories they base their work, you will be incinerated by a barrage of highly refined techniques to attack your objective questions, they will in very sophisticated ways deflect, deny and play the victim to win an argument, to hold their place as king or queen of the mountain."

"Wow, the Narcissists playbook? Even at the level of an Ivy League professor. Incredible! We are all hardwired to act the same way," Mary responded.

"Don't think I'm just attacking academia. The point being, high IQ, high emotional quotient, low ethical quotient, is commonplace here. The highly self-interested can destroy those that are honestly looking for the *real* answers. Yet *here*, being highly Universally Ethical is not a qualification of those in powerful academic positions. They'll even argue what it means *to be* ethical. Many of those that gain power often do it by any means necessary or an unfair bestowment due to pedigree or connections."

"If they truly didn't care for the power in the position, they wouldn't have sought it out, acquired it. They don't just accidentally fall into it as some try to make it appear. I can see why the OCSs have spent their resources and effort developing systems that exclude a pecking order."

"I remember being eviscerated by at least two professors for simple, honest questions; you just learn to nod, smile, and laugh at all their mundane jokes. In the end, the grade is all that matters, so you don't challenge them; you just applaud their half-baked views and get out of the way," Mary said.

"Or the one that hinted if I drive her to the airport, I'd get a better grade."

"Wow! That's something. Our discussion of the three essential bell curves would be incomplete without one final thing, my group prefers a unique model of the three bell curves when analyzing human behavior."

"The bell curve itself? How it looks?" I asked, a little fuzzy.

"Yes, what has been observed about probability, human attributes, and the bell curve is as accurate as a two-dimensional representation can be. But, *true* natural phenomenon needs never to be truncated or abbreviated into two-dimensions. If the model is wrong the predictions and speculations will usually be wrong."

"Well, about half the time," I said with a smile.

"Yes, you're getting it," he said with a smile.

"I guess what *you're* saying is that we're looking at a two-dimensional representation of a bell curve? We need a three-dimensional model. Since you're giving us our three coordinates, the IQ, Emotional Quotient and the Ethical Quotient we could logically create a three-dimensional model," Mary explained.

"We still use the term the three bell curves to describe our three interrelated bell curve scores which are developed upon this three-dimensional model. The three scores are far too inextricably interwoven to be calculated separately. Think of skinny ovoid or an skinny egg with two protrusions."

"Protrusions?"

"Like the rings around Saturn. Let me show you." He took a shiny silver 2-inch top out of his pocket. "We call it, *The Top*."

To me, the glistening silver made this top look almost otherworldly. *The Top* was the bell curve as I knew it and the bottom was a perfectly symmetrical bell curve. It was two bell curves, perfectly reflecting each other.

"You can imagine how with three coordinates it can give you a very concise location, a regional location upon this model. Imagine how similar those scoring similarly upon the three bell curves would be. How identical those within the same region would act. How those within a region of three high scores would be super prosperous and how *troublesome* it would be to visit those with a high IQ, high Emotional Quotient but low Ethical Quotient."

"I could imagine it might be a scary location, a place where a lot of brain power gets used to fulfill unhealthy emotionally based needs and desires. A location where it's typical to find those controlling others through the manipulation of love. A place where you're taught by the larger group to be unempathetic, that your own *greed* is *good* for society. Supported by the group to overlook the suffering of others for your *own* benefit."

"Duplicitous people! One might say," Mary said.

"Dupli what?" I asked.

"It means double-dealing, deliberately deceptive pretending to act under one set of feelings while being driven by another. Yeah… like that? Thank you, GREs, for making me spend otherwise valuable time to memorize words no one else ever uses or knows. It resonates my Narcissistic Drive, gives me a nice false sense of importance, subdues my Feelings of Inferiority," Mary said with a silly face.

“Here, here. The endless hours with word cards. Now we get to walk around sounding like walking thesauruses but *that’s* all,” I said with a smile.

“Since OCSs find related general scientific phenomena to interrelate and parallel with behavior and the human mind, when we find things that are inexplicably interconnected, we become fascinated. We know, the most accurate answers in science bring the most wonderful returns with the least effort.”

“Like you had said, general laws of science have important parallels to human behavior and you also said there are ways a sentient with a human’s abilities should think and act to resonate with the universe. *Unleashing* endless possibilities!”

“Precisely, so we feel the three-dimensional way to predict an individual’s behavior is with the three bell curves scores. When put together they create *this* beautifully balanced symmetrical object. It’s as if this shape is meant to exist within our multi-verse.” He put it on a box top and spun it. “It takes no effort to spin it and it just *keeps* going. Talk about extreme efficiency.”

“Wow! It’s almost like it never wants to stop!”

“Yah…” Mary added, starring at the spinning top.

“This shape, this object, *this model*, has such an effect when interacting with the actual natural world. It’s incredible to think three scores that are derived from this shape, this model and placed within are so natural, understandable and accurate. The truth about the universe is all around *you* if *you* know how to forget what you’ve learned and see things without your Embraced Beliefs Network Cloud guiding you.”

We meandered around the gift shop; I found myself back at the Galton board. Mesmerized by the tiny metal balls all falling into a near-perfect bell curve each time I flipped it, over and over, crazy, bell curve, bell curve, bell curve. This was us. Since we are emotional, incentive, and escape-driven animals, group behavioral outcomes would always be predictable based on probability. I began to see it clearer; over time and in a large unfiltered population, this was what *we* amounted to. Just organisms acting primitive on a Probability Planet. This statistical phenomenon was why some guy in Haiti, a few hours away by plane, was going to die today that was starving to death. A guy that had my scores on all three bell curves. It wasn't because the Christian God didn't love him or because he had bad karma. He was just as decent, thoughtful, and intelligent as me. Staring at this toy, I thought of him and felt painfully disheartened. I genuinely wished I could help him. I wanted to join the OCS far away from here and be capable of making real alterations, not just repeating what we all do. I realized at that moment if my mission was to fully experience, examine, and record the things Wolfzang recognized as necessary and document them as well as I could; I was all in.

"Could you imagine if a group lobbied the U.S. government to spend hundreds of billions on a system that would contradict current educational systems? A system that would oppose ideas to existing bureaucratic governmental organizations? A group that wanted to reengineer systems that have been accepted for — centuries? A group that also wanted to end the meat industry?"

"You'd have — no luck, a complete non-starter."

"There would be no chance. THE Tool needs to be built completely out of view from disapproving eyes yet with intense clarity," Wolfzang said.

"I see, you're walking directly up to some guy that is highly incentivized by the existing systems and saying, 'Look, buddy — we've gotta improve our fundamentals! You think we're getting somewhere, but it's excruciatingly slow,'" I explained.

Mary smiled and said, "Look, buddy!"

"The resistance would be unending by those attempting to sustain their livelihoods. They would have little tolerance to objectively examine a novel system. You would find yourself the victim of endless falsehoods."

"I get it; we avoid objectively reflecting in general, but when it comes to our income, livelihood, no way!" I responded.

"Hmm, I don't blame you for going slowly with us. I'd have reflexively resisted a lot of your points of view after spending a fortune being indoctrinated by our medieval church, I mean, college."

“Within the ethical quotient, an essential sub-domain is the ability to reflect upon one’s Embraced Beliefs Network Cloud and dynamically alter old ideas; it’s an evolutionary imperative to be universally compassionate and willingly examine new information.”

“Wow… I remember so many people that have said, ‘I am who I am,’ or ‘everyone has the right to their own opinion,’ or ‘forget the past, let’s just move on,’” Mary responded.

“The question is, what’s the line between perseverating on the unchangeable past and learning from it not to repeat it? It reminds me of the Reynolds quote, how did it go? ‘There is no expedient to which a man will not go to avoid the labor of thinking,’” I responded.

“It’s all someone else's fault, wounding others, destroying lives, very pitiful and tragic are those that deny and deflect their own mistakes. Severe cases can really destroy and waste what could have otherwise been a prosperous life.”

Making circles with his pointer finger and thumb, then putting them over his eyes and wiggling his head. “A fundamental article we instill in our young is the development of adroit skills of how to be a trusted friend to others. It’s a treasured skill we all must learn.”

“What was all that about?”

“You didn’t think I resembled a vaquita?”

“A whoooo?”

“Oh, yeah, we pretend to be certain animals just for fun. I’ll go into that sometime in better detail,” he said with a smile.

“*Great*?” I said suspiciously with a funny grimace, wondering if this was all just insanity. His peculiar behaviors — rubbing his thumbnail and making animal gestures. Was this all part of the perception research, was this just an eccentric rich old guy, or was this just how all OCSs operated? I began to think of his complex, intricate points and quickly assuaged my own concerns.

“Mistakes are embarrassing. We rarely tell people about our mistakes. Social media has us presenting ourselves, branding ourselves. We try to make ourselves look *perfect*, modelesque, and having fun. Yet OCSs embrace imperfections, the difficulties, and you're nice to yourself the entire time? You're even more accepting of mistakes others make," Mary asked.

"Exactly, mistakes, errors, successes, they are ALL equivalent. You only learn with both. In a few years, you'll meet Anh Cuong Zo, a Buddhist living in Quebec. He'll say to you, 'Mistakes are no different than accomplishments. The stressors and pressures mistakes bring on will increase your escapes. Use your escapes for accomplishing your tasks before your mind makes you think of something less productive."

"Wow, you know what she's going to say to us? That's sooo weird — how you can reference our future like our past?" I asked.

"No… no, that's just something she says," he responded with a smile.

"HA!" I couldn't keep from letting out a gut laugh.

We left the museum and purchased grilled corn and fresh lemonade from a vendor at a street fair.

"The IQ here, the perception of it, needs reexamination. You embrace that the person that acts as a fast European sportscar is brainy. But what if, given a little time, calmness, exploration, and objective examination, better answers can be uncovered? That is, the most effective process for the greatest insight is not argumentative chatter, debate, quips or the quick regurgitation of embraced beliefs but calm, pragmatic, objective examination."

"I can see high-performance vehicles being paralleled to intelligence. A fast car is like a fast-talking, fast-thinking overpowering know-it-all that always assumes that they are the smartest person in the room and has developed many persuasive tools to coerce others to agree with their embraced beliefs. Afterward, you're left wondering if his or her high voltage beliefs are at all *accurate*," I said.

"And also, what if these other cars get to high speeds, can travel much faster than said sports car, and even handle better at very high speeds?"

"Hmm, go even faster and with incredible handling," Mary said.

"During our analysis process, what we call our Obstacle Interventions — we analyze multiple models, then zero in on the specific possible explanations. We enjoy analytically breaking apart our difficulties without competing against each other to win a position. We all win when we examine an unanswered question and open up possible paths to better understand the enigma. When no one in the room is catering to their own emotional drives, it's different. No one speaks to be noticed or jockey's position. *Here*, since 66.6% of the population is more self-interested and can easily convince themselves what's good for them is the best thing for everyone. There is a tendency of undermining those that have a high ethical quotient and high IQ. Even though the latter is often far more capable, just accelerate and maneuver differently."

"This Obstacle Intervention… it sounds like discovery paradise, not an intellectual blood sport."

"We really don't like the term *expert*, but humans are well informed when they have taken the time with a problem and, most importantly, have used imagination to creatively examine and experiment upon the enigma with unique explorations. Experts are not experts because they've been certified, given credentials, or reverberated solidly trained indoctrinations. We don't use credentials or certifications, but for those that do, we see certifications as only an extreme baseline. An elementary understanding of a problem. We're skeptical of those that use it to exude ethos, for they are usually laboring too long under incorrect assumptions."

"Huh, just touting credentials suggests the individual has embraced the process of being indoctrinated. That is a different perspective than *here*."

"I'm picturing a very calm, analytical down-to-earth diverse group. Not a type 'A' intellectual whose hubris is always present and is insistent on winning a good argument, flexing his technical knowledge," I said.

"Robert Goddard, an accomplished rocket scientist, once said, 'It's not a simple matter to differentiate unsuccessful from successful experiments; most work that is finally successful is the result of a series of unsuccessful tests in which difficulties are gradually eliminated.' Like others that made exponential progress, the Tool was formulated upon their… mental processes. It was the *why... the how* he produced his significant derivatives that *fascinated* us. What we found most interesting was his demeanor, the dynamics that occurred in his mind, and *how* he and his wife worked as an inextricable team. There was an optimistic, healthy climate that he set for his entire team. He was a quieter gentleman with a degree of anxiety. Yet, he married the right woman, Esther, a highly intelligent, nurturing person; they were each other's best friends."

"They completely fulfilled each other's Yearning for Emotional Closeness. It might sound so basic, and unimportant, but it's essential, of infinite importance. The human is driven by these deep emotions. As I mentioned at the cafe, Yearning for Emotional Closeness is one of the two strongest drives within the brainstem and limbic system; *If* this Genetically Important Drive can't be calmed quickly, other distractions take precedence, and the mind can be easily overwhelmed by the resonating drive. The majority of great minds have withered, weakened, or become lost because their resonating Genetically Important Drives overpowered them and then redirected them. Robert and Esther had the right mix of amicable personalities. That is, their glasses didn't quickly overflow; their work, the academic pursuits were their escapes. Yet they enjoyed a variety of other escapes; he painted landscapes, played the piano, and she enjoyed photography to soothe the stressors and pressures or peacefully, sometimes — unconsciously wrestle with enigmatic problems."

"That's interesting. They had escapes. Even though academic pursuits of rockets were their escapes together, the other escapes were useful and gave their mind time to unconsciously solve a significant question, and that their genetically important drive, Yearning for Emotional Closeness, was well supported, therefore, voilá… productivity," I said.

“In the newspapers, he was regularly the target of mockery for his ambitions. Yet, in the end, he was quite correct about his pragmatic, objective conclusions — both were such admirable rational, analytical individuals. The Goddards pushed the human race forward.”

We found a bench and finished the last bite of our corn.

“So, I’ll be in touch soon to give more details about our observation down south,” he explained.

“I guess you’ve got to be going. You have some important business to attend to with your colleagues? Probably another Analytical Field Exploration to take part in?”

“Actually, I’m going to see my family later today and wanted to take a shower beforehand. Send me your journal entries; I’d love to see how they’re coming along; we’ve covered a tremendous amount over the last two days,” he replied with a smile; we soon parted.

A few days later, Wolfzang emailed me an article that discussed two gentlemen from a Sante Fe area University that questioned our society's embraced beliefs about life. Their theory vastly increased what could be seen as life to include concepts such as culture, forests, and the economy.

“It’s refreshing here when I see there are those willing to trek new and objective game boards. They aren’t conspiracy theorists, some sort of crackpot wingnut… ideologues. That is, you can’t easily use objective analytical reasoning to disprove what they’re saying. They simply have a different viewpoint than the currently accepted and indoctrinated embraced beliefs, which is more often followed by a reflexive — ‘they’re just ridiculous!’” He wrote.

“I thought you didn’t care for our universities?”

“As with all things, there’s going to be aberrant outcomes in some locations. My concerns with your current universities relate to their internal functioning, exclusivity, and rigid perpetuation of inaccurate group applauded beliefs."

I thought for a few minutes then wrote. "To be on multiple 'game boards,' with conflicting views, doesn't that make the OCSs disoriented?"

"Well, I'm glad you asked. Here are two quotes, 'The world as we have created it is a process of our thinking. It cannot be changed without changing our thinking,' and another, 'The measure of intelligence is the ability to change.'" I knew he was once again quoting Einstein.

I found myself awake at 1:00 am. My mind moved quickly, reviewing past journal entries. Mary awoke. "What's wrong?" She asked.

"What if he's right? What if all of these terrible things — cancer, mental illness, abject poverty, rare diseases, remember that kid I knew, Stephen, with Epidermolysis Bullosa? All sorts of pestilence upon the human race could be cured by traveling down a different road, with systems that don't magnify and repeat the wrong answers, with a different set of fundamental principles that can harness the human's seemingly infinite abilities of our minds? If he's right about our systems, our embraced beliefs are too frequently *wrong*. They're all built upon resonating our Genetically Important Drives. *Here* we *feel* things are controlled, we're the center of the universe, at the cutting edge of science. But, gains are frequently lost by those that contaminate our science. Yet, he thinks we can actually accomplish these seemingly insurmountable feats as a race with significant ease! But it's because of our emotional, incentive, and escape-driven nature, *not* our ability to solve the math and science involved. I think that's exactly what he's saying!"

"I know, *that's* what he's saying — it would be an *entirely* different world! It's all here, there's too much heartache and suffering in our world. If we better understood *why* we do, *what* we do, we wouldn't have so many problems circulating, being rebranded, some so well concealed."

Temporal Forward, Dinner

We continued to walk down the two-tire track dirt road. Twenty minutes later, we found ourselves sitting in very comfortable large Adirondack chairs on a slate patio behind his farmhouse. The grounds were pastures then, in a distance, forest. I could see a stream and a few cows, pigs, and goats.

“I’d never leave this spot if we lived here,” I said.

A rather fit-looking woman with light brown hair and brown eyes walked toward us. She was maybe late middle age, about the same as Wolfzang’s age was *presently.*

“This is Lophochroazang — or Birdie.”

“I’ve been *there* with *my love* so many times when he visited you. You both have extremely endearing personalities; your demeanors are *so* similar to other—OCSs,” she said.

“Wow, what a compliment! So you’re saying you took part in his AFEs with the OCSs vision. The sound, and video quality it's so incredibly clear. You must feel you know us extremely well.”

“We’ve been working on this project for well over a century now. You might recall seeing me once or twice in *busy* places. I’ve been there a few times,” she said.

“Wow!”

Mary looked at her with a blank stare. “*Yeah…* Wow!”

“She’s provided me invaluable support. She came up with the idea of leaving the backpack on the beach with Lincoln's stuff in it; figured it might be perplexing, an amusing mystery to be solved.”

"An amusing unanswerable question or how you… we wanted to see how you coped; it impressed us. It didn't faze you."

"O… K!" Mary said with a chuckle.

"Ha! I guess we were so in the moment when we were driving across the country after receiving the OCS Mental Model that even if our Need to Control the Environment resonated, our minds were so absorbed in the moment we didn't demonstrate any Primary Cloud weaknesses," I said.

"In another timeline, we provided you with all the knowledge of the OCSs, supported you through an Ivy League Ph.D. program, and attempted to play the existing games in academia, providing vast evidence of our understanding of behavior to attempt to persuade the opposing academic 'experts' with antithetical embraced beliefs. Soon our information was misconstrued to the benefit of entrenched academics. When you get a bunch of highly intelligent, highly incentivized, self-interested, well-positioned primitives that want to secure their embraced beliefs as unquestionably correct, you're simply in front of a firing squad," Birdie said.

"That firing squad attempted to convince you and everyone that listened that you or any supporters were suffering from *delusions*, a delusional disorder… The 66.6% primitives can be so cruel if you don't allow them to be right. If you don't get into line far behind them."

"Weird, you say it was us, but in another timeline? You already know how the human-animal works, embracing emotional ideas, then supporting those ideas with facts and getting reflexively frustrated at anyone who—*disagrees*. Why would you waste your time and torture someone like me, like *us*?" I asked.

"The question was—could we empower those few in the necessary positions to develop more research providing evidence to others about the OCS Mental Model and the necessity for an instrument to neutralize our expected primordial responses? We wanted to see if we could find that small percentage within academia to support the novel ideas and plant the seeds *there*, but there were far too many incentives not to believe and pre-existing pressures from coworkers; even if one academic was capable, she worked alongside a more typical primitive. Often several that quashed the idea, made her frightened about losing her coveted position, becoming a pariah and losing future credibility. The Genetically Important Drive, Feelings of Inferiority, would always be made to resonate, in every group, by someone to control the more reflective primitive; each experiment ended with a more pragmatic, objective, enlightened academic *folding* under pressure. Dealing with high IQ, low ethical quotient types is debilitating, even if the desire is creating effective systems for exponential human progress."

"Sure— as would be expected, but what happened to Dan and Mary? Did they go insane? It would have made *me* crazy. I'd be so frustrated at the human race to see those that should support creative, unconventional, well-developed ideas undermine progress. I mean, it must have been a very intensive AFE if you weren't doing it with the same very subtle approach as with us. Rather, taking a more offensive stance," Mary explained.

"It sounds like a painful and intensive AFE?" I prompted.

"Well, it was subtle; we tried to make the necessary alterations just under different circumstances," Birdie said.

"We ended up retiring the gallant but exhausted Mary and Dan to a beautiful home on the coast of Costa Rica overlooking the ocean. You're right; we stressed your other selves out pretty good for over fifteen years with our attempts, then needed to give them everything to enjoy themselves and restrengthen their Primary Clouds. They soon had a beautiful baby girl and lived a happy, vibrant life," Wolfzang explained.

"Whoa!" Mary responded.

"That *sounds*… wonderful!" I said, feeling a little choked up and having a tear in my eye imagining a little girl that looked like Mary.

We were both silent for a moment, trying to take it all in.

"Wolfzang bestowed us with the extreme importance of a robust diversity. Your belief to continually observe when others are acting reflexively homogenous and the clarity of how destructive sameness is to *all* parts of society, science, and discovery. Before him, I never tuned in so clearly how groups are *so* frequently blindly identical. Where, do these established groups expect to get the *fresh* new ideas?" Mary said.

"They all want to be the same back there. Painfully, identical sameness driven by unrealized resonating emotional drives," I added.

"In the end, they're incentivized to limit ideas that are not properly formatted, fitting their own narrow beliefs about how imaginative ideas spring to life," Wolfzang added.

"Their missing out on the accurate aberrant ideas at the far ends of the bell curves. Nearly always, these similar people all grow out of the same soil, breathing the same air, drink the same red fruity drinks," Birdie said with a grin.

"What you're saying, it reminds me of a documentary I watched on quantum theory. They showed a conference of the cutting-edge thinkers. It became apparent that the upper echelon of our time are all a bunch of well-dressed affluent sounding, white male professors that enjoy drinking tea at Cambridge. Only now I saw how absurd it *all* was. What if a true genius was an older woman with an unfamiliar accent, purple and green hair, tattoos all over her face that prefers wearing clothing some would consider otherworldly. Yet, she was truly innovatively solving mysteries by asking unique questions and having curiously uncommon approaches?"

"She'd be ignored or laughed at, never getting a place to voice her ideas," Mary said.

“Or a well-dressed snarky sophisticated professor that astutely plays his part, that simply struggles with his ethical quotient and is happy to take the credit for her *unique* abilities,” Wolfzang responded.

“Why allow your Narcissistic Drive to resonate and be venerated if you’re standing on the shoulders of unappreciated giants?”

We all seemed to giggle in our own way.

I began to notice the patio table; it was quite beautiful by any standards, round, with flat stones in the design of animals.

“What a beautiful table,” I said.

“I designed it, and ACE Meerkat and I crafted it; you’ll rarely find anything but round tables and perfectly square tables here. We found that the little ones within might mistake those sitting at the ends of a rectangle or oval as having certain importance over others,” Birdie explained.

“There are laws against it?” Mary asked.

She smiled, “Laws? Oh, no, nothing like that; we are just opposed to anything that symbolizes a hierarchical social structure. You know your little one thinks independently, and we’re always considering what a situation or environment might mean to our ever-aware, very emotional minds. Hierarchy has a place with data — computing or temporarily organizing things before seeing a more complete view, just not with any of *us*. When you’ve been brought up as we were to use the Doc of the OCSs as a fundamental objective guide, you act a little peculiar to those that aren’t from *here*,” she said.

“Peculiar — maybe? Distinctively rational and unrigid. Objectively incomparable. We felt everything Wolfzang described was unusual but fascinating to us, intriguing.”

“I’d say!” Mary said with a smile.

"We couldn't prove his points *wrong*; they were not outlandish. They were simply different from the explanations that were widely accepted. After reflection and embracing his… your understandings we felt healthier," I said.

"That one article made me *think*… the importance to never allow an individual to act as a guru or authority over another during psychological analysis."

At which time, the family members looked down solemnly as to mourn. They were clearly thinking of the title of that particular article which I recalled to be "Child that Experiences War."

"Since all of your soft sciences are highly speculative the opinions that the psychological field *professionals* would pontificate as assured facts were quite often *inaccurate*. They didn't see the necessity of acting as equals, harnessing each other's imagination to be enthusiastic true observers of the natural world. You're taught to hand over undo power to an all-knowing advisor, to believe someone was *more* accurate about behavior and the mind."

"I know, they often not only happily took the role but he or she reveled in their supposed absolute clarity. We're taught in our universities to demonstrate undo self-confidence. These *therapists* proceed without a true willingness to be reflective upon one's own emotions, their own inaccurate embraced beliefs. They're not attempting to recognize the possible imperfections of their own models of reference. None began with creating a framework of a neutral moderator or facilitator of a multitude of possible understandings. Later to find that so many of their unyielding convictions were simply *wrong*. But there was no getting our money back or telling them that when we later determined how ridiculous their points of view were."

"Exactly, so we had to rethink how to explore emotional challenges, how to effectively perform psychological counseling not allowing the certified *expert* to believe they were somehow *more* accurate than those attempting to be truthful, rational and reflective. Loose speculations by someone acting as all-knowing certified expert can be quite destructive if you are attempting to overcome one of life's emotionally charged personal difficulties."

"Hmm, the zero-hierarchy social belief is far more reaching *here* than just governmental organizations, or social status. I can see it always starts with *how* we understand our mind and *who* influences that understanding and *why*."

"We all appreciate the way you objectively wrestled with our beliefs," Wolfzang said in a warm voice.

"You've been resilient, receptive, and questioned the difference between primitive-centric ethics and Universal Ethics."

"I think if we could just share this culture, these pragmatic, objective, deeply loving beliefs in our time, they'd spread over the globe. They are indeed the best answer I've ever heard to solve so many of the profound issues humanity has always faced!" I said with great enthusiasm.

"We truly see it that way," Wolfzang responded.

"To know the Doc of the OCSs, to feel we're in a land of those that have embraced the need to be pragmatically Universally Ethical. To be around others that have a vibrance, a healthy upbeat nature, your own pendulum is reinforced to swing at a non-erratic calm speed, a reflexive desire to be *optimistic* about others, about the future," Mary said.

"Back there, we glorified the smart, snide professional in a lab coat: pretentious Dr. House, the intensely driven, flawless model-like scientist with no compassion or humor. It's *all* wrong! This permission we gave to intelligent people or those who *think* they are—a free pass to be unflinchingly egotistical. It's just a sign of our primitive nature; another embraced belief that kept us chasing our own tails. Here I feel the highly refined culture. There's calmness, a desire for universal compassion, an ability to think objectively and have others who desire to thoughtfully challenge you to reach ever higher," I said.

"It seems OCSs are the furthest humans that will ever travel down the evolutionary trail," Mary replied.

"Thanks for the compliment. Though for us, it's a little paradoxical. We're pragmatists. You'll find we may have difficulty feeling *'special.'* If you're in a group that insists upon feeling *more* special, more chosen, more unique, it leads to division. Unacceptance of others that are quite equal. Those you can learn from and deeply and equally *love*. Being 'more special,' these types of embraced beliefs are the seeds of a low ethical quotient. One ends up segregating the very similar human animal and other sentients for *imaginary* reasons," Birdie said.

"Another indication OCSs worked hard not letting your Narcissistic Drive resonate and be reinforced," I said.

"I guess *all* of *this* wonder wouldn't have happened if you did things like — *us*. Those from our time would assume *more* competition, *more* force, *more* control over others is how we would accomplish *this*, but quite paradoxically, that's all wrong."

I thought of a news report that said that Elon Musk had told his brain chip company to imagine they had a bomb strapped to their heads to make them work *harder*, faster. I thought… "So gross!"

"We have differences; we can explore them together. But we also have enormous similarities; we all have these minds; we all have these dynamics within the mind. In the end, a true willingness, a yearning to be objective to the true nature of the world and compassionate to all living things is all any sentient race needs to develop the Tool," Wolfzang said.

"Pragmatic, uncontaminated LOVE; *that* is the bedrock of this, this place," Mary said.

“Did I mention this is when we all get naked and start kissing?” Birdie said.

Mary and I looked at each other and said, “OHHH—Crap!”

“HA!” Lophochroazang and Wolfzang both laughed from the gut.

“Just a little levity; we’re not like that *either*,” she said with a wry smile.

“Yeah, we still enjoy the enormous benefits of a deep friendship and a monogamous marriage. AFEs are usually fun — but at times, they leave us breathless, emotionally exhausted. If it was always easy, smooth, those conditions wouldn’t be as authentic. We desire the three-dimensional experience to help us imagine the four-dimensional explanation. Close friends are taught to always be on standby to nurture each other after high-impact AFEs. We want some degree of grind; if we only sought smooth home runs, we would have missed out on so many discoveries; to have your best friend helping you accomplish a task or help you destress after a disastrous situation, it demonstrates how deeply loved you are *here*. After endless situations, truly caring about each other, being there, our love for each other is *unbreakable*,” Wolfzang explained.

“That is so, *so* beautiful,” Mary responded.

Two fit guys in their thirties walked in wearing shorts, sandals, and loosely fitting shirts. Similar to our current fashions. It occurred to me they had a focus on our time and place, which might have influenced their fashion. I wondered if they did it to make us feel more at ease.

“Hey!” They both said.

“These are my sons, *Agalychniszang or Agy, and Crytodirazang or Turt,” Wolfzang said.*

“Hey!” Mary said.

“Great to meet you!” I said, then thought and continued, “You guys are incredibly, like, over a hundred years old? Right?” I said with a smile, squinting my eyes.

“Well, I’m quite a bit more than that,” Turt said.

“Yeah, that's about right,” Agy said.

“Whoa, I thought these are your children?” I said, feeling quite confused by the reply.

“Great stars, that’s interesting.”

“Yes, they are my sons, born a couple of years apart, but Turt, he’s part of a group that’s doing some fascinating work. You’ll get a better understanding of *it*,” Wolfzang replied.

As Mary had hinted, my Genetically Important Drive was indeed resonating, recognizing the foremost challenge was to calmly experience the moment, not to force the pieces together; I accepted I’d be exposed to many things that would take some time to digest. I accepted the answer, soothed myself, and attempted to proceed without looking unnerved.

Possibly to redirect my emotional response, Mary quickly redirected the conversation, “I have to ask, you folks are clearly capable of perfect teeth; what’s up with crooked teeth? Do you OCSs prefer crooked teeth?” Mary asked.

“I guess you could say that we see every attribute a human is born with, hair color, eye color, height, birthmarks, nose shape, ears, are all quite unique and exceptionally beautiful; we’d see having someone straighten crooked teeth as being misguided and conforming, not loving themselves for what nature had provided. If it doesn’t impact one’s health or quality of life, it’s a beautiful characteristic. The question is, what makes one want to be something other than what they are? All animals are quite beautiful without alteration. So is every possible unique human attribute. Beauty is compassion for living things and high scores in all three bell curves, which is obtainable to all. All that matters is that the person is striving to live their healthiest existence. Besides, there is nothing particularly better about straight teeth," Wolfzang explained.

"I like crooked teeth; they're sort of like blue eyes," Birdie said.

"I get that — I once knew a guy that was an extra in soap operas, part of being in the actors' union, he'd travel down the Hudson Line and get small background, walk-on gigs all the time. They made him get veneers on all his teeth; before, his teeth were fine. I heard they do the same thing for workers on cruise ships. Grind down and put veneer fronts on their teeth. I always wondered who helped those poverty-stricken people pay for the grinded-down teeth care after they left the cruise ships' companies?"

"Yet, we are pragmatists. If a condition is less desirable and another was seen as an improvement the individual may opt for a change."

"Besides the teeth, how are you both coping with all this unfamiliar information?" Agy asked.

"Well, our cultural differences, the varying details that the OCS long ago picked up on, this skill to perceptively identify *finite* oddities, not discounting them as aberrant, while continuously reflecting upon our hard-wired drives that perpetuate the wrong answers, our embraced beliefs. Being here magnifies our unwitting lives *there*, our unwillingness to fully inspect well — reexamine clues appearing in the world around us, not reflexively find fault or avoid that which does not align with our embraced beliefs," Mary said.

"The string that pulls down the curtain reveals unexpected truths, our Need to Control the Environment and retain embraced beliefs, being *here* makes it evident how we must continually contort our mind and walk upside down to keep everything the way we believe it *to be*. Yet I guess it's all sustained because everyone around us *there* shares endless inaccurate embraced beliefs," I said.

Looking out into the field at the beautiful cows eating peacefully, Mary said, "It blew my mind when I heard U.S. psychiatrists have a very high rate of suicide. It just seemed like they were all no better than the tonic-selling hucksters of the early 20th century, but buying their own ridiculous pungent elixir as *the* cure. Yet… to be *more* suicidal than the general population?"

"Yeah, that blew my mind. I think that was the string for me too, an end for me and any confidence in the American Psychiatric Association," I said.

"The energy primitives will expend to conceal and spin such pointed evidence is a fascinating study. But think of how entrenched the psychological governing organization is, how many people they control via employment, certifications, credentials, the strength they hold as a controlling monopoly. *They* have the final word on how the mind functions, the perception of the dynamics of the mind and act as a special interest group, cloaked in good intentions, unable, *unwilling* to be questioned by a capable, rational observer. They deem outsider's incompetent, they rely upon internal checks and balances, there are no other truly neutral, independent outside organizations to verify that their conclusions are indeed pragmatic, objective, compassionate, agile and not developed from in-vogue or inaccurate dogmas. They are *the* all-powerful religion of the mind in the U.S. and even beyond in *your* time. If you don't have the keys agreed upon by those in the castle, you cannot enter the castle to help perpetuate and expand the existing doctrines… Besides, as in any large organization with a large population, OCSs would immediately recognize the percentage of extremely unreflective self-interested primitives that must exist within the organization," Turt explained.

"The 66.6ers! Yeah! You'd be unquestionably deemed a complete heretic if you said that back *there*." Mary said with a smile.

"I see. I guess all of this matters to OCSs because you believe progress is based on how capable we are *not* to be emotionally, incentive, or escape-driven. You believe most large organizations end up being *all* of the above. And *that* particular organization has far more jurisdiction and influence than is perceived by most back *there*. You see it as a foundational *issue*, that is, the way a society is taught or trained, to perceive the mind. If this governing organization is set up to determine how everyone perceives the mind but, in the end, misunderstands and misinforms the masses, it produces a society that *is* indeed — emotionally, incentive and escape driven," I said.

"You'd certainly offend *a lot* of high IQ types and receive impressive arguments defending every aspect of their indoctrinated embraced beliefs. In the end, fueled by their resonating emotional drives," Birdie said.

"Hah! Smart people, well smart primitives are just as emotionally driven as any other. Just better able at defending their embraced beliefs," I said.

"Primitives Probability Planet keeps rotating and fueling itself," Agy explained with a chuckle.

"I'd love to know, what other differences immediately stand out to you?" Turt asked.

"There's a feeling of abundance, great wealth, sort of like money is no object to any of the OCSs," I said.

"The richest kings a couple hundred years before *you* lived under squaller conditions compared to your time; those sorts of things just exponentially continued to improve after the introduction of the Tool," Wolfzang explained.

"The little history I know about the OCSs is fascinating; I would love to learn more about how it all began, more about the origins of the corporation?" I said.

"In the beginning, we provided needed products and services around the world cheaper and of the highest quality."

"What kind of products and services did they provide?" Mary asked.

"They followed their interests and determined the needs of the world. If a water delivery, filtration system was needed in some forgotten place we designed it. For some, we provided cheaper greener energy. But it didn't stop there, we continuously experimented with our new fundamental systems to test ourselves and create and innovate."

"All done while we searched for more possible OCSs. Places like Haiti, with people living in abject poverty, had plenty of future OCSs that were quite *accessible* because of the high levels of corruption in the country. We got better at identification and gathering, unobtrusively cherry-picking, and acquiring new OCSs. For every product or service, we offered, we simply used it to refine our systems. We were a different type of corporation and did our very best at concealing our… progress. Envy, after all, vigorously resonates several of the Genetically Important Drives and is a powerful driver of human behavior; *it* can become deadly. Our products and services were impressive; we didn't focus on the innovation as the endpoint. We focused on the intrinsic fundamentals, the underlying mechanics, emotional, and behavioral systems involved when creating the incredible derivatives, continuously cognizant that all of our activities must align with the true dynamics of the mind," Lophochroazang said calmly, yet with an upbeat tone, smiling as she looked at each of us. I couldn't help but to think how she had the ability to embody a balance of warmth and intelligence. Looking at her, her age was simply difficult to determine. Like all the others here, she had a vibrance, a focus on good health, things I had only occasionally seen in others in the past.

"Where you're from, Amazon wanted to be the most customer-centric company in the world. We gained strength because we wanted to align all systems and processes with the true nature of the human mind, customer-centric yes, but we are human-mind-centric and compassion-centric, weeding out ETOs made us infinitely stronger than any other," Wolfzang explained.

"Wow, you showered the mouse with love and affection, removed toxic environmental stressors and pressures, you developed a much more enlightened understanding of what makes a smarter mouse, cultivated perfection of the neocortex network during the mouses developmental period, the mouse no longer spent her valuable mental real estate avoiding punishment, overwhelmed by ancient powerful emotional drives. Then OCSs enlightened the mouse to what the most delicious cheese truly is; discovery and innovation," I affirmed.

Mary chuckled and said, "And a mouse is used figuratively… because?" Then touched my arm with a smile. Knowing I had no good explanation for my silly experimental metaphor, she continued, "If one wanted the experience of driving a Ferrari or spaceship, for that matter, it's quite a fostered desire. In fact, there's a cultivation of continuous new experiences, to happen upon by design, a previously expected unexpected, serendipitous paradigm shift of thinking," Mary replied.

"Wow! Mary!" I said with extreme admiration.

"Early on, our corporation provided skills, services, and products of the best quality, all done with the utmost integrity, all processes inextricably interwoven with the true dynamics of the mind. We used our complete understanding of escapes to harness our mind's focus and create astounding derivatives. This early experiment showed how unimaginably effective we became by following specific fundamentals in the DOC. Everyone involved eventually became quite wealthy, but that wasn't *the* why. There's more to our magic formula. We all desire to be pragmatic, objective, compassionate sentients. We were simply driven to freely exponentially discover and innovate. We needed the instruments to do that. Einstein once said, ‘Compound interest is the eighth wonder of the world. He who understands it earns it; he who doesn't pays it.’ This wasn’t something to trivialize. We studied Value Investing and mastered what would provide us with the means to spread compassion to all living things. This particular Article made us unimaginably capable of funding *everything*!”

“Whoa!”

The family began to wiggle their heads around and tucked in their lower lip. Each making a spitting sound.

“I know this one! Article Llama!” Mary said. We both began to laugh. They all looked a bit nuts.

“Buffett wrote a great article about the Mona Lisa.”

“I never read it.”

“In 1540, Francis I, the former king of France, bought the Mona Lisa for 4000 gold crowns, or about $20,000. If he put that into an investment generating a compounding return of a modest 6% a year, where you are, they’d have 1 quadrillion dollars. The painting is wonderful but not worth nearly that much, even for you.”

“Ha!”

“But, for us — it’s ALL about the experiences,” Turt said.

I thought back to the variety of cars Wolfzang drove, intimations of his desire to acquire unforeseeable experiences.

“I see your point. The lifestyle is quite like being a multi-millionaire back there. We certainly like comfort, the experience of delicious foods, exploring exciting unknown places, the value of expanding our ability to make unexpected connections and *joyfully* replacing embraced beliefs," Wolfzang explained.

"When we stopped focusing on the desire for stuff; when we realized we didn't care anymore to compete for *stuff* and focused on other more profoundly useful things, we focused on having a dynamic embraced belief cloud, becoming Universally Ethical, improving our systems for discovery and innovation, then paradoxically we seemed to have it *all* available to us. Quite a phenomenon, we still see the irony," Agy explained.

"But, far beyond the standard of living we have, the luxuries that are afforded to us, the ease of living, the greatest reward of all is the consequence of our complex systems, the abundant emotional health we feel by perfectly resonating one of the two strongest Genetically Important Drives, the Yearning for Emotional Closeness," Lophochroazang said.

"That genetic drive in our brainstem and limbic system, once you know it's all there, you begin to observe it. You see the formulaic production around you; those that know how to resonate it for profit sure do an exceptional job. You know, the Mortimer Mouse movies, someone *always* dies. Different imaginative story, same resonating drive. The corporate execs, writers, directors all know that's the secret formula for the success of a movie. The storyline changes, not their desire to resonate *that* powerful emotional drive," Mary said.

"I think, I sort of get it. It has to do with emotional connections, feeling alive because you feel so connected to the people around you, people you care about. You never feel alone or disconnected, and that is what this *place* is all about. The Primary Cloud becomes intensely healthy, the absolute highest degrees of executive functioning, capable of being dynamic. Thereby, you can fully experience being alive! Compounded by the mastery of escapes. Since you have mastered the use of escapes, you can fully harness their power. Everyone can be as intelligent as Einstein," I said.

“Also, you’re not blindly directed by your Genetically Important Drives that reflexively fuel your embraced beliefs,” Mary added.

“Exactly, it’s the OCSs ability to truly feel love, to give it and receive it with *no* contamination. Have you ever seen a Christmas photograph of a family that you know is being abused by, say, a toxic parent? They’re all smiling in the Christmas picture next to a tree, but there are so many underlying, repressed, painful feelings behind and concealed with smiles. What if those smiles were truly real? They had no concealed emotional wounds, no scars, and there was no walking on eggshells. There was just true deep love and affection for each other. A love that they could rely on day after day, morning after morning, night after night, no false pretense, no deception to keep the parent’s false reality perpetuated,” Birdie explained.

“I can see it. The lack of appreciation for the importance of deep connections is *everywhere*; it’s *ubiquitous* back there. When I was a kid growing up in Queens, I’d go to Manhattan and see the nannies in the parks watching the *rich* kids. You knew they were *rich*, they were always well dressed, and the nannies would always be from *far* away. Struggling to survive, these nannies work as underappreciated servants, often being underpaid, mistreated by the kids' parents, and even mistreated by the kids. Those that should appreciate them the most treat them as disposable. *Who* would want to give their love to others under those conditions? It’s *all* an act, there is no deep love, deep affection for the kids. But these wealthy families that we all aspire *to* don’t value this cultivation of love. So, these throwaway servants that are there while the kids are developing present the kids with faux smiles, hugs, and affirmations of love. Then the parents wonder why the kids have problems, need to be medicated. There’s a complete disregard for the necessity of a *real* long-standing, loving, nurturing connection. Some of these *parents* couldn’t even identify what that would look like as they look out of the large windows from their super expensive, hugely impressive apartments centrally located,” Mary explained.

"In defense of these *rich* people you do sound a little jel a bit green-eyed monster about their *nice* clothes and *big* windows," I said smiling. "Admittedly, I too would never have connected this emotional need generated deep within the mind with scientific advancement, multi-verse travel, or a healthier society," I said.

Wolfzang smiled and nodded.

"So the fact that any OCS can charter a boat anywhere is great, stay at the most luxurious hotels in the most expensive cities, but the unalloyed love you have for each other was the reason it all occurred in the first place," I said.

"That *is* it!"

"I remember Ayn Rand in an interview once said something like, 'If you love everyone, you love no one…' I'm embarrassed now to admit it felt right. I agreed with her," I said.

"Sounds quite two-dimensional. Our love is based on honesty, compassion, and a desire to help each other reach their highest potential in all three bell curves; we have plenty of love to go around. Those we spend more time with get a richer, deeper love. The friendship and committed endless history of support develops a deeper dependent love beyond the love we have for other OCSs, but it's a very real love for them nonetheless."

"For so many back there, religion is where love is found, used by many religious organizations to control its followers. That love for each other is rarely found in the science lab, in the research and development labs. It should be since the human-animal is involved, but it's falsely removed."

"Hmm, quite interesting. I've seen *those* religious groups. They support each other blindly, endlessly, have such blind eyes to money trails. The love in those religious organizations is harnessed to be powerful. To cleanse the love of its hidden impurities, to remove the concealed incentives, then adding that intense appreciation and affection for each other to the research and development labs. Correctly resonating our Yearning for Emotional Closeness during the discovery process would change *everything*! To add uncontaminated love to the lab, would, I guess *did*, supercharge the race," I said.

"Wow! I can see why scientists back there might have avoided such things, just sensing the power of love in those sorts of groups. The emotional voltage must seem overwhelming, uncontrollable, and ungovernable. Do you all work on the same projects as a… group?" Mary asked.

"I think you hit your mark; what we love most is talking about our AFEs and getting others' objective insights on each," Turt said.

"Your timeline has some significant challenges. Yet it is one of the closest to our own and sometimes has been our own. You'll find many OCSs considering ways of coaxing the Tool out early."

"Growing up here, every day we were told about one AFE or another, how it affected their embraced beliefs, how they went wrong, what they did right," Agy explained.

"Wow, that's so much different from my experience. My father's opinions reigned supreme. I was disrespectful if I ever questioned his all-knowing, self-assured points of view. I never heard him once mention he was ever wrong about anything," I said.

"The other day, I was doing an AFE located a few decades before your time, observing a small-town hate group. It's quite comical to see their monthly meetings. They started the get together by calmly discussing the type of fern to put in the front of the lodge; then they discussed some repairs to a road in town—one of the members is also the highway superintendent; then they proceeded to discuss whose wife made a better key lime pie. Next, they talked about a fishing trip, and *then* they focused their attention on one of the few black men in town. Not unlike them, the poor black man is simply poorly educated under his limiting circumstances, nothing else. It was merely a group with nothing going on, nothing healthy to challenge themselves with, nothing to feel accomplished about. They each had weaknesses in their Primary Clouds that allowed their own Feelings of Inferiority to overwhelm and pain them. So, this complete unawareness of their own emotional drives caused a need to have this powerful, Genetically Important Drives subdued. So… to fight their Feelings of Inferiority, they picked one rather helpless minority to abuse in order to feel better about themselves. It was all quite painful, yet ridiculous when you observed it up close. They needed to resonate their Narcissistic Drive any way possible," Birdie explained.

"Hmm, that's how they were trained long ago to do it. Find someone they can feel better than, then resonate their Narcissistic Drive. It sounds like some sort of twisted group therapy."

"Exactly. Also, they just didn't know how to use their escapes productively; they were never taught to reflect on their mental dynamics to reflect and guide the mind's attention. I guess you can live, but the quality of one's own life is diminished. Not thinking about the dynamics in the mind, I wonder if there is a way to identify the most reflective in that group and attempt to process him?" Agy asked and looked at his mother.

"Ha! We were processed!" Mary said with a robust laugh.

"One AFE I was working on recently was dealing with your current *identification* and *response* to extremely self-interested primitives, that is, the terrible outcomes when incorrectly dealing with an unreflective, highly self-interested primitive," Turt said.

"Narcissists or what Wilcox calls Narcs!" I said.

"Hah! Yeah, Narcs!" Mary said giggling.

"Quite right, I befriended a group of therapists that were focused on creating interventions for narcissists and their *families* — well, a Narcs *victim*."

"Ha!" Mary and I both laughed.

"One narcissist can infect, wound, and weaken so many family members. One Narcs dysfunction can ripple through *time*. They harness ETO's that those that don't understand the mind are so vulnerable to be sucked into. Those taking part in the cutting-edge therapy embraced the words of the leader. Devotees or trainees were indoctrinated with strategies of intervention by an acclaimed, absurdly venerated Dr. Weinstein. You know the type, Ivy League Ph.D.. His money-making scheme was skillfully shrouded under the pretense of altruism, science, and psychology. All of his theories were artfully complex."

"Like Wolfzang pointed out, that's so much interwoven in science back there. If it was *real*, it could be described in a down-to-earth readable inexpensive book or books, not an expensive drawn-out *training* that takes years to acquire."

"Well for us, *all* rigidly developed elongated certifications raise immediate concerns," Birdie added.

"This PhD was clearly an unreflective Narc himself, yet so charming and incredibly often combatively self-confident. To rise to the top back *there*, you gotta do the necessary intellectual slaughter of those that question your embraced beliefs. Who wouldn't believe him? He sounded *so* sure, never a moment of reflection publicly or privately. But that's the way you're taught to be a *leader* in a society that thinks two-dimensionally. His followers or sycophants fully committed to and embraced his regurgitated unremarkable in-vogue slightly different methods and any other *thing* he muttered. He had tapped into funding streams of large not-for-profit cashboxes designed to repeat fallacious societal norms. Funding groups that were indeed highly profitable for each's very *own* executives. So, *this* well pedigreed thought leader positioned himself and

now controlled the livelihood of *so* many. His newly unwitting disciples were forced to sign ten pages of contracts, including non-disclosures. He desired to and controlled them *all*, utterly fixated on controlling his intellectual property, he had *no* interest in discovery or innovation. He thought and acted as a money loving, ethically challenged lawyer. 'Do not say you had your own ideas, don't discredit my genius; otherwise, you'll be *sued.*' They all believed his work was *so* groundbreaking since others in their circles mindlessly nodded and applauded. Many professors in universities that wanted to be *relevant* jumped aboard feeding the ceaseless discussion."

"Joining the conversation," I said.

"All of his work was developed upon a number of idealistic, embraced two-dimensional misconceptions. It was all heavily chart and number driven. The charts and data were communicated stylishly, perfectly formatted, with his disciples always insisting everything was *clinically proven.* His scheme included confronting, forcing, training, referencing social cues of each other family member, and getting an admission of the cruel behavior from the high conflict individual while simultaneously trying to get the Narc to reason and empathize," Turt said.

"But… that's the thing, *right*? These Narcs, they wouldn't be the way they are *if* they didn't have a weakness in their Primary Cloud and could reflect on their thoughts and behaviors?" I said a little confused.

"Ha! As if you could *train* a person to empathize without a complete understanding of psycho-dynamics," Mary added.

"They sound cult-like."

"He's subtly and not so subtly coaxed his followers to get him nominated for the Nobel Prize."

"WHAT a NARC!"

"HA!"

"Wolfzang has helped apprise us of our inaccurate understanding of what creates one, a Narc. He really drove home their ubiquity in groups and how it has a much larger impact on our ability to arrive… *here*," Mary added.

"Quite the point, So… this doctor from Columbia tried organizing each family to act as a team to intervene. He recorded everything and then had his certified sycophants charge enormous amounts to provide over-analysis to the families. Within the families, there was always at least one well-concealed family operative, a narcissist's flying monkey that quickly flipped back and forth depending upon the circumstance; there would never be any consistency in working as a team against the toxic individual in these extremely conditioned and endlessly groomed family dynamics. After all, you have an intelligent Narc strategizing control of these people day and night; they've spent years strengthening the webs. They know each victim's weaknesses. The amount of energy they're willing to spend is unfathomable; no paid *professional* could compete," Agy explained.

"The term shit-show comes to mind," I said with a smile.

"Yet the trauma the Narc had once experienced was never exposed, confronted, symbolically dealt with; there were no attempts to strengthen the Primary Cloud to reflect upon the effects of the powerful Genetically Important Drives, there was no attempt to break down the walls about what had happened to *them* to be overwhelmed by their own Need to Control Others," Wolfzang said.

"The Narc simply returned to their highly lucrative patterns since the underlying trauma and weakening was never dealt with appropriately," Birdie explained.

“Here… *here*, watch these! Some interviews I worked on,” Turt said, sounding exuberant, clicking his thumbnails together, then rubbing his right thumbnail.

The OCS Vision started, “The way we do it is we try to get the narcissist individual to discuss their behaviors. Then confront them, use logic to prove their behaviors are destructive,” a woman in her early thirties with brown hair in an unmemorable dark red, very business appropriate dress explained.

“How long have you been doing it?” Turt asked.

“Almost two years.”

“How’s it going?”

“Yeah — no, it’s extremely challenging.” She explained with trepidation. “They seem to act willing, but further along, show significant resistance.”

“It almost sounds like they’re solving a puzzle, taking time to develop a defense.”

“I don’t know, most point the finger at me and try to blame me for provoking others and taking the daughter, the son’s side. They usually try to question my credentials, my background, attempt to find a weakness that they can exploit.”

“Now watch this response from her ten years later.”

The unfortunate woman gained 50 pounds; she went from being a rather healthy-looking young woman to a woman that looked like she was well past middle age and significantly overweight. Clearly neglectful of her own well-being over the past decade.

“Do you still practice the same methodologies? How’s it going?”

"Great! I really believe it helps a *few*… as long as we can reach a few just for a moment and give some of the victims a bit of happiness."

"Does that 'bit of happiness' have any longstanding actual impact on the victims? How about professionally… has it been a good career for you?"

"Following Dr. W's program, I've established myself and have a nice home."

"She's… entrenched," I muttered to myself.

"Is it quite stressful to perform… these methods?"

"I've been suffering a lot of my own depression issues. But! The clinical, empirical data demonstrates they are less likely to be diagnosed with a narcissistic personality disorder after the intervention. So it works! This is without question the best evidence-based practice there *is*!" She said with an unbelievable degree of enthusiasm. To me, her statement seemed endlessly rehearsed in her mind for delivery to paying clients and ended up conditioning her beliefs as well.

"You believe it's been clinically proven?"

"YES!"

"Do you think you can change them?" They both fell silent.

"I thought I could, but no, I think Dr. Weinstein is downright wrong on that account. He still insists he's right, and so many not in my position fully support him, but I've been through it endless times; I've attempted to bring it to his attention, and he ignores my points and redirects me nearly always saying I'm doing some minor detail wrong. He's actually gotten hostile with me when I attempted to demonstrate a few concerns. The clients *all* seem to go back to the original patterns even after we set boundaries, reason with them, get them to admit and… show empathy."

"Do you actually think the individual does empathize with those in their family? Or are they just putting on a show to deal with the situation, the group? Could they see everyone as a pawn?"

"I don't think anyone could definitively answer *that* question, but some seem to — care. At least momentarily."

"You once said that they point the finger and blame you. Do you think that could have a great impact on you on an… unconscious level? Resonating your Feelings of Inferiority which you carry home with you? Impact all parts of *your* life? My institute believes food is an escape used to sooth the emotional drives. Some foods will act as a depressant, some a stimulant, chemically reducing stressors and pressures. But importantly they absorb a part of the attention. Weight gain needs to be viewed as symptom of what's going on in the mind."

"You think my eating is related to this *job*?" She said. I could see her own little one asking with pure sincerity.

"Overeating is far more emotionally linked than recognized *here*. It's that you're overwhelmed by your emotions. If you weren't overwhelmed, you wouldn't reflexively attempt to calm yourself with an absorbing, mood-altering depressant. You've conditioned yourself to overeat to get through it all. It's a clue that you have to explore without fear or favor for this entire commitment."

"But… I like helping people?"

"Maybe you do, but maybe the storyline you've embraced has significant deficiencies."

"No one has ever put it that way. I mean, all jobs are stressful… right? I don't know why it's getting to me. Maybe it wouldn't bother someone else?"

“Has the Dr. ever suggested that his intricately trained consultants might be put under undo stress for prolonged periods of time? Using inaccurate methods even though he’s worked hard at establishing it’s all evidence-based work. I’m sure you had to deal with a lot of cruel narcissists that have directed their venom at you. Could it be, if you recognized some of it does resonate deep in the mind no matter how stable you perceive yourself, especially with the volume of work you perform, the number of narcissistic webs you are required to navigate through? By rattling them, you’re *not* teaching them what you think you’re teaching them. Instead, you’re only teaching them how to better prepare for you the *next* time. This ceaseless stress… Well, could it be affecting a deeper part of your mind, one you may have an obligation to protect like you would a two-year-old child?”

“Yes—yes, you’re so right. One profoundly narcissistic mother even wrote a grotesque lye-filled letter to the state about me trying to have my credentials taken away. I was trying so hard to be a support to that family. One son was being profoundly abused, every movement that poor kid made was scrutinized. Why she was so fixated on him I’ll never know. I gently worked with them for months. You could feel her hatred toward me. Trying to help them long-term, but she literally attempted to destroy me and stain my qualification with lies, all because I attempted to get her to reflect on her intensively controlling nature, her own very real behaviors. She was destroying everyone in her ‘*family*.’”

“What happened?”

“Her attempts to soil my credentials didn’t work in the end. But I had to deal with the blindness of state workers. The state bureaucrats were oblivious to the hard work I do and the level of mental illness I’m exposed to every day by such —*people*. One state administrator that questioned me actually perceived her as *the* victim. She was extremely persuasive; those in the credentials oversight office aren’t exactly digging that deep. They think everyone has a right to their *own* opinion. Who do they want to upset, some intensely hostile woman playing the victim or an easier target that needs to get into line and not rock the boat."

"At that point, did the brilliant *Dr.* back you up?"

"No, funny you should mention *that.* It's a good point; it has all left me perplexed and frustrated. It still irks me a couple of years later. I've really considered quitting, but don't see other work that would pay as well. He blamed me for pushing her too hard. When others in the state started to question this approach, he said I should have suggested she needed a higher level of care. Whatever *that* means?"

"Terrible! How misguided! Would you recommend this work, your position to anyone you care about?"

"What an interesting way to ask the question, No — NO way in *hell*! I'd tell them to avoid it like a terrible disease."

"Have you ever thought you must care about yourself? You must stop embracing this belief and find a better way to spend your life. A healthier environment to be in every day, the one you must show compassion toward, is hurt by such *toxicity* if you accept it or not. The little one inside can only give you subtle hints that go unheeded — life is brief."

At that moment, her face went pale. She had an enormous change in her complexion as if her eyes exposed her very own two-year-old. Her eyes shut for a moment, "I think I can't continue. It's unhealthy for me, *thank…* you." I could see it. It was her little one speaking, coming out of the darkness; the little one wanted to protect her from the concrete walls she hit against every day. The socially acceptable absorbing food she ran to instead of alcohol, which would act as a depressant and soothe her, was a detrimental escape. The incorrect embraced beliefs she fully committed to ruining her one life. Ruining one day at a time, slowly — continuously, breaking her apart.

The video transitioned to another man sitting in a cafe wearing a blue button-down shirt with the top two buttons unbuttoned. He also noticeably overweight and exuded an aura of frumpiness.

"How has Dr. Weinstein's methodology been going in practice?"

"It's paying the bills. I have a large caseload; he's been in a lot of interviews promoting his *wonderful* work, there has been a high demand for the work. People are *starving* for any support they can find dealing with toxic family members, you know, the high conflict type. They just want to do things like *normal* people get to do."

"Hmm, it sounds like he's vigorously marketing his… creative method. But for yourself? How have you been, do *you* find it stressful? Over the past few years? Do you have any health issues?"

"Well, you're paying for *this* interview. But my health issues are really unrelated. I guess I've had some health problems. I struggle with an ongoing drinking problem. My *wife* thinks it has something to do with depression; y'know, *but* my Doctor agrees it's a type of genetic predisposition. A neurological issue I have. Something about my receptors not functioning accordingly, it does drag me down a bit. I guess it makes me tired, sort of lethargic. Now I've been taking anti-depressants."

"Do you think these high-conflict, intensely self-interested people could be impacting you?"

"No. Well… I guess it could have some minor relationship, but I don't let it affect me."

"Would you recommend this line of work to a loved one?"

"Interesting question; **NO**, I have a high tolerance for this stuff; it doesn't *really* bother me! But I'd never want my kids to do this."

“Have you ever considered a healthier line of work even though it pays well?”

“Financially, it’s hard to get out. I intend to retire in about nine years. I get calls a lot. This program is well known, has a lot of funding and support, people are desperate for some sort of help, there’s a real demand for this *evidence-based* intervention.”

“In-vogue-funded-opinion-based,” I thought to myself.

“Try to look deeper and see if it’s impacting you. Nine years is a long time to deal with this every day.”

With a slight scowl, “I can’t! I have bills to pay, a family to support,” he said with frustration.

The OCS Vision went off, “I can see how incentives drive dogmas and methodologies, these professionals, their ‘clinically substantiated beliefs,’ are emotionally defended. It’s amazing how unscientific it all looks when you see it isn’t real or working, how this is so pervasive through our society that needs to gyrate from in-vogue broken dogma to in-vogue incomplete methodology, these soft science methodologies have more to do with what gets funded, what’s currently caught wind,” I said.

“All the while, proponents using intelligent-sounding scientific terminology such as ‘evidence-based practice,’ ‘clinically tested,” “empirically substantiated,” to sound sophisticated, sciency* and support their opinions, competitively out talking others, clearly, having financial motivations to strategically promote the ‘innovative, groundbreaking approach,’” Mary said, staring out at the distance, apparently pondering the conversations.

“Always seeing the behavior as two-dimensional, not three-dimensionally driven, supplying numbers and charts to defend and perpetuate,” I added.

“We never just see the one aberrant behavior as confined to the individual, for instance, a serial killer; we see someone that had countless horrific events occur during childhood. We are aware of those adults during his developmental process that never protected him, that were disconnected from him, that wounded and weakened him, a large number of those around him that rationalized turning a blind eye,” Agy said.

“Not getting involved,” Wolfzang added.

“Our hardwired—ness probably exacerbates such things?” Mary said in a ponderous voice.

“Hmm, I think I see what she’s saying. I guess if part of the dynamics of the mind is to act as a defense, redirecting us, and remain concealed to help remain calm during stressful social situations, we are dealing with that, or the fact that we will emotionally defend embraced beliefs reflexively. We become *frustrated* to keep our beliefs intact, our environment controlled, but then — we’re always dealing with the 67% primitives that are more easily motivated by self-interest and will sell an idea if they are appropriately incentivized to do so.”

“I suspect the same is true for more than just psychological *groundbreaking* methodologies back there; all market-driven industries magnify the high IQ, high emotional quotient types to persuade others so they can get *the* cheese.”

“Are you two *sure* you’re primitives? Dad’s not playing a practical joke… right? Challenging us to pick out an OCSs from a primitive? You seem so much like everyone else *here*,” Agy explained with a smile.

“Ha! What a thoughtful compliment.”

“Wolfzang has the right touch; he used practical explanations to describe the world in your way. He resonated our Yearning for Emotional Closeness; it was so powerful to the two of *us*; we came from such dark rocky places. Little by little, we became thirstier and thirstier to understand what Wolfzang knew. It was almost a debriefing after years of family members, friends, coworkers, bosses, acting self-interested — irrational," I said.

"The way you resonate each other's Yearning for Emotional Closeness, the way all the OCSs have learned the value of harnessing that *one* immensely powerful genetically important drive, and now can fuse it into your science and technology pursuits rather than pretending like it doesn't impact everything the human-animal does, that's likely the most extraordinary cultural difference," Mary said.

"I had once heard that religious groups like the Jehovah's Witnesses will ostracize anyone who leaves the group. Some religions use that all-powerful behavioral drive to control and cripple — SUCH a *cruel* practice for those that have a pretense of love," I said.

"Not here; it's like leaving the smog of the city behind and entering a huge beautiful fresh forest, breathing in the crisp, fresh morning air; the lungs can almost get overwhelmed by the amount of healthy oxygen available," Mary said.

"The attributes you both exhibit make it easy for us," Birdie explained.

Mary slowly began to appear disquieted, clearly recalling each step we took since we set foot on this enigmatic land. "Everyone is sooo warmhearted *here*. It's not the synthetic *plastic* love, the pretend friendship a consumer gets when buying *stuff*; it's the real uncontaminated desire to fulfill each other's Yearning for Emotional Closeness," she said, looking blankly off into the distance, once again gazing toward the beautiful cows in this perfect bucolic setting. She then turned to me, her eyes slightly glistening, her head slightly quivering, and said, "It's REAL! They accomplished something far more elusive to us than multiverse travel," She said, as she placed her pointer finger in the corner of her eye disposing of a tear.

Feeling the magnitude of her thoughts, I replied, "I'd have to agree with Mary. You're all so down-to-earth. I don't think it's going to change either; no one has come off as pretentious or smug, acceptance of equivalence pervades the very breathable air. You have vastly more knowledge than us, and *you* can teach *us* so much. Yet no one acts like they are intellectually, emotionally, or ethically superior to us."

"It's palpable. It's not in *your* creed. You're all so vastly intelligent; you know it would all work against you, against the exponential progress you're capable of. You're not thinking we're just specimens to be probed. You're not thinking my shirt is stupid, that I'm a dumb primitive, or that you're God's chosen people… far superior to us. You're not thinking that you have more money, so you're the upper class. If you had *those* thoughts intruding into your thoughts, you would sense you were resonating your emotional drives and then realize the destructive nature that line of thinking can produce. You're taught all of those biases are not aligned with universal compassion; *trust* is the derivative," Mary said softly with immense adoration. Gazing at her, I comprehended this was all from her own little one.

"You all truly care about *us*; we both left home so young to get away from our out-of-control families. Here no one would ever want to leave. Here, love is clean and pure. It's a true understanding of the human mind, not a disconnected data-driven clinical view of human behavior," I said.

"Trust… *is* the derivative," Mary repeated clearly organizing her thoughts.

Wolfzang's family calmly listened. No one attempted to interject opinions and make points. No one was attempting to guide us or sound smart. It was as if we had reached the zenith with their support, and now they simply allowed the transformation to occur.

"We can't pay you money; we can't be a part of the church where you're attempting to gather a group of unquestioning followers. The bigger flock, the more strength, the more money… the better. There is nothing to gain from *us*, yet you just see us, the young children within *us*, *pure* and *innocent*," Mary said, a tear clearly visible. I put my hand on Mary's arm.

I felt it too, "It's possible to see everyone as a beautiful innocent two-year-old. The elderly man dressed in homeless clothing, the woman of a different nationality in clothes that look otherworldly, and the donkey walking down the road. The competitiveness we're cultivated to have, back there, the dehumanizing climate we are taught to encourage and perpetuate. The every man or woman for themselves belief, which we euphemistically call individualism — it's all contaminated with deeply flawed embraced beliefs, beliefs we defend reflexively… emotionally defended beliefs."

"Well, to get here, it was like everything else, trial and error, but the direction was based on the correct underlying assumptions; our founders struggled and had many bang-ups, unexpected pitfalls to traverse," Wolfzang said.

Like Facebook's old motto, "Move fast and break things," Mary responded.

"Yeah, like Hawklung," Agy said with a smile.

Birdie let out a bit of a chuckle, then explained, "Hawklung was one of our early founders. She attempted to create an oversight commission to police the Doc of OCS. Argued our AI was not advanced enough and that it would need a human to temporarily organize and run the systems. She said the individual needed to be highly specialized to pick out the very subtle clues that demonstrated ETOs. Like so many who desire power, they themselves buy the lie and conveniently conceal their own ambitions for power with what appeared honorable intentions. She said, 'Only *I* can do this job!' We quickly caught on to the fact that she was attempting to control and coerce others by wielding power over other OCS, all masked with our own Articles and ETOs. Once she was in, she attempted to convince, cajole or use any trick to stay in power. For a few months, she became a powerful czar to police the Doc of the OCSs. But since our underlying systems before her were designed to neutralize any perceivable hierarchies, she was quickly identified and removed from the position while retaining any innovative ideas she might have been developing."

"Which were actually quite meager," Wolfzang added.

"Those reaching for power are often cloaked in admirable intentions," Agy repeated, nodding his head.

"Hawklung, ha! How the hell did she get her slimy little fingers into that position? *Here*? The OCS detest all hierarchies?" I asked.

"Growing pains, many originally were pulled out of the horrific despair, nearly everyone who joined up knew ahead of time what they were joining. They were completely committed to the ideals; some brought their own weaknesses within their Primary Cloud that needed to be strengthened."

"We're all a bunch of enthusiastic problem solvers; our systems simply became stronger. That was our magic. Each time we came upon a Hawklung type, we would learn strategies of responding, strengthening our systems so a similar sort couldn't do it in the future," Turt said.

"It was like developing an immunity to a virus you fought off?"

"Great point, one might say. We embraced those that showed us our own weaknesses. We only developed stronger systems because of them," Agy explained.

"So, with Hawklung, what did you do? Did she lose it all? Get kicked back out into the cesspool we know as modern-day life?" Mary asked.

“Since we see people in a three-dimensional light, those with such issues are *not* acting because of a chemical malfunction but because of weaknesses in the Primary Cloud nearly always induced during development. So, she was provided our rehabilitation process, compassion, and we developed a better understanding. Identifying why her Primary Cloud was overpowered by her resonating Genetically Important Drives in her brainstem and limbic system, the Need to Control Others, the Need to Control the Environment, her Narcissistic Drive and the Feelings of Inferiority. Once we understood her childhood, worked on her recovery with symbolism, role play, and our own versions of rational therapies, she made astounding improvements.”

“We are so proud of altering our embraced beliefs and discussing those *changes* that it’s *all*... different for us. We allow our Narcissistic Drive to resonate, feel immensely proud of ourselves for improving ourselves. It subdues our Feelings of Inferiority.”

“*Huh*! I’d think you’d never let your Narcissistic Drive resonate, *but* OCS’s always surprise me with their finite distinct beliefs. You folks are pragmatically Universally Ethical. There are few essential moments to feel you’re the best and most wonderful for accomplishing something so resoundingly impressive unlike billions of primitives that had proceeded you,” I said.

“Well… it’s not that we feel better than all the billions that couldn’t do it, we allow ourselves to feel like we’re heading toward the unequivocable truth and resonating with the universe. We are headed toward becoming… truly enlightened. We *understand* what a very small percentage of all humans have been given the soil to accomplish something so once *unimaginable*. We feel *exceedingly* grateful to have built our *thoughts*… our logic upon systems that can transform us into something… magical.”

ACE brought out a tray of silver goblets filled with what appeared to be a green beverage. The goblets each had a different scene of animals frolicking. Mine had jungle animals with elephants, snakes and long-legged birds. Mary had forest animals, I could see a bear, beaver, and a frog. Next to the goblets was a snack platter that appeared to have French fries and some sort of fried tofu with an orange-colored dip.

"The drink has kale, ginger, apple juice, mango, and dates," Ace-Meerkat said, then he turned and walked back to the house.

"Thanks!" all the family members said with upbeat exuberance.

I sipped from the large ornate goblet. The taste was *incredible*; it wasn't *just* a delicious drink, the OCSs prided themselves on delighting and absorbing the senses. Many times, I remember loving my first sips of cola. Releasing an, "*mmm*," right after the highly caffeinated, high fructose, cold bubbling beverage went down my throat. I could only speculate on how the chemists created such an addicting unhealthy drink that we could drink endlessly and never tire. As for the OCS's wholesome, harmonious green drink, this surprising explosive taste momentarily consumed a part of my attention. It occurred to me that if a race was all about truly healthy absorbing escapes, foods and drinks like this must be part an essential art and science.

"There were others like her; I remember learning about a couple of early OCSs that gained prominence attempting to be financial watchdogs; they were simply contrarians desirous of being a committee that reviewed all OCSs financials, so, rather than letting them have the control, we simply developed a sophisticated alternative system in which we randomly generated other OCSs to audit financial work in case there ever was any such malfeasance. Later it was clearer. They were simply creating unnecessary subjective criticisms."

"Hmm, what Wolfzang calls over-analysis."

"Exactly, even though there were a couple of them, they too, were all found to have weaknesses within their Primary Cloud."

“Behaviors are a symptom of what’s going on in the mind, not a product of a neuro-chemical malfunctioning,” Mary said.

“You got it. It made their Genetically Important Drives attempt to control *the* show. We pride ourselves on being highly skilled and organized, always on the lookout for those that are concealing emotionally driven motivations.”

“I could see how a group of OCSs might make concerns seem—*genuine.* They themselves believe their own ambitions aren’t stemming from resonating emotional drives.”

“But again, we’re in love with the *unusual.* Since we never force fit, always love to examine and explore the… atypical. So early on, when we found highly intelligent, extremely emotionally aware amongst us that still succumb to their resonating emotional drives we realized it was essential to develop a skillset to continuously reflect upon ourselves and others. For its far too easy to be seduced by ourselves and by those that can’t even imagine that they are *indeed* acting upon, often with astonishingly complex rationalization, but still driven by their Genetically Important Drives.”

“You say it was a group? Water finds its own level. I suspect, those with weaknesses in the Primary Cloud are often emotionally driven and frequently drawn together,” I said.

“Quite right! So, something like high voltage angry types seems to attract,” Agy replied.

“Hmm, how does the saying go? ‘He who controls the money supply controls the nation,’”

“James Garfield!” the family said in unison.

“Ah, to have enlarged caudate nuclei.”

“I could see it all sounded quite reasonable, having intense checks and balances. *Here*, no one group has a special position over others. The position is executed by an unnamed individual, sometimes AI, that will soon relinquish control to the next and are evaluated for their own ability to be pragmatic and objective,” Turt said.

“Since humans are emotionally, incentive and escape driven back then we had to accept the power of those that *were* involved with finances.”

“I once again could see how my fellow primitives might think you’re a bunch of anarchists, but that would be entirely missing the point; it's just a more complex form of checks and balances aligned with an acceptance of the OCS Mental Model,” I said.

“Right, without acceptance of the human animal’s complex but predictable emotionally, incentive, and escape-driven behaviors, we couldn’t so concisely prepare for and overcome our own shortcomings,” Agy replied.

“Crytodirazang and I are playing at a concert tonight. We should probably leave soon, so we don’t have to rush, I can continue to show them around.”

“You should hear these two play,” Birdie explained.

“That’s amazing to be talented in so many things,” Mary said.

“Well—we think anyone can become quite skilled in anything after a mastery of the OCS Mental Model,” Turt explained.

“Yes, but don’t instruments just come naturally to some? I once read an article that said people that were good at math are good at instruments,” Mary asked.

Turt smiled, “Here, we have found it’s about learning how to engineer and harness escapes, and anyone at all can become a world-class musician, mathematician, programmer, or accomplished artist. Using escapes to decompress from stressors and pressures absorbed during AFEs. Quieting the mind and being in the moment is essential. If you can't quiet the mind, that alone is an important symptom to investigate," Turt explained.

"From a young age, we train the mind to use many desirable escapes and we're always in search of possible new ones, as our interests take unforeseeable paths," Agy added.

We both realized we had limited time to eat. So we attempted an accelerated, sophisticated approach. Yet we both wanted to be uninhibited and began a frenzied gobble. I recalled a few years ago. We were invited to a friend's house; they had a platter full of cheese and a bunch of fruit sodas. I loved the sodas, and Mary fixed her attention on the cheese and crackers. After we left, we realized we embarrassed ourselves and laughed; I must have chugged five of their sodas, and Mary ate most of what was on the platter meant for five. Whatever it was, we never heard from those '*friends*' again. We promised each other to be a little less glutinous during social visits in the future, but here, the OCSs food was just — *so* good. The breaded seasoned tofu had a ranch dressing dip. It reminded me of the chicken wings I would get late nights in New Paltz years ago. Though I purposefully didn't bring it up, I thought of the OCS cultural beliefs and their equivalence to living things. I reflected upon my complete disregard at the time of what I was eating and how indifferent businesspeople mass execute those emotional little creatures by the thousands with engineered ingenuity, perceiving the beautiful little beings as inanimate *things*, forcing them to survive just long enough in horrifying conditions.

Temporal Rewind, Southern AFE

I continued to transcribe the journals. Attempting to examine these constructs his group held as fundamental axioms. The Embraced Belief Cloud Network, aka *the* book, the three bell curves, the glass of water, escapes, the Genetically Important Drives. Why he believed each played an essential part in our academic assignment now in our minds labeled, "How to change large scale behaviors with minimal effort."

"What are you doing?" Mary asked. She'd noticed I was sketching on a notepad I'd collected at the opulent hotel on Crosby Street.

"I'm beginning to wonder *how* I'd want my metaphorical book, the book that he uses to represent the Embraced Belief Cloud Network, to appear. I'm trying to imagine how I'd make the front and back cover, the spine, and the pages in between. I want to create it slowly, over time, so I know it's perfect. This is really a sketch of the binding."

"That book, I can see the power they get from it. It's a fascinating ingredient to understand *him.* A communication to the deeply rooted parts of the brain that responds to repetitive training and symbolism. But they know exactly what and why they're crafting the book. The act of creation is symbolic, then the ability to see it, hold it."

"Accelerating the ability to alter a belief quickly, seamlessly, and hunting the inaccurate, intricate but overlooked ones down."

"The essential ability to give the Embraced Belief Cloud Network a comprehendible form, so they can completely envision and reflect on their *own* book every day."

"His group needs to wear a shirt that says, "I'm from the Vac-Plat, I'm sorry in advance, my intentions are good. I might frustrate you, I'll try to conceal my thoughts, but we attempt to examine embraced beliefs… Again I apologize for any aggravation I may cause you. But if I cause you too much vexation, you may want to look into it."

"Uh-hah! Would all that fit? It'll have to be an extra-large. I can see why a group with such practices needs to be in stealth mode. If his beliefs are indeed accurate and if you went around questioning people on their religious, academic, or political beliefs, they'd want to clobber you. Why waste time dealing with such needless drama?"

"He'd said their kids create art projects that represent their metaphorical book. It's an essential practice for them at a young age."

"That's a cool design for the binding, sort of a galactic feel with planets and bell curves."

"It only makes sense that we usually choose the easiest answers. Like those underpaid, overworked, disgruntled woman at the *daycare*. 'Let 'em cry it out!' It was easy for them. Our emotional drives resonate, generate a response, a feeling. We have a belief then we defend that belief with logic. When something is undemanding, we buy in, easily accepting it."

"I think I get what you're saying; if we agree with an idea, it's easy we go on resonating our Narcissistic Drive. 'We smartest monkey descendants ever!' We all seem to believe ourselves the authority of accuracy. But if it's conflicting our current embraced belief, it might make us feel less intelligent. Thus, resonating our Feelings of Inferiority, Need to Control the Environment, Need to Control Others. If it's a demanding question, not linked to our escapes, we might be reflectively resentful. It resonates one of the two strongest Genetically Important Drives: Resentment of Demands."

"Even in our psych and education classes, they're all leaning toward nature, not nurture, as the answer to the debate."

"I wonder why we believe that? From a business sense, our market-driven economy has a lot of pharma companies that benefit from the nature, chemicals in the brain going haywire view; the budgets spent propagating that belief is actually boggling. To them, everything is chemical and biological. I hear commercials all the time that seem to suggest our behaviors all have a chemical basis behind them and can be helped with the right pill. Can you imagine how those continuous positions reverberate onto the medical world, into the education world, and into mainstream embraced beliefs?"

"Hmm, the funding is there to sell an idea. So you think it's pharmaceuticals first and then all others downstream? The idea humans are emotionally, incentive, and escape driven would be absurd to them."

"Because of the strong influences on our society, that nature or nurture debate is a hot-button topic. It should be an easy discussion. But it's not; it's an explosive topic for many. One of those things you gotta stay away from, like politics or religion."

"It's become evident, the OCSs believe very little has to do with genetics or neurological malfunctions and a *lot* to do with environmental impacts."

"They see that as immensely impacting our future prospects. So many I know put on the show that they're open-minded, progressive, but when you scratch the surface, you begin to find someone that is very good at buz words, defending an idea, but are actually quite rigid with beliefs they cultivate."

"Yeah, I'm going to be careful with this axiom. Those I know, too many people believe it's all nature, all a chemical issue. It's emotionally easier to think something other is impacting who we are; we don't have to have this deeper understanding."

As he had requested, I emailed him the transcribed journals we now obsessed over. As I agreed, I kept our conversations precisely as they happened, careful not to doctor my opinions to make them what I believe he wanted to hear or for us to look *smarter*. When we returned to the possibility that this all could still simply be a sociological perception experiment, we appreciated our responsibility to adhere to the original agreement. It made us a little uneasy that he was privy to the fact that we thought he was a time traveler or even possibly a conman, but, as he mentioned, we needed to be completely honest with our thoughts; otherwise, he couldn't use us for this academic research. Additional emails focused on our trip down south; he suggested: "It's simply to introduce you two to someone that's part of the same perception experiment."

We started at 5:00 am and drove down the intensive Interstate 95, with occasional bathroom and snack stops until 7:45 pm. When we arrived, we were both exhausted and checked into a clean, blue-grey-painted motel where an older woman with impeccable clothing and an immaculate beehive hairdo stood behind the counter. She was very business-appropriate and quickly handed us the keys. I felt like we walked right into the 1960s; even the photos in the office were black and white. I couldn't help think of the Pearl Jam song "Elderly Woman Behind the Counter in a Small Town." Wolfzang had made the reservations for us. A few years before, we had read about bed bugs on a previous trip down south, so we did our routine inspection of checking the bottom of the mattress for blood streaks. The place was exceptionally immaculate for being quite dated; still, the sink, bathtub, and fixtures looked brand new, but from 60 years prior.

The following day was sunny, and the mist was rising from the grass; the trees around the motel had a large amount of Spanish moss hanging. A novelty I'd only seen in movies, I found myself pulling and probing the plant to pass the time as I waited for Mary to get ready, then meet with Wolfzang at a local diner, which I could see several blocks away as I pulled the vines.

"Don't touch *that*! I know you're a New Yorker, so you don't KNOW! That stuff is full of MITES and LICE! I'd get away from it if I were you!" The elderly woman, originally behind the counter, yelled from the office door. Feeling a bit embarrassed, I simply said, "Sorry… Thanks!"

Mary and I walked over to the diner where Wolfzang was already sitting. He was reading a newspaper, looked up, and said, " Glad you both made it; I bet you're both tired from all the driving yesterday. I'll be right with you; I just wanted to finish this; I have an article for you both to read," he pointed to the paper.

Coffee and tea were both already sitting at our spots, along with Wolfzang's newspaper he wanted us to read, so we both started reading as well.

Sadly, it was the heartbreaking story about a mother that committed suicide after her young daughter was killed in a mass shooting a few years before up North. Not the painfully grim way I usually preferred to start a Sunday.

"Why does this terrible shit happen? That poor little girl, those beautiful little children, that poor woman having to wake up every day, she must have thought about her daughter's murder every day… all day. How could she not stop thinking about it? She would have had so many painful visions. It must have been hell for that poor woman," I said, feeling great pain thinking about the little girl and her mother. Pain oozed in my body like poison.

"How is this gun shit going to end? With these mentally ill assholes that shoot people, innocent people they don't even know? Why is it happening?" I asked; as positive as an impact as Wolfzang had had on us, it wasn't enough for this. There was still part primitive in me that felt total disgust for the monsters that inflict pain and suffering on others without the slightest empathy for the harm they cause. The situation being children made it even more heinous.

"You're facing a mighty gun industry with many highly incentivized self-interested people supporting the industry. But that's not it; there's more about guns. Otherwise, after all this loss and sadness, things would have changed." He paused for a moment and put the newspaper down, taking a sip of his coffee. "It goes deeper than the availability of ridiculously destructive weapons; there's a much larger emotional drive and misconception that needs to be explored about why people are drawn to such a — needlessly deadly device."

"I think I get it. Guns are not just an object like a toaster or metal shovel; they are impacting our minds in some way that makes us very emotionally unstable when we think someone is going to take them away. I can already imagine how they may be resonating the Genetically Important Drives of the brainstem and limbic system," Mary explained.

"That's extremely insightful. It's true; guns resonate so many of the drives in the brainstem and limbic system. They absorb the person's attention; then they become an escape in so many ways. The mind uses them to decrease stressors and pressures," Wolfzang explained.

"How do they become an escape?" Mary asked.

"The gun lover gets a powerful, easily available escape. The mind can focus on something familiar that is absorbing it. It gets time to decrease stressors and pressures, time dilutes stressors and pressures. Guns become the focus of so many *fantasies*. It becomes an intellectual, academic fixation. The mind can be absorbed by the types of guns, the history, the mechanics, the art of use. As you know, resonating the Genetically Important Drives is extremely reinforcing. One may fall into a fascinating fantasy world, and the person feels powerful, wielding the gun over those that make him or her feel powerless, even if the other isn't fully aware. For the weary, depressed, stuck primitives, it is an extremely reinforcing available escape."

"Wow, guns are such a *mental thing*; I've never thought of it that way. Just thinking about them now, they are symbolically meaningful, and like you said, symbols and symbolism are the language of the brainstem and limbic system," I responded.

"All types of practice is repetitive training; practice teaches the deeper part of the mind to perform reflexively, thus communicates with the inner mind. The more absorbing due to the resonating emotional drives, the more likely something becomes an escape."

"Hmm, guns are a *mental thing*," Mary said, sounding reflective.

Putting down the menu, he smiled and nodded at the waitress.

Then he continued, "Altogether, they are hugely symbolic. The dynamics that occur in the mind because of them are quite impressive. They resonate the Genetically Important Drives, the Need to Control the Environment, the Need to Control Others, and the Narcissistic Drive, yet they help to calm Feelings of Inferiority. So, since the need to use an escape is as important to the human mind as water is to the human body, the use of guns as an escape is often vigorously reinforced, conditioned, and classically, to be used to absorb the mind and reduce stressors and pressures."

"Classically conditioned, I remember you saying *that* about escapes, but how with guns do you think?" I asked.

"The mind feels its stressors and pressures, the glass of water rises, maybe the person is mistreated, a boss, parent, coworker, TV show resonates Feelings of Inferiority; as you know, the mind is reflexively redirected to what absorbs its attention, and for some folks, guns do it best."

"Wow, no wonder OCS have advanced; that's — incredible; we're all hardwired with the same mental dynamics, just different escapes depending on our environment," I responded.

"That's amazing! So to some, guns are like candy to the mind, so reinforcing. Just the thinking about them absorbs the attention, then becomes an escape. *If* you try to remove an escape, you'd better replace it with something just as entrancing to the mind, *just* as reinforcing?" Mary responded.

“Exactly, unbelievably powerful to the mind and very available,” Wolfzang responded.

“Hmm, absorbing is reinforcing. As you’d said, if it takes time, absorbs the mind to some degree it can fit this definition of escapes.”

“What would you like?” A 60-year-old woman with well-kept make-up and long silver antique earrings, wearing a once-white apron stained with what appeared to be coffee, asked in a kindly grandmotherly voice.

“Double order of grits and any fruit you might have my dear,” he replied.

“The same,” I said

“Same,” Mary said a moment later.

“NO, meat? You guys *got* allergies or… something?” She asked.

“No, no, we just like grits a *lot*,” Wolfzang responded.

“My grandson’s got a lot of allergies; he doesn’t eat meat either, sometimes he says he doesn’t like the texture, the blood bothers him — such a sensitive, smart boy, he’ll get over it, I’m sure. The doctor says he’s got the *sensory* issues,” she responded, then went to another table to take the order.

Wolfzang continued, “If you are living a life where everyone puts you down, you are never appropriately deeply cared for, cared about, then told to act tough, told not to feel your very real… exceedingly powerful emotions, you can’t reach your fullest potential as a sentient, you become stuck repressing and battling what's going on inside.”

Waiting for a moment, looking out the window he watched a car pulling up alongside the diner.

“So — paradoxically, when you ignore, neglect your emotions, you become emotionally driven,” Wolfzang said.

“That is soooo true — if you come from a place where you're supposed to be tough and not care about your emotions, you simply end up being emotionally driven,” Mary responded.

“I can see that if you’re repressing, attempting to ignore, not confronting these normal resonating emotions deep within, they end up dictating your actions!” I responded.

“Hmm, I can see why that’s important to you when understanding large-scale human behavior.”

“Exactly. Those emotional drives of the brainstem and limbic system are a huge driver of human behavior. Without a complete acknowledgment and understanding, you’re doomed to be a slave to them.”

A large balding man in his late 60s, apparently the cook, brought out our plates, himself wearing clothes far more stained than the waitresses. “Here ya go! We had bananas and blueberries, strawberries for y’all. Since you guys like fruit, want some freshly squeezed orange juice?” He said pleasantly in a deep voice, all the while breathing like he just finished a long run. His unshaven appearance, his overall aura, something about it, just made me think of a cigar.

“Sounds great!” I said while Wolfzang and Mary affirmed with nods; within moments, the cook returned with our orange juice.

We sat quietly, taking in the authentic Southern atmosphere and enjoying the fresh, very pulpy orange juice, our fruit, and grits, to which Mary and I added sugar.

“The man I’d like you to meet today, look beyond what you see, try to perceive him the way the OCS would,” he explained.

"Like an emotionally, incentive, escape-driven two-year-old?" Mary responded with a smile.

"Well — yes, but we wouldn't feel superior with that perception. We see all humans that way; my wife, my boys, I see them that way. They see me that way. We're always listening for clues for when that part of the mind is speaking," Wolfzang responded.

It occurred to me that by immersing ourselves in different cultures, such as visiting indigenous communities in the Brazilian rainforest or connecting with the Amish community in Pennsylvania, we may gain insights into their unique worldviews. The goal being to empathize with their perceptions and beliefs, attempting to understand their truths on a deeper level. Yet, the OCSs beliefs were all objective, pragmatic, so far rational, intricately developed, and solidly understandable. Just different, we couldn't disprove them. Yet, it wasn't the way one might say we couldn't disprove God; we weren't buying into superstition or some faith-based set of beliefs. Each step we took was an objective examination of a part of his particular understanding of the natural world. Thus far, just a uniquely highly refined examination, sometimes intersecting our beliefs, sometimes paralleling our understanding of the world and human behavior. Since I was in no way suspending disbelief, it seemed unique, unlike another perceivable sociological experiment easily imagined. All other cultures with faith-based ideas seemed easy to walk away from in the end, but these embraced beliefs were challenging and changing us — *forever.*

"I'm excited about today's field observation," Mary said.

We took another 20 minutes and finished the meal, then Wolfzang paid for the check at the register. We were traveling into the backcountry of South Carolina; Wolfzang was sporting a black Ford truck about ten years old with Kentucky license plates, which we all climbed into. If I asked him where he got the pickup, he'd say, "From a friend." The question was moot; however, it was clear his choice was made with great precision.

This place was timeless; life hadn't changed very much in the last hundred years. If you put pictures of some of the country folk from the early 1900s next to images of their offspring of today, one would think no time had passed.

The dust kicked off the road behind the tires. We passed many shacks and mobile homes that were beat up but had nice trucks, boats, and ATVs outside. A peculiar phenomenon for people living in otherwise squalor. One couldn't help to think that the credit companies were effective at finding people others had long ago forgotten. We passed several sizeable beautiful homes down long driveways that were unquestionably once working slave plantations.

We soon pulled up to a rusted mobile home, immediately taking notice of a speed sign riddled with bullet holes and a large confederate flag laid haphazardly on top of the roof, hanging and flapping in the wind. A large chicken coop was beside the house, the chickens scurrying around the front yard. Left to my own devices, I would have sped up and kept driving; the place looked beyond creepy — dangerous.

Wolfzang began, "This is going to be a long-term friendship for the three of you. In the future, you'll actually become terrific friends. Paul's father came from a long line of men with little hope of pulling themselves out of poverty. Paul was told throughout his childhood he was an idiot — worthless. He had no choice but to embrace these cruelties as facts."

"It's in his Embraced Belief Cloud Network. He has that stored as fact; that's so… sad," Mary responded.

"His genetic drive and Feelings of Inferiority resonated when his own father repeatedly told him, in a cruel self-assured way a parent can, that he was dumb, 'a retard.' His father showed a great disdain for people with more melanin than him."

"You mean black people?"

"Yes, and whenever Paul agreed, his father showed less hostility toward his own son, less hatred, and even some interest in him. It was a type of reinforcement; the alarm clock would stop ringing. At that moment, there was a bit of relief. Indeed, the only happy memories he had with his father were when they were agreeing on hating," Wolfzang explained.

"Wow, that's — terrible, such a dysfunctional group," I said.

"I can see that kind of thing perpetuating over generations. Some piece of him wanted to love his own father."

"Now, he feels terrible about himself. His Feelings of Inferiority are always being resonated, his weakness, wounds long ago burned into his Primary Cloud, and now it's easily overpowered. Still, his Narcissistic Drive energizes and fights it, 'yeah, I'm poor, but I'm far better off than those black people,' or so he attempts to rationalize," Wolfzang explained.

"Really, you say we're going to be friends with this guy? He sounds — horrible?" Mary said.

Pausing for a moment, all three of us got out of the truck.

"If Paul didn't genetically need to feel superior in some way, driven by his Narcissistic Drive, which is a natural Genetically Important Drive in all of us, if Paul didn't have such strong Feelings of Inferiority reinforced by the conditioning of his father and many others when he was young, then Paul wouldn't be a racist."

I attempted to avoid the chicken poop all over the front walk or the ruins of a front walk, now mostly fragments of slate rock covered by dirt.

"If Paul felt good about himself, he would work through some of the nightmares his parents subjected him to, the wounds they left him with. Once you get to know him, you will see a man with an above-average IQ, an above-average emotional quotient, and an above-average ethical quotient. I've quietly tested his resilience. He has the ability to reflect objectively, and *that* is the golden ticket. I can work with him."

"That's all it takes?"

"Well, I had to acclimate him. Give him the vision that there is a healthier possibility for life. I've given him undeniable clues. He's opened the doors; he hasn't locked them to keep me out. If I show someone a better way and the walls go up, the defenses are propelled against me it's immensely more difficult. But he and the both of you are showing the willingness necessary for friendship and a full examination."

I considered what we must have said in the beginning for him to have seen us as capable enough for this research.

"I remembered seeing Carl Sagan on the tonight show saying, 'What distinguishes one human being from another in terms of intelligence is probably very little to do with heredity and an enormous amount to do with the environment.'"

"Wow, so even in a place like this, you can find the flowers growing out of the rocky mountaintop?" Mary asked.

Wolfzang knocked on the door, and a slight knock rattled the entire door frame, which showed the quality of the straw house this *pig* lived in.

A "KEEP OUT!" sign, including pictures of old revolvers, hung in the front window.

"When Obama was president, Paul had no money, yet he gave whatever he could to the NRA to fight against anti-gun laws. When Trump was president, Paul and others like him gave much less to the NRA, and the NRA suffered financially," Wolfzang explained.

"Obama being black and supporting anti-gun regulations must have resonated the emotional drives, Need to Control Others, Need to Control the Environment, Narcissistic Drive, Feelings of Inferiority," I explained, impressing myself by being able to rattle off most of the list he gave us in the bagel cafe.

"Come in!" Paul yelled. Wolfzang opened the door and we walked into a tiny very foul smelling living room.

"Just a minute; I'm on the shitter! Just wait a minute! Jesus Christ!" At that moment, I realized this would be a completely immersive field observation, a true AFE; we were becoming one with it. It would be a muddy, messy, authentic three-dimensional experience. There was no clinically calm, quiet, safe office here where certain emotional drives would be aided, abetted, and applauded. We were absorbed in the moment; there was no high-minded speculation or argumentation with like-minded homogeneous academics using rarely used vocabulary to compete and impress each other for positioning; it was an absolute desire for objective examination and discovery.

Paul appeared out of the dark of the hallway. Wearing a tank top, spotted with grease or maybe oil and carrying a beer can, which quickly made me take notice of the many beer cans scattered around the inside of this… home. "Well, well, if it's not my space alien friend and his experiments, probably Yankers. Let me get something for you out of the truck," Paul said and squeezed past us to get out the door.

"This guy is freaking intense!" I said.

Mary, standing in the living room, was clearly fascinated by what she saw. She visually inspected each piece of the room like a crime scene detective scouring the room for clues.

"Most primitives are *biased*. They just happen to conceal their biased thoughts and beliefs better than Paul. But, I assure you, in a short time, Paul will even be amazed by his current embraced beliefs."

"How Wolfzang? How can you change a man? Especially a man like *that*?" Mary asked.

"The first step is always seeing if someone can be dynamic with their embraced beliefs. Everyone has their walls, their blind spots. But… If you first filter out those that show intimations and traces, a willingness of reflexive reflective thinking, *then* you can start to strengthen the — *individual* by providing them emotional closeness, showing them compassion for their — unfortunate situation; their past. Proving things can be amazing, can be different."

"I see, then like us, you can start to give the details for what is going on, leaving it up to us to observe your information in real-time, in the world around us," I said.

"Precisely, these things, the guns, the bullet holes, the beer cans, the mess, it all doesn't matter, what he says doesn't matter, it's all symptoms and indications of what's going on inside of him, as long as he has shown some essential qualities of a willingness to reflect on his own thoughts and behaviors — objectively, as he has, there is infinite promise."

"Like Einstein said, 'Not everything that can be counted counts, and not everything that counts can be counted,'" I said.

"Where did that guy go? He's not like doing something weird out there?" Mary asked, appearing a little uneasy about her surroundings, giving a feeling that she feared being shot. The bullet shells around his living room made me feel the same.

"As always, you're here to see what an AFE is, to begin to use them accurately, and take it all in as a neutral observer; you must find it within yourself to make all your interactions genuinely compassionate and upbeat. Low-key, unobtrusive is also essential. If you do, other primitives will be much more willing to connect, and you will get a much clearer picture," Wolfzang explained.

Paul returned wearing a belt diagonally across his chest, no doubt a gun holder behind his back. Quite a way to make his guests feel at ease, but in his world, it was something to be admired. "Look, I found this rock in the woods, over near the large pond," Paul explained, looking like a kid during show and tell; his eyes just beamed with pride. It was a smoothly rounded-looking rock the size of a softball that clearly must have been some sort of a geode. I began to see his childlike wonder and that he might be different someday.

"Wow, indeed, that *is* impressive. May I open it?" Wolfzang asked.

"I don't reckon how ya gonna do that? But yeah, sure *spaceman*, let's see what's inside," Paul responded.

Wolfzang pulled out a small hammer, something resembling a reflex hammer, from a doctor's office. It was pure silver but had a tip on it that might have been a diamond itself and a small cylinder on the top, unlike anything I'd seen. Wolfzang placed the rock on the floor and, with three very concise hits, broke the stone perfectly in half, revealing an inside adorned with tiny crystals.

"This is Dan and Mary from upstate New York; you three are going to be good friends in the future and do some eminently important work. I thought you could just meet briefly today and get a little acquainted with each other."

“Northerners, I heard about you guys; I’ve seen pictures and videos of that… city. The smells must be just terrible, with all those — people. I hear you can’t even carry your guns there; what if you get mugged by one of those drugged-out Mexicans?” Paul asked.

I thought, “This place smells like crap and body odor. Standing next to a homeless guy smells better than this place,” but instead, I calmly responded, “Yeah, muggings by anyone is a thing. We’re sort of an equal opportunity uptight couple in that way, we avoid anyone that looks like trouble on a quiet street, avoiding streets when something looks a little strange. We’ll quickly walk the other way, take a fast corner.”

“Would you like a beer? I got some venison stew; it’s great stuff.”

“I’m good,” Mary said.

“Do you have some soda?” I asked, trying to be friendly without having to drink a beer this early in the day.

“Can of cola, OK? You’ve got some kind of digestive problem? My uncle makes a mean shine that you can try too.”

Not wanting to appear aloof but not wanting to drink this lunatic’s moonshine, I quickly responded. “Yeah, stomach problems, it would probably burn a hole right through me. I’d spend all day on your toilet,” I said in a cheerful voice. Realizing how he never bothered to ask Mary if she wanted the poison.

“Get me a shot; I’d be happy to give it a try,” Wolfzang responded in his most masculine voice.

We took a seat on his couch, which was clearly several decades old, plaid cushions, wooden armrests, a relic from the late 70s.

Grabbing an old cast-iron pot, he poured a glass that could be smelled across the room of sweet corn and yeast. He opened a top cabinet revealing his very cluttered cupcake, cookie, devil dog, potato chip-filled cabinets to grab a Sam-W-Mart can of cola.

I had to give Wolfzang a lot of street cred; he calmly drank the whisky as if it was a fine wine.

“So you know our friend is not from here?” I asked, looking at Paul.

"Sure, we've known each other for a couple of years now," Wolfzang explained.

"Yeah, something like that *hammer*. This guy has some mad shit. Only a space alien would have his stuff. But anyway, you know how the government is. We honestly shouldn't discuss his tech with anyone."

"Their job is to journal about their perceptions, contrast them to my own societal viewpoints during the reexamination, document their own immersive interactions, and give complete descriptions of how they felt. Thus, describing the Tool I've told you about," Wolfzang said, looking at Paul.

"Sheesh — that sounds more complicated than I thought!" Mary said with a smile.

"All for this sociology experiment to make large changes in human behavior with subtle, intricate efforts," Paul said.

"Ooh… you've heard that — too. You know that?" I said, floored at the details this unstable man understood, the wide swing in the dimensions of his personality.

"Your whole family lives close by?" Mary asked.

"Yeah, I see them all the time; my cousin is an ass. My sister is just like my mother. I like crap food like everyone else, but she's gonna get a belt around her stomach to make her stop eating; she's like 400 pounds."

"Yeesh, that has gotta be terrible," Mary responded.

"My grandmother died last year. Too much smoking and a bad heart. She was the glue, what kept the family together," Paul explained.

"Are you close to your father?" I asked.

"Well, between you and me, the guy has got some big problems. He's into the whole white supremacist stuff; he's an unhinged extremist. I loved shooting my guns with him; like we really got along when we were shooting, but the racist shit, it was always too much," Paul explained.

"Whoa!" I gasped.

"Sounds like the shooting was when you bonded. When you resonated your Yearning for Emotional Closeness with your dad. That must have been a huge push for your love of guns — shooting."

"I guess, but I don't know, Wolfzang said that before. Lately, dad's crap just got worse, you know, some of that stuff is a little too far, like I know these guys in town, and they're ok. I guess they're not that smart, but they're actually kind of nice. Besides, my grandmother never liked all that hate," Paul explained, then left the room for a moment.

"As you can see, my friend Paul is a man torn between worlds," Wolfzang explained.

"Do you guys wanna shoot my AR-57?" Paul asked from the other room.

I had shot a gun over my own hot-headed uncle's house; it sounded like a unique experience; besides, Wolfzang was with us. We weren't in any danger with this maniac.

"Suurrre?" Mary responded, clearly feeling the same.

He went down a skinny hallway and returned a minute later with an Uzi-looking gun raised above him to the right side; he looked F-ing frightening. I was about to say this is all insane; we're out of here! But Mary looked less concerned, and Wolfzang looked quite relaxed. Looking at them, I decided to continue. The three of us followed him out the skinny back door of this shack trailer, down three rusty metal stairs, onto a path, and into the woods. It was getting creepier and creepier.

After a couple of minutes' walk and a few mosquito bites, we came to an opening in the woods. Fifty feet from where we stood, there were six silhouette posters, the kind right out of a shooting range. Two of the posters were never used; the rest were bullet-riddled, focusing clearly on the head. It became clearer this guy lived in his imagination, dreamed of and prepared to kill, and I was glad I didn't live anywhere close to him.

Wolfzang handed us earplugs. Paul didn't wait for a second more.

TAT.TAT.TAT..TAT...TAT...TAT.TAT.TAT.TAT. I don't know the difference between a semi-automatic and an automatic, but there is clearly no reason to differentiate. The sound was non-stop. Suddenly Paul, the guy that lived in squalor, spoke like a highly educated, well-informed guide, “The crest is a solid piece, the utter finest alum, the bolt is one-piece quite easy to clean, look here, you can see. The barrel is threaded into the receiver. The ejector sits right here. There is a very low pullback to this magnificent model; it’s likely the most accurate model — from my own experience.”

“Oh, my god Paul, if there is ever a war, call me. I’d be needing to know you,” I responded, trying to make light of his scary killing machine.

“Why don’t you try it?” He said, looking at me.

I took the gun and pointed it at the silhouette targets. As a kid, I loved fireworks. I remembered how I would keep them in my bedroom drawer and think about them every day for weeks until the Fourth of July. Sometimes, I would take them out just to look at them, to smell them. I recalled a feeling of exhilaration, a visceral feeling of power and control over what I perceived a mighty explosives. This immediate activity began absorbing my attention completely; I was there at that moment. I wasn’t thinking of anything other than hitting the target. After emptying an entire cartridge, which Paul quickly reloaded for me, my thoughts shifted. I thought about what Mary might be thinking. But then my thoughts went right back to TAT,TAT,TAT,TAT,TAT,TAT ...TAT,TAT. I thought about how he must have felt as he imagined shooting those that belittled and criticized him; I began to understand him better. He was clearly capable of much more, just reduced on every occasion by this — place… these people in his world, never feeling accomplished, an intelligent but stuck guy, capable of not being a bigot. Like a guard dog with huge teeth, barking and biting toward those 100 feet away passing by on a sidewalk, practicing for a future opportunity to sink his teeth into someone. I could feel the gun pushing back against me. It was a symbolic action that gave real sensory input, and as Wolfzang had revealed, symbolic activities are how to communicate with the brainstem and limbic system. I imagined how each bullet coming out could take a human life, and this machine was designed and sold to do so; yet, the sales and marketing department would use the pretense of protection. Undoubtedly there was a lot to take in. At that moment, more than ever, I realized why Wolfzang was so insistent that we did more than just talk about stuff in a comfortable, clean, air-conditioned setting. His point being, we must continuously be vigilant of and overcome the assumptions reinforced by our emotional drives; a deep sense we already *knew* it all. I could see if we didn't visit Paul, but read a description of him, my own biased opinions would have remained. There was infinite importance that we talked with him, that we felt the walk down his backwoods path. We needed to hold and feel the weight of the gun and the sounds of the bullets hitting the targets. It was all necessary to fight our Narcissistic Drive communicating to us through visceral emotions. The feelings that equate to, "I already know that. That would be *sooo* trivial." I thought back to a 33-year-old psychology professor that would, when questioned, without hesitation, condescendingly speak down to the class and regularly subtly and creatively reminded us of his pedigree from Yale; he was far too smart to ever actually take part in something so rudimentary. At that moment, I embraced the OCSs absolute necessity to master the dynamic Embraced Belief Cloud Network and the importance of adroitly studying the finite details of Analytical Field Explorations as essential for the exponential discovery and innovation process.

Looking over at Mary, I gave a signal it was her turn.

"My cousin's a girl. She shoots pretty good," he said, handing Mary the gun.

Mary held the gun, put on a pair of goggles, and began shooting. TAT,TAT,TAT,TAT,TAT,TAT.

"WOW! That's CRAZY!" Mary said. Mary became immersed. Immediately she showed far better accuracy than my initial attempt.

TAT,TAT,TAT,TAT,TAT,TAT,TAT.

"It was great meeting y'all, Wolfzang's other guinea piggies. I don't got much more time, I gotta get to my real job," Paul said.

"On a Sunday, where do you work?" I asked.

"I cut down trees. I got a job to finish."

I realized it took someone with some substantial skill using machinery to clear the area we were in. He had invested a great deal of time in creating this sanctuary, this place he could symbolically deal with his pain.

"That must be an exciting job. Climbing and cutting trees down, I was never great with heights," I said.

“It pays the bills. My boss is a dick, so I’m looking for a different job, but this area ain’t got a good economy.”

“Right — it must be hard, to find other work around here?”

“Yeah!”

With that, we all walked back to his shack.

“Thanks for showing Dan and Mary around. It was essential they met you and had an opportunity to try your gun. I’ll be in touch with you.” Wolfzang explained and then handed him an envelope, which we knew was his cheese. Payment for a request to show a couple of Northerners how to shoot a gun.

“Yeah… call me soon.”

We got back into the truck.

“Soooo, what the hell was *that*?” Mary said jokingly.

Wolfzang smiled. ”It was the real thing. There was no censoring his world. You saw it for what it genuinely was, not the assumptions, speculations, or two-dimensional conclusions one might have of an individual in a cultural group while seeing a truncated news report.”

“I get that. At first, he was one creepy dude, like a murdering nut job, but over our visit… he began to make more *sense*.”

“You see the gun, you see the shack, you hear his biased views, but these things are symptoms of something else going on within the mind. The next question to ask is, can he exponentially build upon his reflections and alter his life’s direction? Can he objectively reflect on his thoughts and feelings? And that question takes specific skills and fine-tune listening done systematically.”

“And, *we* clearly must have passed that test. I’m still amazed we’re all going to be friends in the future,” I replied.

“Through *him*, see yourself. You are both still primitives; you *also* have the tendency of being an incentive, emotionally, and escape-driven animal. *Still* vulnerable to the hard-wired fact that primitives come to an emotional belief, embrace it, and then use logic to support the belief.

Before our next visit, in the interim, your task is through him; see yourself."

There was something profound in what he was saying. We *both* took note. We continued to travel through the backcountry, then calmly said our goodbyes as he dropped us back off at the motel. Paul was such an enigma wrapped in a caricature of a hillbilly; he captured our thoughts for days after that. Clearly, he was capable of reflective thought. Otherwise, Wolfzang wouldn't be wasting his time. Paul showed us reasonable intelligence. What would cause a man to be such an outward degenerate, the flag, the beer cans, the guns? He looked like a completely hopeless case to the two of us. I found myself asking questions I didn't expect to ask myself, namely, to a Universally Ethical alien, what unbalanced behaviors would I exhibit? What kinds of blind spots do I have, moving across time on this train with my cultural group? Sure, I wasn't running around making racist remarks, waving threatening weapons around to be an alpha male. Yet, how am I unknowingly a product of my environment? How are those around me reinforcing me to act certain ways? What am I doing that is just as ridiculous to someone that would have a completely pragmatically objective, neutral view of me?

A week later, we found ourselves back at home flipping through channels and found PBS news hour.

"Our next expert is from the Institute for the Resolution of Gun Violence and Remediation of Criminal Firearm Possession."

"Wow, what a complexly intricate name?"

"Hmm, maybe they're trying to be pragmatic, concise, objective?"

The expert spoke for a few minutes. Her main point revolved around internet chat rooms where future shooters congregate. Recognizing that young males are more likely shooters. Anger issues are fundamental to understanding gun violence.

"Wow. repeat, applause, talk about symptoms, repeat, applause..."

"It's like she's afraid to ask the real three-dimensional questions. I wonder if she'd offend typical PBS viewers if she posed deeper questions. But, she likes being on TV, she enjoys being the face of that organization, she doesn't want to lose her coveted position, so she becomes a mouthpiece just performing the job of distributor of confirmation bias?"

"She seems to think some elementary detective work to identify possible shooters was enough to change the deeper behavior when it's a much deeper dive into our current insanely strong psychological dogmas and embraced beliefs about the mind that are constantly perpetuated here."
"Yeah, she kept referring to the symptoms, certainly a starting point, clues that something is going on in the mind. It was a two-dimensional not three-dimensional examination of the *why*. There was no *unique,* genuine, imaginative, well-developed explanation for an attempt to tackle and transform those involved."

"What about Einstein's quote, "We can't solve problems by using the same kind of thinking we used when we created them."

"Right, I think Wolfzang would ask, 'What are these shooters' family life like? Was there a true deep loving connection? Was there abuse? Was there continuous subtle abuse, was love a commodity used by a parent to control? What was their childhood truly like? How was their Primary Cloud weakened? Why are they overwhelmed by their emotional drives? After we see *symptoms*, can we identify how to strengthen their mind before their emotional drives and embraced beliefs cause great harm to others? What are those around them like? Those that are possibly perpetuating, enabling the weaknesses? Why are guns an escape, and how to replace them with a healthy escape?' But perhaps Wolfzang's most poignant point about behavior is that our understanding of it is truncated, two-dimensional, and fundamentally inaccurate, yet fully embraced and extensively built upon. Consequently, many of these shooters are medicated by professionals who have a fundamentally flawed understanding, which only further deepens the shooters emotional disconnect."

"Huh, I'd love to know what the real medication history of the shooters has been. Even make that a law to make that particular detail publicly known. What the medication history was leading up to the shooting? It might give the pharma industry a new responsibility."

"Hmm, but *here* the people that think their intellectuals gain guru status spend all the time fighting the nuances of the obvious symptoms, spinning around unessential details, sounding super intellectual, feeding their own Narcissistic Drive, getting applause, putting on a dance to keep their highly incentivized important positions."

"You're right; there was no deeper discussion, just superficial applause of the painfully obvious."

Mary thought silently for a moment. "Are we from here any longer? Do we still want to be here?"

"Everything looks much different."

Endnotes

Some quotes by historical figures are difficult to trace. This author has earnestly attempted to give appropriate credit to the true source. After thorough research, it is clear many of Einstein's ideas and statements have been widely disseminated and paraphrased over the years.

1. Pg 67. "Stay with a problem longer." Albert Einstein.

2. Pg 73. "Science is more than a body of knowledge, it's a way of thinking. A way of skeptically interrogating the universe. With a fine understanding of human fallibility." Carl Sagan" *The Charlie Rose Show*," May 27, 1996.

Definition

Sciency- when an intelligent person refers vaguely to an expert, real or unreal resource. Sounding highly intelligent, still being vague, thus believing they won the argument but simply protecting their embraced beliefs in a reflexive manner. Thus remaining emotionally driven, but sounding *smart*.

Excerpts: Doc of the OCS

Article Goose used for Foie Gras

Humans are capable of exponential progress by inventing new technologies and making scientific discoveries. We are intelligent enough, but the human-animal is hard-wired to be emotionally, incentive, and escape-driven. Acceptance of human dysfunction and the genesis of said dysfunction are essential for us to reach our next step. We must understand what drives the dysfunction, identify common and predictable dysfunctional behaviors. Then, develop systems to efficiently neutralize dysfunctions but retain our deep compassion and each's very own essence, creativity, and individuality, harnessing our imagination to the fullest. We are not conformists and have not developed the Tool to create a society of like-minded identical sentients. We work to become a beautifully compassionate race of free-thinking individuals that will resonate as a positive force within the multiverse.

Expected Toxic Outcomes are repeatable dysfunctional behaviors seen throughout human societies and throughout human history. They are the behavioral products of the Genetically Important Drives within the brainstem and limbic system intermixed with incentives and embraced beliefs. It is important to recognize that the list of ETOs may sound colloquial or somewhat trivial; they are anything *but*. The physiology and neurological processes involved have evolved over hundreds of millions of years and are quite astounding. Throughout human evolution, behaviors that occurred due to Genetically Important Drives within the brainstem and limbic system have had a significant positive impact on human survival…

Article Orchid Mantis

During the genesis of this document, we are not yet capable of saving every life form that crosses our path. We are objective, pragmatic, and Universally Ethical. We are not well-meaning idealists that stumble over our own good intentions. While traveling, we may kill insects, and during construction projects, we may inadvertently and unknowingly kill tiny living things. As our technology improves, we intend to address our fully accepted inadequacies and improve our ability to be compassionate to all living things.

Article Spider

All articles will have some degree of flexibility. There will always be exceptions to every rule; we believe overly rigid rules in the long term can negatively impact an outcome. There is always something on the far ends of the bell curve worth reflecting upon, investigating, and learning from.

Article Vaquita

Repression of pain and the weakening of the Primary Cloud is often more effectively overcome by examining the facts with someone you trust. Trust is inextricably interwoven with love. You must trust others won't use bang-ups, hang-ups, and mistakes against you. We must be honest, pure, and compassionate toward each other to support a robust Primary Cloud network. Trust starts with kindness to our own little ones, on guard against any negative self-talk. You need to be able to walk away from things and trust yourself.

Article Llama

For a strong long-term economic outlook, all OCS must develop a mastery of acquiring compounding interest.

An in-depth mastery of business economics through the lens of value investing that considers the fundamental health and culture of a company, including identification of any systemic ETOs. An objective sophisticated examination of balance sheets, underlying assets, and long-term advantages that may produce substantial compounding returns. Importantly, we are a race of compassionate innovators, not a race of money lenders that will enslave others for our own compounding interest intentions.

www.ingramcontent.com/pod-product-compliance
Lightning Source LLC
LaVergne TN
LVHW010549160826
845677LV00013B/3053

* 9 7 9 8 9 8 8 7 1 7 6 3 8 *